MATT MILLER IN THE COLONIES

Book Two: Prophet

MARK J. ROSE

The Skydenn Looking Glass
Simi Valley, California

The Skydenn Looking Glass
508 Longbranch Rd.
Simi Valley, CA 93065

Printed in the United States of America

Library of Congress Cataloging-in-Publication Data
Rose, Mark J., 1965 –
Matt Miller in the Colonies : Book Two: Prophet / Mark J. Rose.
ISBN 978-0-9975554-3-1
1. Science Fiction. 2. Historical Fiction.
Title: Matt Miller in the Colonies: Book Two: Prophet

Second Edition

TWO BODIES IN A FIELD

Anne Morris reached around to ease the backpack from her daughter's body and pushed it clumsily toward the pile she had made of their possessions. She lowered Sarah back onto the ground and shook her gently. She was startled when her daughter took a violent breath.

"No!" the girl screamed.

"Sarah, honey, wake up!"

Her daughter's eyes opened. Sarah looked at the sky, then around where she lay, and then to her mother. "Why are we in a field?"

"No idea," Anne replied.

"Where's the car?"

"Don't know."

"Were we robbed?"

"I have my purse, jewelry, money...fur," Anne said. She shrugged her shoulders.

Sarah struggled to sit up. "God, my head's pounding," she said. She motioned to her backpack. "There's water in my pack."

Anne reached to drag the backpack to them, unzipped it, and moved the textbooks aside. She handed the bottle to her daughter. "It'll be dark soon," Anne said. She grabbed her purse, pulled out her phone, and hit the emergency button. The phone beeped, so she touched the button again, but she got the same result. "There's no service."

"They guaranteed these to get a signal everywhere," Sarah said.

"Can you stand?"

Sarah attempted to get on her feet but fell back to the ground. "Maybe not," she gasped. "My head hurts."

"Mine too," her mother said. "Either way, we need to walk." She grabbed her daughter's hand and pulled upward. The teen was shaky but managed to stay on her feet. Sarah held her mother's shoulder and stooped to pick up her backpack. Her mother reached to grab her fur coat and purse. Anne went to put her coat back on but thought better of it. "It's warm," she observed.

Sarah stopped to scan the forest. "The trees have leaves."

"What?"

"Look around," Sarah said. "They're green."

"They're pine trees."

"They're oaks," Sarah corrected. "They're already bare at home."

Anne shrugged again. "We need to find a phone signal."

"It'll be scary out here in the dark," Sarah said, looking around at the thick woods.

They started walking to what looked like another clearing and stumbled onto a dirt road. "That was easy," Anne said, relieved, but then she stood perplexed. "Which way?" She pulled her phone out and checked again for a signal. "Nothing."

"There's a sign ahead," Sarah said. "Probably says Argentina."

"Argentina?"

"Where else could the season change from fall to summer?"

"Let's get to a landline and call for help," Anne said. She scanned the trees. "None of this feels right."

Sarah focused hard to read the sign. "Philadelphia, one mile," she read. "You'd think we'd be able to see the city."

"I see buildings," her mother replied, pointing. They increased their pace toward what looked like a town.

It was dark by the time they faced a rough-hewn grey building with a wooden sign reading "Beaufort's Inn" dangling from a crude metal chain. "An old-time inn," Anne declared with a smile. "They had one of these in Ithaca."

Sarah inspected the street as her mother was talking. It was lit by soot-stained lamps. "Is this what they mean by a gaslamp district?"

"I don't know," her mother replied, still scrutinizing the front of the building. "If it has food and rooms, maybe we should stay the night and figure things out in the morning."

"There has to be cell service here," Sarah said.

Her mother pulled out her phone and dialed. It beeped again. "Your father probably wouldn't answer even if there was service," she said. "We may be on our own tonight."

"Like most nights," Sarah quipped.

"What d'you want from me?" Anne said, irritated, as she pushed open the door of the inn. It was lively inside, with more people than they'd expected from the dark exterior. There was a hostess dressed in a colonial costume behind a counter.

"Can I help you, mum?" she said.

Anne pushed closer to the front desk. "We were robbed. Can I use your phone?"

"Oh dear, robbed, you say? We'll notify the sheriff in the morning," the hostess replied. Then she noticed Sarah. "Oh my!" She waved frantically at another woman in a colonial dress who was waiting on a table. "Annabelle!" she cried. "A blanket from the cupboard, quickly! They've been robbed!" Both costumed women had gone into a panic. Sarah stood there, confused.

"Find a blanket," the hostess repeated. "Poor girl had her dress stolen!" Annabelle, a chubby young woman, hurried to the closet, grabbed a blanket, and wrapped it around Sarah's body. Sarah stood stunned through the entire process.

"'Tis a cruel world where a robber thinks naught of leaving a lady in her pantaloons," Annabelle said.

"Pantaloons?" Sarah questioned. "This is a put-on, right?"

"No, 'tis a blanket," Annabelle replied. "I'm sure there's a dress we can lend somewhere in the closet. There are things people never come back to claim."

Sarah and her mother waited for her to return with a dress. It took some acrobatics for Sarah to slip it over her head while still covering herself with the blanket. When she was done, she stood there wearing her new dress on top of her school uniform with the blanket dropped at her feet. The costumed women looked at her with pleased grins, happy to have averted a major crisis.

"That should do until you get a proper dress," the hostess said from behind the desk. "Poor dears!"

"Thanks," Sarah said. She was feeling groggy and wondered if this all really made no sense or if it was because she was so tired.

"We need a phone," her mother said to the hostess.

She gave Anne a puzzled look. "Are you recently from across the ocean?"

"No," Anne said. "Why would you think that?"

"Your words," the woman replied. "'Tis not Philadelphia, to be sure."

"We're not from Philadelphia, in any case," Anne said. "We're from Oak Ridge, Tennessee."

"Welcome to Philadelphia, present circumstance aside."

"Do you have a phone I could use?"

"I don't believe we have this foon," the hostess replied.

"You don't have a phone we can use," Anne asked, "or you don't have a phone?"

"Should you see one," the hostess said, still perplexed, "you're most welcome."

Sarah, who had been taking stock of the surroundings, turned her attention back to the desk. "It fits the theme," she said to her mother. "You don't make all this effort to look old-time and then have people sitting around talking on cell phones."

"We've rooms," the hostess said. "You don't look like no beggars."

Anne's head was pounding hard and she was having trouble focusing. "We've got cash and credit," she said. It was a struggle to say the words clearly through the pain.

"Your coin all stolen, then?"

The smell of the food was making Sarah hungry, and she needed to get off her feet. She spoke up, trying to ask as nicely as possible. "Can you show us what would be acceptable payment? We'll make sure you get paid for the room and some food."

The hostess pulled out a thick wooden register and set it on the counter. "Put your name, colony, and mark saying you'll make good on your four-shilling debt," she instructed.

"Four shillings?" Sarah's mother asked.

"For the both of you; meals tonight and tomorrow morning," the hostess said. "'Tis a fair price."

Sarah poked her mother gently in the side. "'Tis a fair price," she repeated. "Sign so I can sit down." Sarah's mother looked around for a pen. There was a quill next to an inkwell. She pulled them close and filled out the ledger.

"Four shillings *is* a fair price," Anne said. "I apologize. I'm very tired."

"We understand, mum," the hostess replied. "We're used to weary travelers. Gather yourselves in your room, then come for a meal. Your humor will be much improved with a full belly."

Annabelle motioned and they followed her through a hall lit by oil lanterns in sconces. She carried a candle into their room, guarding it with her hand as she reached to place it on a worn wooden writing table that separated two simple beds. The writing table had an inkwell with a ragged feather quill and a printed piece of paper that was folded in half. The beds were made up with woolen blankets and quilted pads for pillows.

"'Tis a half shilling for another candle, should you desire," Annabelle said. "They're costly as of late."

"We're fine," Anne replied as she looked around.

"Come downstairs when you're ready to take your meal," Annabelle said. "I apologize for what you've endured this night. A mother and daughter robbed and abandoned in the street? What has become of this fine city?" She left, closing the door behind her.

Sarah and her mother stood there bathed in the flickering light of the candle. Sarah eased her pack down to the narrow swath of bare wood floor between the beds and took a seat. Her mother sat facing her on the opposite bed. "What's going on?" she asked her daughter.

Sarah was trying to adjust her position to relieve the tugging of the dress on her shoulders. It had been a long time since she had worn a full-length dress. "I have a new dress," she said. "It smells like dust, but it fits."

Her mother stared blankly at the wall, hypnotized by the candlelight that danced about the room. "The leaves are back on the trees," she said. "We're in a place called Philadelphia that doesn't look like Philadelphia, and we're staying at an inn that only takes coins." She reached out and touched Sarah. "This isn't a dream?"

Sarah rolled her eyes and reached over to pull the paper from the corner of the writing table. "*Philadelphia Gazette*," she read. "It says August sixteenth, 1762. They make it look so real."

"We might as well go down for food," her mother said. "Maybe it'll help my headache."

They stood up and went into the hall and down the steps. The dining room was bustling with activity. Another costumed woman, a waitress, noticed them and pointed to a table. "Sit there, mum," she said. "I'll be over." The room was dim, lit only by the warm glow of the oil lamps.

Sarah took inventory of the faces around them at the wooden tables. "Do you think everyone here's an actor?" she whispered.

"We're the only paying customers?" her mother asked in disbelief.

"Nonpaying customers, actually," Sarah reminded her.

"We're somewhere else," her mother insisted. "Or sometime else."

"Mother, seriously?"

"I remember leaving the hotel to pick you up for school," Anne said, "then nothing."

"I remember standing outside your car," Sarah replied.

The waitress was at their table. "Two ordinaries?"

"What's an ordinary?" Sarah asked.

"Lamb, carrots, and potatoes. The ale is excellent."

"Two ordinaries and two ales," Sarah's mother said, smiling at her daughter. "I'm sure it won't be your first." Sarah remained silent.

The woman returned almost immediately with the drinks, set them down, and left to get the food. "They're not going to ask for my ID?" Sarah said.

"I told you," her mother replied. "We're someplace else...sometime else. Seasons don't change while you sleep."

"Mother," Sarah replied. "There's an explanation."

"Ask the waitress when she comes back."

"Ask her what?"

"The paper upstairs said it was 1762," Anne said. "Ask the date."

"She's going to say 1762," Sarah declared. "It'd be silly to not stick to the story."

"Everyone here's an actor?"

Sarah looked around. "That would be pretty hard to believe," she admitted.

"Wait until the morning before asking questions. I'm too tired for a surprise."

The waitress was setting the food on their table. "Here you go, mum. Anything else?"

"Yes," Anne replied. "We were robbed this evening and need to sell items to travel home. Where should we go?"

"What would you be selling, then, mum?"

"Jewelry, mostly."

"Reed's," the waitress said. "It's a walk down Market Street, perhaps fifteen minutes. They trade in gold, gems, and such."

"Thanks," Anne replied. The waitress turned to attend another table.

"You think we're going to walk fifteen minutes down the street and not get a phone signal?" Sarah said, exasperated. "And then you think we'll need to sell our jewelry?"

"I don't know what to think," her mother replied.

PART I.

PILGRIM

CHAPTER 1.

MATT MILLER

The horse knew the way, so Matt let him steer as they rode the few miles from the Taylor farm into Richmond. Thunder was a powerful chestnut-colored thoroughbred that Matt had met on the first day that he woke up on the Taylor farm. They had become comfortable companions during the time that Matt was learning to ride, and Matt was grateful to have been able to find enough money to buy what some colonials would describe as a "rum prancer."

Despite their snail's pace, Matt still reached Richmond in plenty of time to meet the couriers he'd hired to deliver him safely to Philadelphia. As he approached the city, he saw a man sitting on the bench outside the silversmith's. It seemed too early for a random townsperson, so Matt considered that he might be a representative of the men who would escort him to his new home.

Matt looked again at his wrist. He wore a Rolex he'd bought with the signing bonus from the job he'd landed after graduate school. Matt grew up with very little money and had dreamed of the day when he'd finally have cash in his pocket and could start his real life. Ultimately he'd come to find that his concept of "real life" consisted of not much more than purchasing an expensive wristwatch and a new car. He remembered the sense of disappointment when he finally put the watch on his wrist and realized that he didn't feel any different. It was like any other watch in the end; it told you the time. He considered himself fortunate now, though, because it was self-winding. A battery-powered watch would've turned useless in the eighteenth century. He needed this to last a lifetime.

Matt was close enough now to see that the person sitting on the bench was Grace's brother, William Taylor, the man who was responsible for introducing him to Richmond society. Matt waved as he approached. "Glad to see you, my friend," Matt called. "I appreciate your coming to say goodbye." Matt dismounted and tied Thunder to the railing outside the silversmith's door.

"I'm not here for you," Will said with a wide grin on his face. He stood, pulled an apple out of his pocket, and held it out to the horse. "Only a cruel man would steal you away from your dog," he said to the horse. He scratched Thunder's head with both hands and watched with satisfaction until he finished the apple. "Grace claims I care not, but I'm going to miss this boy."

"We'll be back," Matt said.

Will let go of the horse and turned to Matt. "How was Grace with your leaving?"

"I'll miss her," Matt said simply. "You see my escort?"

"They'll arrive ere long," Will replied. "They pass through every other Monday after sunrise and make a fair racket." He reached into the leather bag on the bench and pulled out a large silver flask. "A gift of Irish whiskey from Graine's father. He said to share it only with men of the first quality." He handed the flask to Matt. "Mother give you victuals?"

"Plenty," Matt replied. He pointed at the large sack hanging from his saddle.

Will laughed. "Fortunate that you have a large horse."

"Thank Mr. Martin for the whiskey," Matt replied. "How's Graine?"

"We've discussed an engagement. I'd want you to have some role in the wedding."

Matt was flattered. "I don't know what to say."

"Graine expects you to return. She has some conviction you'll win my sister's hand. I haven't the heart to tell her you have but two pence to rub together."

"For once, you're wrong," Matt said. "I'm a wealthy man."

"You got your price? Then your success is assured!"

"Who knows?" Matt replied doubtfully.

"Have you learned nothing in Virginia?"

"I know what you're going to say," Matt said. "Trust in—"

"Must I pound this into your skull?" Will said. He picked up his foot in a kicking motion to imitate Matt's tae kwon do skills. Matt stepped away in mock defense. "Do you believe God rolled you under a bridge in Virginia for you to repair to Philadelphia and forget us?"

"God rolled me under a bridge?"

"How else would you end up there?"

"You people always catch me at my worst."

"We see it upon your face," Will proclaimed. "Know anything about grapes?"

"I like wine," Matt joked.

"There's a parable in the Gospels. After the grapes are harvested, you cut the vines back. They look as if they should never grow again, but they do. One year, I didn't trim the vines, and you know what?"

"Oh gee," Matt said. "What?"

"You jest, but we only had a third of the usual crop."

"So I'm being trimmed?"

"I should think down to the stalk," Will replied, chuckling. "There'll be fruit…in the end."

"You can't relate every life experience to plants."

Will put his palms up in a "What're you going to do?" gesture. "We're farmers, not Greek philosophers."

"Send me a note when you decide the wedding date," Matt said. "I'll want details on the clothes and the dances. Showing up to a party is never enough with you people."

Will nodded. "Take care of Thunder and return soon." They shook hands one last time and Will grabbed his bag and walked across the street without looking back. Matt took his place on the bench to wait for the people who would take him to Philadelphia.

CHAPTER 2.

ZEKE WILKINS

The man hopped down and shook Matt's hand, staring at Thunder. "Name's Zeke Wilkins," he said. "He's a beauty. You interested in selling?"

"He's my only traveling companion," Matt said, laughing. "Probably not."

"Never seen a finer animal."

"He's a Taylor horse. One of the owners works there." Matt pointed to the building across the street where Will worked as an accounting apprentice. "Tell him Matt Miller sent you, but be prepared to pay a fair price."

Zeke nodded as he looked over at the accountant's office. "Mr. Berkley told me you're traveling to Philadelphia," he said after a moment. "Mail's going as far as Wilmington. 'Tis two guineas to guarantee your passage."

The fact that they wouldn't be going all the way to Philadelphia was news to Matt. "How far from Wilmington to Philadelphia?" He didn't like the idea of traveling alone with all the gold he had in his bag.

"Two days. Those aren't dangerous roads."

"I'll make it," Matt said finally. He didn't have any other option for going north, so he handed the man the two gold coins.

"You're responsible for your own meals and lodging. We've arrangements with inns along the road. We'll only assure your safety if you hold the same lodgings."

"I'll sleep where you've arranged," Matt said.

"You armed?" Zeke asked, scanning Matt's body.

"No," Matt replied. He had his Walther in a side holster, but it was small enough to hide under his jacket.

"I expect little trouble, but we're armed to protect the mail. Leave it to my men."

"Fine by me," Matt replied. "I'm an apothecary, not a soldier."

"An apothecary? That's like a wizard, right?"

"More like a businessman. Either way, I'll let your men do the shooting."

"We expect to reach Fredericksburg early tomorrow."

Matt pulled the sack of food from his saddle and walked to the first of the three wagons. He nodded to one of the men driving and tucked the sack into a safe spot in the back corner. Before stepping away, he reached in for the three ripe pears Mary Taylor had packed, handed one to each of the drivers, and put the other in his pocket. Both men smiled and mouthed thanks. He turned around, untied Thunder, and mounted up. Zeke took a position at the head of the wagon train and waved his hand forward, and all the wagons started moving. One of the drivers directed Matt behind the second wagon, and Matt guided Thunder into the spot when the space opened. Four riders on horseback brought up the rear.

They traveled quickly out of the city and then for almost an hour in a neat line until Zeke waved for the train to slow as they traversed a rough portion of road. Matt took care to ease Thunder around the deep ruts to avoid twisting a hoof. When they'd cleared the holes, Zeke rode back along the line and talked to everyone as they continued down the road. When he got to Matt, he said, "How goes it?"

"Fine so far."

"You have water?"

Matt pointed to the canteen attached to his saddle.

"I can see that you're not used to spending a full day in the saddle. Ride in the wagon if you become weary." He pointed at the second wagon with his whole hand. "You can tie your horse on the back."

"I'll be fine," Matt said.

"If you nod off and hurt yourself falling," Zeke warned, "we have to leave you at the next town."

"I've got nothing to prove," Matt replied. "If I get tired, I'll go to the wagon."

Zeke nodded and rode off to talk to another driver. He lingered at the rear with the men on horseback until one was convinced to take his place at point. The man waved and smiled at Matt as he trotted past. When the rider made it to the head of the line, he raised his hand and the wagons started moving again.

They rode for two more hours until they came into a clearing that overlooked a large shimmering lake where they stopped for lunch. They lined the wagons up in a row under the shade of some large oaks and the men began unharnessing the horses so they could graze in the field between the camp and the water. Matt led Thunder down to the lake to drink and then let him join the horses that were happily grazing on fresh plants. Matt stood in solitude for a moment to watch ripples pop in the smooth, clear water as fish snatched insects from its surface. A few colored leaves had already gathered along the lake's edge, and they rocked back and forth as the water lapped at the shore. The leaves reminded him of the fact that it was almost fall, and he confirmed this by breathing in the smell of autumn that floated on the cool midmorning air.

Matt made his way back to the camp, grabbed bread and beef jerky from his sack, and sat next to one of the drivers on a stool that had been set out in front of the wagons. "I'm Matt Miller," he said, extending his hand.

"John Stewart," the man whistled through missing front teeth. "You going to Philadelphia?"

"That's right."

"Whatcha got waitin' there?"

"Starting an apothecary business," Matt replied. Matt had a degree in pharmaceutical chemistry and had done research for a big drug company in his own time. He knew how to synthesize a few different medicines that he thought colonial people would buy, and this was his plan for becoming wealthy enough to ask for the hand of a prominent Southern woman.

"You a medicine man?" John asked.

"I guess so," Matt said, laughing. "I kinda like the sound of that."

John gave him a wide toothless grin.

"You do this trip often?" Matt asked as he bit off a piece of jerky.

"Every fortnight." John pointed. "That's my brother there. We make good money working for Zeke. He keeps us out of trouble so's we can keep some of our money too."

"What kind of trouble do you get into out here?"

"It's when you're in town that you kin spend all yer money on wrangling and drink," John replied. "Zeke fines us if we get too wild."

"Seems pretty strict."

"Wakes us at sunrise," John added, "so we gotta take quiet at a decent hour."

Despite the fact that Matt had very little in common with the man, he talked with him for the entire break. Like everyone in the colonies, John had an interesting story.

"You ask a lot of questions, Mr. Miller," John finally said.

"You can call me Matt. Or medicine man, if you prefer." He laughed.

"'Twas only a jest," John said. "Zeke says we're to call passengers Mister or Ma'am."

"Fine by me, *Mr.* Stewart," Matt said. He saw John smile again.

"Mr. Stewart," John repeated to himself. "Sounds like a gentleman."

****

Zeke whistled loudly to signal the end of the break. They picked up camp, gathered the horses, harnessed them, and took the trail in less than fifteen minutes. Matt's butt was growing sore, but he still felt attentive and strong in the saddle. It helped that they took breaks almost every hour. The sun was low in the sky when they rode up to the crest of a hill that overlooked a large and swift-flowing stream. Zeke gave the signal to stop and the vehicles were moved into a half circle along the perimeter of the space where they would camp. Two men tied their horses and walked away to get firewood. Two others left with wooden buckets to fill with water, and another took a rifle to hunt. A gunshot rang through the valley and a small doe was soon rotating over the fire.

As the men ate, they passed a bottle of rum and traded stories about Richmond. They told a side of the city that was less respectable than the version Matt had experienced during his time with the Taylors. "Jake just bought a horse near Richmond," Zeke said to Matt. He pointed across the fire to a bearded man wearing a tattered leather hat.

"Cost me a pretty penny too," Jake replied. He looked uncomfortable being the center of attention.

"Where'd you buy him?" Matt asked, hoping this wasn't going to be a conversation about the Paynes.

"Payne farm," Jake said. "Cost me twenty-five pounds. Hard earned, that was."

"You paid twenty-five pounds for a horse?" another man said.

"Been saving," Jake replied. "'Bout time I had a fine animal."

Matt tried to stay silent, but the questions were screaming too loudly in his head. "They have many fine horses at the Payne farm?"

"I thought you'd know," Jake replied. "Man named Levi said he knew you."

Matt looked at him with some surprise. "I do know Levi. How'd my name come up?"

Jake glanced at Zeke like he was in trouble. Zeke glared back. "What'd I do?" Jake asked. "He asked me about where I was ridin'."

"How'd my name come up?" Matt repeated.

"Can't remember exact," Jake replied. He paused, trying to think. "I mentioned that we were taking a man north who was staying at another farm. He said your name like he was your fellow. He is, right?"

"Was his nose still black?" Matt asked.

"Mostly yellow, like he was healing from a fight," Jake said. Matt nodded.

"You had something to do with this?" Zeke asked.

"He wanted to kill me."

Jake looked Matt up and down and said, "This Levi Payne was a big, strong-looking man."

"I held my own," Matt said, smiling.

Jake shook his head. "I meant nuthin' by it. Acted like your fellow, he did."

"No hard feelings," Matt replied. "I can't imagine there's a problem with him knowing about my journey." Even so, Matt couldn't keep himself from looking out over the valley for travelers. He caught himself. *There's no way Levi Payne has the time to follow me to Philadelphia.*

"I apologize, Mr. Miller," Zeke said. "I'm unhappy with Jake's want of discretion."

"It was an honest mistake," Matt said. "I expect discretion, though, if we work together in the future."

"I'm sorry, Mr. Miller," Jake replied. "I was a fool to mention your name."

****

Zeke roused them at sunrise. They wolfed down food, hitched the horses, and soon were moving along a well-traveled dirt road. Matt was in a thoughtful trance for most of the morning. Something about the rhythmic walk of his horse or the relative quiet of the surrounding woods enhanced his ability to explore the possibilities of his future in the colonies. This, combined with some dramatic views of the Virginia countryside, was enough to bring back the optimism that had eluded him since he had been forced to leave the woman he loved behind.

When Matt wasn't contemplating his future, he was talking quietly to Thunder, much like he had done with Scout, the Taylors' dog on the farm in Richmond. Matt had shared a barn with the dog while he worked on the farm to help bring in the hay. Matt had never had much experience with animals growing up, but his time with Scout gave him a new perspective on the therapeutic benefits of having a live set of unjudging eyes staring back at you while you pondered your future.

Matt felt some sense of déjà vu when they finally rode up to Fredericksburg, a Southern city situated on the Rappahannock River. The familiarity he felt was either because the city reminded him of Richmond or because he'd seen Fredericksburg in his dreams. The dreams came every night now and were growing too vivid and prophetic not to take notice of. He'd wake and try to remember information that he could correlate with future experiences, like seeing an oddly shaped tree or the velvet dress of a woman. Sometimes, though, his dreams would come rushing at him during the daytime and his mind would be saturated with indistinguishable pictures flashing like a high-speed camera. He'd have to consciously back away from the bursts to stay in the present. So far, he'd been able to force the visions out of his head, but he had a fear that they would someday overwhelm him.

As they entered Fredericksburg, Zeke rode along the line of wagons, chatting to each driver. "This is where we sleep," he said to Matt. "There's a corral at Danner's Inn. The horses and wagons will be under guard."

"Sounds good," Matt replied. He was anxious to walk on his own feet.

"There's a doctor we've used along the river," Zeke said. "Name's Hugh Mercer should you desire intercourse with another medical man."

"I'll go say hello once my horse is settled."

By the time Matt took Thunder to the corral, Zeke was already talking to one of the attendants to arrange accommodations. He waved back at the wagons. Each of the vehicles pulled over to the front of the corral along the fence, and the men unhitched their horses and led them to the gate. A few of the animals trotted around the perimeter, happy to be free of their bonds. Others headed to the feeding trough to focus on the hay.

"This is where you're staying," Matt said to Thunder. He led the horse over to the corral gate, pulled off his saddle and blanket, and removed the bridle from his mouth. He smacked his flank and the horse trotted happily to join the other animals. Matt lifted his saddle onto the wooden rack next the others, hung the blanket so it could air, placed the bridle on one of the hooks above, and then walked around to the front of the inn. He arranged for a room and then wandered tentatively out the door into the city of Fredericksburg.

CHAPTER 3.

HUGH MERCER

Matt's only memory of Fredericksburg from his history classes was that it had strategic importance during the Civil War. He knew nothing about the city during colonial times. The innkeeper gave him directions to find Dr. Hugh Mercer, who would hopefully have a better disposition than the last scientist type he'd met, a man in Richmond named Benjamin Scott. Scott had proven to be a disorganized lunatic and left Matt with a very bad impression of the state of apothecary in the eighteenth century.

Matt walked through Fredericksburg's business district, passing a number of shops until he was in front of a two-story white house with a sign beside the door reading "Major Hugh Mercer, Physician."

A Scottish man greeted him when he walked through the door. "Welcome to me shop, lad. I'm Major Hugh Mercer."

Mercer was nothing like Matt had imagined. He was young, with a head of dark curly hair and a narrow face. Matt wouldn't have described him as handsome, but he wasn't ugly either. He had an upright stance and a firm handshake.

"Good day," Matt said. "I'm Matt Miller from Richmond."

"How can I be of service, Mr. Miller?"

Matt inspected Mercer's office as he answered. The room contained the requisite plethora of bottled natural medicines filling the wall shelves, along with the round glass aquarium of thick black leeches that was the centerpiece of every eighteenth-century apothecary. Matt couldn't keep himself from wrinkling his nose as he dragged his gaze across the slimy creatures to look back into Mercer's eyes. "I'm traveling to Philadelphia to start an apothecary business. One of the men I'm with suggested I visit you."

"Always glad to talk to another medical man," Mercer replied. He stepped forward and inspected Matt's face. "Almost healed."

"What?"

"Someone punched you in the face," Mercer said.

Matt had thought his injury from the fight with Levi Payne was no longer visible. "That happened weeks ago."

"'Tis easy to see," Mercer proclaimed.

Matt shrugged. "I had a run-in with the town bully."

"Did you win?"

"Hardly. Broke his nose, though."

Mercer gave him a satisfied smile. "What brings you to me shop?"

"I'm interested in picking your brain," Matt replied.

Mercer considered the phrase. "You desire to ask me about my medical experience?"

"I learned apothecary in China," Matt lied. "I don't know anything about doctoring in the colonies and would appreciate your advice."

"I heard the Orientals poke you with needles," Mercer replied.

"They do," Matt said. "People say it works."

"You'd let them prick you?"

"I'd try my medicines first."

"What ailments can you cure?"

"Fever, headache, pox, swelling in the muscles, and morsel."

"Morsel?" Mercer said with interest.

"The medicine prevents wounds from festering. You don't have to amputate."

Mercer put a smile on his face. "I'd much like to hear of this medicine. Would you be available to sup at my home this night?"

"Of course," Matt replied. "Name the time."

"I should say in one hour," Mercer answered. "My wife is away this evening."

"I need to let my traveling companions know I'll be gone," Matt said. "I'll be back." He shook Mercer's hand and went to go inform Zeke of his plans.

****

The sidewalks were substantially more crowded than when he'd entered Mercer's building, so Matt found himself having to step out into the street to move around people who had gathered in front of the shops. The people were polite and would step aside and say "good day" as he passed. Matt felt some bounce in his stride, either in anticipation of his meal with Mercer or just because he was getting caught up in the festive nature of the city. He smiled at almost everyone he passed.

The smile remained on his face until about midway through his journey back to Danner's Inn, when two men, one very tall and the other short, stepped out of an alley as Matt passed. They matched his pace almost exactly, and he had the overwhelming feeling that they weren't behind him by chance. His constant premonitions about events and the people he met frustrated him because they were stronger than déjà vu, but too weak to provide certainty. Did these men attract his attention because they were strange looking, or had he actually seen them before in his rapid-fire visions? Just as he had convinced himself they were following, they disappeared.

****

Matt found Zeke and his men sitting inside the tavern at the inn. "Good afternoon, Mr. Miller," Zeke said.

"I won't be joining you tonight," Matt announced. "I'm having dinner with Hugh Mercer."

"A curious discussion, to be sure," Zeke said, smiling. "He's recently returned from the war."

"That'll be something to ask about," Matt replied. "I'll be back here to sleep."

"Take care walking about," Zeke cautioned. "We had travelers behind us on the road today. I've no reason to believe they're connected with Jake's indiscretion, but…" He shrugged.

"I'll keep my eyes open." Matt thought again about the two men in the street, trying to remember something from his dreams. Instinct caused him to look around the tavern and scan the faces at the tables and congregated around the bar. He had the sensation that a man had been staring at him, or would in the future. Turmoil took over in his head as he tried to sort it out, and he had to force himself back to reality. "Good evening, gentlemen." He bowed slightly and left.

Matt walked around to the back of the inn to check on Thunder and then inspected the wagons now guarded by Zeke's brother and another man. Everything looked in order, but Matt still had to force himself to turn and walk away. It was a bad feeling. The contents of his pack felt too important. The fear of everything disappearing paralyzed him. He looked around and got the feeling again that someone was watching. *This damn money's making me crazy!*

Matt had a small fortune in his bag, about five years' salary for a colonial man. He'd been stunned at the price he got for the gold class ring he had carried with him from the twenty-first century. But now that he was on the road, the money made him nervous. Matt wondered if other people who had come into large amounts of money unexpectedly experienced similar feelings. He'd heard stories of lottery winners declaring that they were happier before they'd won. More than a few ended up with less money and fewer friends than when they'd started.

Matt's steps became lighter the farther he got from the corral and the money, and he started looking forward to asking Major Mercer about the French and Indian War. He wanted to ask about his experiences as a physician and especially treating war wounds. He expected that Mercer would have a considerable interest in penicillin, since many soldiers died of infection from initially nonfatal wounds. Preventing infection using an antibiotic like penicillin would give war injuries a chance to heal without amputation.

The front door to Mercer's store was locked when he arrived, so Matt walked around to the back. He could smell meat cooking as he moved through an alley between a thick white fence and Mercer's building. He came upon a large garden in the back of the house where a grey-haired woman wearing an apron over a faded, off-white country dress trimmed in red was stirring a pot over an outside fireplace.

The woman looked up from her pot and spoke to him through smile lines. "Good evening, handsome," she said in a thick Scottish accent. "Might you be Mr. Miller?"

Matt smiled. "I am. I've come to sup with Mr. Mercer."

"The other side of the house, then," she replied, pointing. "Supper will be served shortly."

Matt looked over to where she had pointed but saw only where the lawn wrapped around the house. He had to walk a little further to see Mercer sitting at a wooden picnic table. He was staring off into the distance, smoking a cigar. He stood as Matt approached.

"Mr. Miller," Mercer said. He reached out and shook Matt's hand.

"I'm happy that Zeke suggested we meet."

"I don't believe I know this Zeke," Mercer replied.

"Two brothers, Ezekiel and Robert Wilkins," Matt explained. "They take the post up and down the coast."

A bell seemed to go off in Mercer's head. "Man came in here with a broken arm." He took another puff. "Cigar?"

"Sure," Matt said, accepting one. "I don't know the first thing about them, though."

Mercer spent the next couple of minutes explaining the finer points of cigar smoking. It struck Matt as ironic that Mercer took the same approach Matt had when teaching Jonathan and Jeb Taylor how to use a toothbrush, but the two skills were on the opposite ends of the spectrum when it came to oral hygiene. "'Tis the best leaf in Virginia," Mercer said when Matt was finally able to light his cigar.

Matt nodded, taking a mouthful of smoke. He'd smoked cigars on two occasions with friends in college but had never been serious about it. Too much grief went with smoking. Someone was always standing around doing an exaggerated waving motion to keep from getting cancer from secondhand smoke. One thing Matt did know for sure as a scientist was that the chronic use of tobacco was the worst thing you could do to your body.

"This tastes good," Matt said. Despite all its negatives, smoking had social benefits that he wanted to take advantage of this evening. Just this once, he'd live dangerously and smoke a cigar with a colonial man before dinner.

"So you're starting an apothecary?" Mercer said.

"That's the plan."

"Why Philadelphia? You could do this anywhere."

"Philadelphia is my hometown and I couldn't stay in Richmond."

"Some father chased you away with a musket?" Mercer said with a sly smile.

"Why does everyone in Virginia assume the worst?"

"Because your story is not a simple one," Mercer declared.

"I've fallen in love with a Richmond woman," Matt explained. "I don't have the means to support her, so I need to go away and make my fortune."

"There *is* a lady involved," Mercer said. "Now your story becomes interesting."

Matt was quiet for a moment as he wondered how much he should say, and then the words came out of his mouth. "Her family found me under a bridge. I don't remember how I got to Virginia." He was trying to keep as close to the truth as possible.

Mercer gave him a satisfied smile. "Tell me more about this young lady. I admit to some trouble understanding my own bride."

"Someone in Virginia asking my advice," Matt said. "That would be a change."

Mercer gave Matt a knowing grin. "Virginians expect to lead. 'Tis at once irritating and attractive. Why else should you cross the colonies only to return?"

"She's a beautiful woman."

"From a strong and proud family?"

"Yes," Matt said, resigned.

"She...they...her church, her city, and her friends. The Old Dominion runs deep."

"Maybe." Matt hadn't thought about it until now. He'd been through Virginia in his own time but had never appreciated that the state had been at the heart of both the American Revolution and the Civil War.

"When the trouble starts, as I imagine it will," said Mercer, "'twill be because of an insult to Virginia."

"What trouble?"

"The king and his taxes," Mercer said. "How else will he pay for his wars but with Virginian silver?" Mercer hesitated as if he was trying to read Matt's face. "I'm no fan of the king."

"If I could predict," Matt replied, grinning, "I'd say that the colonies will, someday, break free from England."

It was exactly the right thing to say. Any suspicion Mercer had about Matt's unexplained appearance in Virginia melted away like the candle that lit their conversation. They talked late into the night.

CHAPTER 4.

PREDATORS

The remainder of their journey to Wilmington was uneventful. They slept twice more in camps on the trail and then at inns in Alexandria and Baltimore. Matt decided that he wholly preferred a bed to sleeping under the stars. There were bugs in both situations, but they were worse outside. By the time they reached their final destination, Zeke's men were ready to celebrate. Their job was done and they had a two-day break before they had to shuttle mail back to Richmond.

Zeke and his crew persuaded Matt to spend both nights "relaxing" with them in the tavern. A two-day layover in Wilmington hadn't been in Matt's plans, but it was a good idea. He was grateful not to spend another day in the saddle. His mild hangover notwithstanding, he left Wilmington refreshed and ready for anything Philadelphia could throw his way. He planned to extend his journey over two days so that he would arrive in Philadelphia with plenty of daylight to find food and shelter for himself and his horse.

The road was crowded on the way out of Wilmington. There was a train of four wagons in front of him that was slowly growing larger. The people in the wagons turned to look as he moved closer. He matched their pace for a few miles, and when the road widened, he flicked Thunder with his heels and guided him around the wagon train. He exchanged waves with the drivers as he passed. The road ahead was smooth and clear, so he kicked Thunder up a notch and soon left them far behind. He slowed only to look at the occasional autumn-colored trees peering out from still-green surroundings.

The cool breeze hitting his face as Thunder moved along the road reminded him that he was making good time. He looked up into the sky and his body surged with optimism. There was no hurdle he couldn't overcome. He would take Philadelphia by storm. His grin was still on his face when he came out into a clearing where the Delaware River Valley opened up across the horizon and the water glistened in the morning sun. The road dropped off sharply to his right, and he was conscious of keeping the horse from wandering too close to the precipice. Thunder began to act nervous as they trotted along the narrow road.

"Calm down, boy," Matt said. "Not the best place to get jittery." Matt felt some anxiety, too, realizing that he had no idea how to calm the horse other than to pass along this section of road quickly. There was an area ahead where the path moved away from the cliff into the woods. Matt patted Thunder on the neck, hoping to settle him. "Simmer down," he said, but this only seemed to irritate the horse more. "Not much longer until we get to the trees," Matt whispered, more for himself than the animal.

Thunder bucked slightly, slowed, and then stopped altogether. Matt watched some rocks vibrate loose from the horse's shuffling and tumble down over the cliff.

Thunder kept wandering close to the edge, and his agitation made it feel like he could flinch enough to take them both over.

"We'll walk," Matt finally said. He dismounted on the left to keep the animal between himself and the cliff so he could pull Thunder back from the edge. It wasn't a sheer drop to the river, but falling over wouldn't end well for a man or a horse. Matt stepped to the front and pulled Thunder forward by his bridle. Thunder jerked his head upward and nearly dislocated Matt's wrist as he pulled the reins from his hands. "Cut it out!" Matt said, grimacing in pain.

Matt tried to remember back when he'd ridden the James River Valley with Grace. They'd been high on the ridge overlooking the river, and Thunder hadn't been scared of heights or of the water. Matt tugged again on Thunder's bridle and managed to convince him to move forward. They'd gone about twenty more yards when Thunder stopped abruptly in his tracks and bucked his feet into the air.

"It's easier to go forward than it is to go back, dummy," Matt said, looking behind the horse. He tugged hard again on the reins, yanking him forward. The horse reluctantly walked another ten yards. "Almost there," Matt said, trying to reassure Thunder as he tugged downward to keep the animal's front legs from leaving the ground.

Matt looked over his shoulder, resolving to pull Thunder the remaining twenty-five yards. The horse bucked and Matt repeated his motion to the ground. Thunder stopped and yanked Matt backward. He bucked again, whinnied loudly, hissed, and snorted. His feet left the road as he stared over Matt's shoulder. He whinnied again as he kicked into the air. Matt saw the reflection of movement in the horse's eyes too late. He turned to catch a glimpse of one man's face as another swung a club silently into his head. Matt recognized the face from the pub in Wilmington. Matt collapsed onto the ground next to his hat and his world went black.

He started moving through the time tunnel of his visions. Pictures surrounded him, moving faster than he had ever seen, and then abruptly, they were gone, replaced by nothing but white. Matt would remember this moment many times over the course of his life, knowing that he'd experienced death. He came very close to letting his life end as he lay there, comfortable and warm.

"What happened?" he asked into the white light.

His own voice answered. "Someone tried to kill you."

"Can I stay?"

"You would let your life go so easily?" the light asked.

"Life is so damn hard," Matt answered.

"A life worth living is always hard," the light said.

"Too hard," Matt declared.

There was hysterical laughter from the light. "You would squander it all after being given so much?"

"Nothing was ever given," Matt said coldly.

"Breathe," the light said.

"What?"

"Breathe, if you dare!"

Matt felt the breath enter his body, and his inner vision was gone. It was replaced by an intense pain in his head. *I knew this was a mistake.*

"You idiot," he heard a man with a very deep voice say. "Mr. Payne said don't kill 'im."

"Didn't swing that hard," another replied. "It's his own fault."

Someone kicked Matt in the side. "Wake up!" a man said.

Matt opened his eyes and hissed in pain.

"Stow it," Deep Voice said.

Matt heard Thunder neigh loudly, then snort, and then came the sound of struggling.

"Shut him up," Deep Voice said toward the man holding the horse. "We're supposed to kill the animal." Matt heard struggling again and then blowing sounds from the horse like loud bellows.

"Ain't gonna kill 'im," another said. "Prancer like this—I could get twenty pounds."

Matt looked up at the man hovering over him and whispered through his teeth, "You hurt my horse, you're dead. I swear—" The man kicked him hard in the side. Matt's breath left him again and he had to focus on filling his lungs with air.

"We should kill *you*," the man said.

Matt heard Thunder whinny and snort. There was struggling again, then another high-pitched whine and more snorting.

"Saddlebags are full," one man said.

"We split it when we get back to camp," was the reply.

My money! Matt thought briefly of how David Taylor, Grace's uncle, had tried to convince him that his success shouldn't depend on the money in his bag. Lying on the ground, unable to move, Matt laughed aloud. David's experiment was about to become reality.

"What're you laughing at?" the man said, looking down at Matt.

"This animal won't shut up," another whispered loudly. "Them Quakers gonna hear this racket." The horse responded by rearing on his hind feet and screaming.

"Hold him," Deep Voice said. "How hard can it be?"

"This horse is off the hooks," another said.

"We quit the road," Deep Voice instructed, "and circle 'round them Quakers." He looked down at Matt. "Dump him over the side. Fall will kill 'im and look like an accident." Deep Voice gave a clever smile to his partners and said, "We kin divide the swag first chance we git." Matt tried to sit up, but Deep Voice kicked him again. "You think you're gettin' up?" he taunted. Matt became aware of the two other men moving close and then felt them grab him. He struggled as they pulled him to the side of the road. One punched him, and immobilizing pain shot through his head again.

"Levi Payne says good day," Deep Voice whispered in his ear. "He don't take kindly to people interfering with his trade. You hear?"

Levi Payne?

"I said, you hear?" He smacked Matt's face.

"I hear," Matt gasped.

****

Matt was in free fall as they threw him over the cliff. The drop should have killed him, but he landed in a thick clump of trees that had been growing unseen from the road. The vegetation broke his fall, supporting him briefly, and then he tumbled like a rag doll down onto the riverbed, hidden from the road.

CHAPTER 5.

SCOUT, PART I

Scout had watched people come and go on the farm ever since he was a puppy. He'd grown used to the strange men who would gather from time to time, and it became a game to dodge them as they went about their activities. He'd growl when they came too close, even at the ones he knew weren't a danger. The Taylors were his pack, and the strangers had to learn quickly that it was unacceptable to threaten the pack.

As he watched them carry the young man into the barn, the place where he slept every night, Scout immediately sensed that something was different. The man didn't smell like anything Scout could recognize. It was as if he didn't belong to anyone's pack, anywhere. The young man had no recognizable scent, and the only way Scout could tell he was a man was by seeing him with his eyes. The young man was almost transparent, like he'd appeared from a stream of water or from nowhere at all.

They'd treated him differently right from the start, and Scout knew that it must be because they couldn't tell from his scent whether he was good or bad. Unlike other strangers on the farm, the Taylors accepted the young man almost immediately, especially Grace, the young woman. Scout had watched her, too, since he was a puppy. She spent almost all of her time with the horses, undistracted by the men they brought to the farm to be her mate. Those men had smelled of desire and fear.

When this new young man arrived, Grace acted differently, stopping often to watch him as he walked about the farm. When she talked to the young man, Scout could hear the strain in her voice. It was like the voice she used when she chased him out of the barn, but different in some way the dog didn't understand. It was confusing when Grace spoke to the young man. Her voice sounded angry, but she didn't smell angry. She smelled like when she spent time with her favorite horse, the speckled one she curried and brushed every day. She smelled of hunger and attraction when she was around the young man. He smelled of nothing that the dog could recognize. The man's scent was colored grey.

Scout's sensitive nose allowed him to swim in the smells that surrounded him, and they gave him a more complex picture of his environment than could ever be obtained by sight. As a puppy, he knew every one of the animals and humans on the farm by scent. As he got older, he learned to build a detailed picture of their movements and moods by the multilayered smells that intermingled through the barns and fields. His nose told him when they were scared, or angry, or when they were sick. When someone cut himself on a fence or a stone, he knew exactly where the blood flowed. This young man was a mystery, though, because nothing about his scent was familiar. His was like clear paint on the vast canvas of brilliant, colorful smells that made up Scout's universe.

Why had they accepted him, then? Were they as confused as he about how to treat this stranger? Scout had growled at him those first days on the farm, like a child scared of the shadows the moon created. He didn't know how to treat a shadow that looked like a man. But, as the young man spent more time with the family, Scout began to recognize his scent, and then he didn't seem so strange. The young man named Matthew was becoming part of the pack and they began to feel safe around him—except the young woman, who still had smells of stress and arousal. Scout wasn't surprised when they paired off as mates.

Scout stood next to Grace on the day that Matthew left on Thunder. He was struck by the saltiness of the tears in Grace's eyes and could smell her sadness. This confused him, because tears in Grace's eyes usually came when she smelled of anger. Scout thought nothing of it when Matthew and Thunder rode away. Members of his pack often came and went, and this was no different. Scout had been a puppy the spring Thunder was born and they'd played almost every day since then. The dog stood by Grace when Matthew left. She didn't shoo him away as was her habit, so the dog followed his instinct to comfort her until they returned.

Scout had expected them to come back before dark, as they always did when they left early in the morning, but they hadn't. The dog slept in the barn himself that night, waking often to listen for the young man. At sunrise, Scout squeezed through the small opening in the barn door and sat facing the road, watching, but Matthew and Thunder still didn't return. He waited there each day looking out into the horizon.

Grace would come out in the morning as Scout sat in the road. She would pet him and speak softly, as Matthew had often done. Scout could still feel the grief in her as they both looked into the distance. The dog was over-joyed on the day that Grace called to him to go riding. They repeated this ritual over the week and the dog began to look forward to their rides. He ran alongside her just like when he, Matthew, and Thunder had chased her across the Richmond countryside. Still, though, Scout checked Thunder's stall every morning and the hay barn every night and their emptiness would make him feel sad and alone.

One night he noticed that he could barely smell Matthew in the barn. He walked to the stall and he could only just smell Thunder, who had once been one of the brightest colors on the canvas of his world. Barely any evidence of their existence on the farm remained. He went out that next morning and sat waiting and watching the horizon, like the days before. Then it occurred to him that they were vanishing, and that if they waited any longer, there would be no scent for them to follow to find their way home.

Grace stood on the porch watching Scout that morn-ing. He turned to her once, then decided to run. He'd find Matthew and Thunder and bring them home. He stood up and started down the road, glancing back only once to see her on the porch. She watched with crossed arms until turning to her father, who had come out to join her.

"The dog's gone," she said, nodding to a dust cloud in the horizon.

"He'll be back," her father replied. "He's chasing an ani-mal or something."

"No," she said. "He's been waiting there every morning for Matthew and Thunder to return. He's gone to find them."

"I've seen him sitting there," he replied. "That doesn't mean he left to find them."

"He went to do just that," she said. Her voice was without emotion, and her father remained quiet. He too had watched the dog every morning, wondering if he might leave.

"I pray he'll be fine," her father said simply.

"Me too," she replied.

"What is it about that young man?" he asked, staring at the tiny dust cloud. He wasn't looking for an answer. "Sometimes I think we would've been better to have left him under the bridge." He smiled softly, looking at her and wondering her reaction.

"Me too," she replied, though not as convincingly. "You didn't, and now I pray he returns with his horse and his dog." Her father remained silent. The situation was too complicated for him to pray for anything except guidance and that his daughter would be safe and happy at the end of all that he'd started by lifting the stranger into his wagon.

CHAPTER 6.

RUM QUIDDS

"Told you he'd be quiet," the shorter one, Ephraim, said. "You woulda kilt him. He's mine. I'll get a fine price." He had tied Thunder to a tree with a rope next to their other horses some distance from where they set up camp. Now that they were no longer near, Thunder had stopped straining against the rope. They could see him stooping down regularly to graze on the grass and leaves that surrounded the trunk of the tree.

"We split everything three ways, even the horse," said the man with the deep voice. They called him Samuel, and sometimes Sam.

"You woulda kilt him," Ephraim repeated. "Not me, though, I knew."

The taller one, Myles, spoke up. He towered over the others by almost a foot. "It doesn't matter, Eph," he explained. "We all helped. It's always been three ways."

Ephraim was silent for a while and then said, "Well...fine."

"Three ways," Samuel repeated in his deep voice. "That's how we always do it. Plenty for everyone." They looked down at the saddlebag and the tricorner hat lying at their feet. Samuel reached from his seat on the log and pulled the saddlebag into his lap. "Bag's heavy."

"Three ways," Ephraim emphasized. There was indignation in his voice, and it was evident that he was still bothered by having to share the horse. They were used to Ephraim's tantrums, so ignored him. Samuel unbuckled both sides of the saddlebag as the other two looked on in anticipation. He pulled out the first item.

"Three ways for sure with this one," Samuel exclaimed. He held up the silver flask. The others cheered as he opened it and took a drink.

"Pass that 'round," Myles commanded. "Startin' our celebration early." He grabbed the flask and took a long swig as his companions watched, then howled like a wolf. "Oh, that there's good!"

"Three ways," Ephraim repeated. He reached out for the bottle and took a drink, coughed, and handed it back to Samuel. Each had another pass before Samuel looked again into the saddlebag. The others drank again as he began to pull out the items and set them on the ground. They giggled like children as each item joined the pile. "Them's some queer stampers," Ephraim said, looking at Matt's hiking boots. He took another swig and passed the whiskey to the tall man.

Ephraim and Myles smirked at each other as they watched Sam unpack. Only the two of them now shared the bottle, and each made sure to drink as much as he could every time it passed. Samuel finally looked up, realized his partners were drinking without him, and reached out his hand. "You drank it all, you bastards!"

Ephraim and Myles beamed, then turned serious as they looked back at their partner sitting on the stump. Much of the clothing and gear from the saddlebag was now on the ground. "Aw, hell," Myles exclaimed, "you can take more for your share cuz'a the bottle."

"Damn right," Samuel said in his deep voice. He took a long last swig of the whiskey to finish it off. "What we got here?" he said as he pulled out a small package wrapped in cloth and bound in twine. "'Tis heavy."

"Statue, maybe," Ephraim declared, "or figurine." He was already slurring.

"What the hell's a figurine?" Myles asked.

"You know, like a small statue," Ephraim explained.

Samuel eased the cloth away. To everyone's astonishment, fifteen gold coins dropped onto the ground. "We got the prize, boys! Fifteen joes!"

"Rum quidds, that is," Ephraim slurred happily. He smacked his tall partner on the back.

"Gimme here," Myles said. "I want my five now before they go."

"I want my five and them stampers," Ephraim said, pointing to Matt's boots.

"Hold on," Samuel instructed. "There's more." He looked inside the bag for a moment and then unloaded the rest of the gear on the ground. For emphasis, he shook the saddlebag upside down.

"Any more gold?" Ephraim asked.

Samuel sorted through the items. "No more packages." There was folded clothing, another leather bag, white bottles with labels that had been removed, a small transparent box containing oblong figures stacked in a row, a mess kit, and a few other miscellaneous items that didn't look the least bit interesting to any of them.

"That rascal probably had more gold," Ephraim said. "We should've checked his pockets."

"Them Quakers was almost on us!" Myles exclaimed. He was also now slurring from the whiskey. "We quit the road just in time."

"We should go back and check," Ephraim said.

"Too far," Samuel replied. "I say we go to town, sell the horse, and celebrate!"

"I'm all for that," Myles declared. "I want the eating kit, the hat, and my gold. None of them clothes will fit." He grabbed the items and scooped up five gold coins from the dirt.

Ephraim reached down and picked up the boots and the shoes, some of the clothing, and his five coins. "Having one of them high-borns tonight," he declared.

"We even, then?" Samuel asked. Clothing, bottles, and other items remained on the ground. His partners were distracted with what they'd already taken, and both nodded that he could have what remained. Samuel swept the small items, mostly uninspected, back into the saddlebag. He stuffed the folded clothing in there too and then checked that he had covered the second cloth-wrapped package at the bottom. He had used his hand to keep it in the saddlebag as he pretended to empty its contents on the ground. From the weight, he was sure the package contained more coins. Samuel smiled, thinking of how easy it had been to fool his partners, and he brimmed with excitement over spending the next few days in Wilmington. He'd eat, drink, gamble, and find himself a strumpet to warm his bed.

Samuel buckled the saddlebag, stood, and said, "Let's go, boys. They're waitin' for us in town." He looked toward the horses and set off for the clearing. Myles and Ephraim followed him in a fit of laughter. They were drunk and had nothing on their minds except anticipation of the next few days.

"He's gone!" Samuel exclaimed. His partners stopped laughing as they looked around for the horse. When they got to the trees, Ephraim reached down for the rope that had held Thunder. It was chewed through. He looked around, but the horse was nowhere in sight.

"Can we find 'im?" Ephraim asked.

"Nah," Samuel said. "Could be anywhere." Samuel knew they could track the horse, but he was eager to go into town, find a room, and check the contents of the second package. "Let's forget 'im and go have some fun."

"I'm all for that," Myles repeated. "We were gonna shoot him anyway."

"I reckon," Ephraim said reluctantly. He looked down at the coins in his hand and suddenly cared very little about searching for the horse. "There's a high-born waitin' for me in Wilmington. Got my name on her bosom."

"Let's get moving," Samuel said to his partners, who were now stumbling drunk. It wouldn't take much for their pockets to be emptied once they got into town. He didn't feel guilty about cheating them. They knew nothing about the finer things in life.

CHAPTER 7.

THUNDER

The horse knew there was danger ahead as soon as they passed the wagons. He was genetically programmed to recognize the essence of a predator. He couldn't understand why Matt kept pulling him forward on the edge of the mountain. The sounds and scent that rode on the wind told Thunder there was harm ahead. It was something the horse had sensed a hundred times before from the mountain lions, wolves, and coyotes that lingered around the farm. He'd been helplessly confined in his corral as predators circled, and he was always relieved when the dog arrived to force them back into the trees.

Thunder thought about Scout, who could smell a predator better than a horse and had always protected the farm from marauders. The dog was also better at communicating with humans. If Scout were here, he'd have barked and growled to warn Matt. Thunder had tried his best, but the young man hadn't listened. He didn't understand a horse kicking and snorting like he understood a dog's barking.

The predators hadn't taken him far enough away to forget where they threw Matt over the cliff. Thunder looked back at where they were before the predators tied him to a tree. It hadn't been hard to chew through their rope. Now that he was safe, Thunder put his nose into the wind and smelled where they'd already been. He'd find Matt and bring him home to his herd. Thunder forced his nose higher as he trotted along the road, then looked around, trying to remember if he had passed this way.

It was hard to recognize the scents as the wind blew stronger, and at one point Thunder lost his way entirely. He stopped, grazed on tall grass, drank from a cold spring, and nearly forgot about Matt. But another air current brought a hint of recognition and he was reminded of where he should go. Even the sounds of his hooves hitting the road were familiar, and so his excitement increased. This was the place where they passed the wagons and then where the road overlooked the river. It was where he'd first known there were predators waiting. *The predators of men are other men.*

The horse left the road over the embankment and stutter-stepped down the face of a steep hill. One time he lost his footing and almost tumbled face-first into the ravine, but he knew to compensate by shifting his weight to his back legs. He righted himself and continued down to the riverbed. The water had receded during the hot summer, so it was easy to walk along the gravel. Matt's scent was strong now, and Thunder saw him ahead, lying with his face on the ground. The predators hadn't finished their job. He was still alive. Thunder wondered briefly if Matt would turn into a predator if he met those humans again. The horse had seen this before when men would fight. Both would act like killers and be covered in blood.

Matt had one eye open as Thunder approached, but then the horse saw it slowly shut. Matt moaned and then was silent as he returned his face to the ground. Thunder could hear his breathing coming in fits and starts. The horse stooped down and nudged him gently in the side using his nose. There was no reaction. He nudged Matt again, hard enough to lift his body up off the ground. The young man's breathing pattern changed with the nudge and Thunder heard him mumble, but he went quiet again.

Frustrated, Thunder shook his head back and forth in a wide motion and snorted. He trotted away for ten yards and whinnied loudly. He heard Matt sigh and then go silent. Thunder snorted again and clicked his hooves on the gravel, hoping to stir him, but it had no effect. He thought of Scout and how he might attract a man's attention. He remembered the dog nipping at the horses' legs when he wanted to get them moving. Thunder walked to Matt, stooped down, worked his way under his coat, put his hindquarters in his mouth, and closed his jaw.

"Ouch, damn you!" Matt yelled. "I'm awake."

Thunder stepped back and whinnied. Matt picked his head up off the ground to look at the horse. He had thought Thunder was a hallucination. There was a searing pain in his head and his vision was blurred. Matt reached his hand up to his mouth to feel his teeth and was glad to find them all still there. A painful smile filled his face as he wondered how he'd react the day when he found some missing. He moved his hand to the pain in his head and felt a large, tender lump; they'd hit him hard. He checked his hand, but there was no blood.

"Glad to see you," Matt said. He strained to smile again through the pain in his skull. He was fighting to stay conscious. "I thought horses only came back...in the movies."

Thunder shook his head in approval and let out his customary "Thpfft." Matt could see the frayed rope around the horse's neck.

"You got away," Matt said, grimacing as he pulled himself to his hands and knees. His head pounded harder. The horse walked forward and affectionately nudged Matt with his nose. Matt lost his balance and went over on his side. "Hold on, you crazy animal," Matt said through unbearable pain. "I'm glad to see you too, but you gotta let me get up!"

Matt grabbed hold of Thunder's saddle and pulled himself to his feet, then slowly got one leg up into a stirrup as the horse leaned low beside him. It took some time, but eventually he was straddling the horse. Matt said a prayer for the strength to stay in the saddle. He was slipping away and worried he wouldn't be able to hang on. The pain was so great that he began to wonder why he'd gotten off the comfortable ground in the first place and the desire to slip back down to the dirt was almost overwhelming.

With Matt on his back, Thunder slowly rose to full height and turned to walk along the dry edge of the river. He went past where he'd come down the embankment and glanced up for some easy path to the road so he could return the man to his herd. It was too steep, so he continued to follow the riverbed. Thunder could feel Matt tugging at his mane to keep from falling and so he tried his best to walk smoothly.

The horse wandered for more than an hour along the river, losing sight of the road they'd used when they met the predators, hoping to find a path that would lead to the man's herd. The predators came to mind and Thunder worried briefly that he might be taking Matt back to them. He put his nose in the air and smelled. These were different smells than where they had tied him. *What's that?* Other horses were nearby. *A mare!*

Thunder forgot entirely about the man on his back as he followed the scent of the horses. He looked ahead and saw a road that nearly touched the river. He stepped onto it to follow the scent that was growing stronger. The mare almost took his thoughts completely, but he remembered the man again and forced himself to walk gently.

As he rounded the bend, a farm came into view. It looked a lot like his home, where Scout lived and where he met Matt. He had liked it when Matt scratched his head and brought him apples. He'd take him back to his herd, and then he'd find the other horses. Her scent was so strong! Thunder walked through the front gate of the farm and felt the man shift and wake again. He walked with Matt slumped over on his back, past the barns, past the men working on the farm as they stared, and then to the front of a large white farmhouse.

Stooping down, Thunder let Matt fall gently to the ground and heard him groan. The horse stepped back, put his head in the air and whinnied loudly. Men all around the farm stopped working to look toward the sound. The farmhouse door opened, and a sturdy and confident middle-aged woman stepped out onto the porch. She looked down at the man in their courtyard and the large chestnut-brown thoroughbred standing behind him snorting protectively. She turned around and put her head into the doorway.

"John, you better get out here," she said. Her voice was calm, but loud. "The Lord has sent us a surprise."

CHAPTER 8.

JONATHAN BOYD

"I'm alive," Matt said to the roof of the barn. Sunlight was streaming in through the open windows. He pulled himself up to a sitting position and his head exploded in pain. He reached up to feel the lump and then looked at his hand. There was still no blood. He recalled riding into the farm though a gate and looking up to see a sign that said "Boyd Farm."

Where's my horse?

Matt remembered falling to the ground, and then not much else. He looked around the barn and felt a certain comfort at being on a farm again, though building a tolerance for waking up in unfamiliar farm buildings was probably not something to brag about. He reached around to take stock of his possessions. In his experience, farmers had a nasty habit of confiscating weapons before they let people sleep in their barns. The Walther was still at his side, but his knife was gone.

"You're awake," a man said, standing at the barn door. Matt stared up and squinted, trying to see his face.

"Thanks for getting me off the ground," Matt replied.

The farmer laughed. "We had to do something. That horse of yours raised a stink."

"Where'd he go?"

"Outside in the corral, pacing. Got wind of my mare again."

Matt moved himself slowly off the bench. He was dizzy and felt like a dagger was being driven through his head. He almost fell and had to steady himself. The farmer saw this and walked toward him. Matt tried to stand confidently as he approached and reached his hand out to shake.

"I'm Matt Miller," he said.

"John Boyd. What happened?"

"Someone hit me with a club on the road. They threw me over a cliff, took my horse and all my stuff. My horse came back for me and I found myself here."

"I thought horses only did that in the storybooks."

Matt agreed with a painful smile. "He saved my life."

"Stay afoot with a head wound," Boyd said. "Can you go see if you can calm your horse? Come over to the house after, and my Maggie will bring you victuals." They heard Thunder whinny loudly. "Is he always this loud?"

"Something's got him excited. He raised a stink before I got robbed, too."

"It's the wrong time, but my mare's in season. I've a proposition when we sit." Boyd turned to leave and Matt followed him slowly out the door. The sun was still low in the sky, and it was cool, so the grey wood of the farm building was still dark with dew. Fresh smells of morning surrounded them. Matt pulled his jacket sleeve up and was relieved to see that his watch was still on his wrist. *Half past seven.*

Matt walked by a pigpen with a trough that was surrounded by snorting pigs and then to another fenced pasture that bordered a grey barn. The barn had a few wagons stored inside, along with plows, shovels, and steel tools. Matt could just see the hay stacked against its back wall. Thunder stood waiting for him at the edge of the pasture as he approached. Matt reached up with both hands to take his head and scratch the animal vigorously.

"Man, am I glad to see you. I'll be back. These look like good people." Thunder was glancing occasionally at the lone mare over in the other corral. "You may meet her soon." He patted the horse's head one last time.

Boyd was already at the table when Matt reached the house. There were fresh vegetables, warm chunks of stewed beef, and bread. Matt sat down and Boyd pushed a plate in front of him.

"Suppose you need a stud for that mare," Matt said.

"How much?" Boyd asked.

"Just your help. Maybe a day or so here to recover."

"I don't expect payment for helping a man in need," Boyd said. "I'd pay a fair price."

"I'm going to find the men who did this to me and get my things back. My money, my clothes, everything I owned was in the saddlebag they stole."

"I'll not take part in retribution."

"Not retribution," Matt replied. "I want my stuff back. There was a lot of money in that bag. I can't imagine those men went very far before stopping to spend it."

"There'll be more money."

"They stole medicine, too. I could help a lot of people with what was in that bag." They heard Thunder whinny loudly from the corral. "Let him in with the mare," Matt said. "Your hospitality's enough. He has good genes."

"Genes?"

"Breeding." Matt got up and Boyd followed. As they neared the corral, Matt called for Thunder, and he came trotting over. "We have someone for you to meet," Matt said. He led him over to the gate that Boyd was unlatching. "Do the deal," Matt said as he smacked him on the rump. The horse bounded into the corral and slowed as he walked toward the mare. Boyd waved one of his sons over, took him aside, and talked to him briefly.

"Henry will ensure neither is hurt," Boyd said. "Shouldn't take too long." He motioned and Matt followed him back to the table. "Give me a price. I don't want that foal tainted."

"Get me back on my horse tomorrow with supplies," Matt said. "It should take them a few days to spend two hundred pounds."

"You were traveling alone with two hundred pounds?"

"Trying to get to Philadelphia," Matt replied. "I had an escort from Richmond to Wilmington. The men who robbed me followed us from Richmond. They were hired by a competitor of the farm of my betrothed." It was a white lie; he hadn't even gotten permission to court Grace yet, let alone marry her.

"They did this because you worked on another farm?" Boyd looked doubtful.

"Long story."

"Harvest is over," Boyd said. "We have time."

Matt told Boyd as much of his story as he could while the man listened intently.

When Matt was finished, Boyd said, "The contents of that bag will bring the prosperity you require to ask her father?"

"Sounds outrageous, I know."

"I'll have your word that you'll do no harm to those men."

"I'm only interested in my saddlebag."

"Tomorrow, then," Boyd said. He looked over Matt's shoulder. "Here's my Maggie."

Matt turned to the woman who had been the first to see him when Thunder dropped him in front of her house. She was in a blue-and-white farm dress, walking purposefully toward them. Her dark hair, peppered with grey, was pulled back in a loose bun and framed a face that was just starting to smile. Matt stood up and introduced himself.

"I'm Margaret Boyd," she said. "Feeling better?"

"Very well," Matt lied. His head felt like it was being squeezed in a vise. "Thanks for taking me in."

"That animal of yours wouldn't stop his racket," she replied. "He had everyone on the farm coming to see."

"He's a keeper," Matt said. A twinge of worry went through his body. He wondered how he would care for the horse with the few coins that were left in his pocket.

"We'll eat around three," she said. "Rest in the shade until then."

Matt looked to John Boyd, who was still sitting. "If it's all the same," Matt replied, "I wouldn't mind doing some work here on the farm. It will help clear my head."

"Know anything about fences?" Boyd asked.

"Built one last week," Matt replied.

"You can help my boys out in the west pasture," the man said. "Won't pay much."

"Just get me back on the road tomorrow."

CHAPTER 9.

SCOUT, PART II

Scout ran as fast as he was able until he recognized the streets of Richmond. The dog had been there many times riding on the wagons his family took to the city. He could no longer smell Matthew, but Thunder's scent was still on the ground. Other smells were brighter, and he lost the horse's scent at almost every turn, but then he'd catch it again and continue. He trotted through Richmond, dodging pedestrians. Horses passed, confusing him with their strong odor. Then he came to a bench that smelled of both Matthew and the Taylor son, Will. Scout loved the Taylor son, who had always taken care of him. He followed his scent across the street to a building.

"Scout," he heard, and then a door opened and Will was calling to him. "Scout, what're you doing here?"

Scout looked around. He'd moved farther away from the horse's scent now and knew that if he went to Will, he'd try to take him inside. He looked at the brother briefly, to acknowledge him as a member of his pack, and then he turned to run again.

"Where're you going?" Will called out, but Scout didn't look back.

****

The trail of the horse and man was weak inside the city, but as Scout neared its edge, it became stronger, and this was enough to keep him on his path. It led him to creeks and watering holes that Matthew and Thunder had visited. The dog stepped from tree to tree trying to interpret their scent. He got nothing from the layers besides the fact that they'd been there, and so he turned and moved on, hoping to find more detail in another resting place.

Scout lost them briefly in the next city. The town was filled with many colors stacked heavily on top of each other, and he became confused. He could no longer be sure if the aura was from either the horse or the man. Lost in the city, with no direction to travel, he crawled under a house and slept. When the sun rose the next morning, he sniffed the air and the faint trail was there again. He followed it outside the city and it became strong. He grew excited and moved faster. Scout got hungry on that second day and caught a rabbit. He ate almost all of it and napped in a small cave out of the sun. He was soon on the road again, following their trail. After a while, their path was obvious to the dog. They'd taken the road north.

Many travelers were on the road, and the dog did his best to avoid them. Scout would follow the scent into cities when necessary but would usually use the bustle and confusion during the day to sleep. It was easy to crawl under a house until the sun went down and he could track them without being blocked by people, horses, and wagons. He avoided humans when possible, except when he came across a butcher. He smelled the fresh meat inside and saw the man peering through his window.

"Shoo," the man said, leaning out his door. "Go away, you dumb dog."

Scout sat on his hind legs. He got impatient and barked.

"Now he's barking," a young girl said.

"He's a stray," the butcher replied. "Ignore him and he'll go away."

Scout barked again. The girl came out into the yard in front of the butcher shop.

"I think he's hungry," she said. "He has a collar."

"Leave him be," said the butcher.

Scout raised his paw to the girl.

"Father," she said, "he wants to shake."

"Stay away," he called from inside. "He looks dangerous."

She walked up to the dog with no fear and took his paw gently in her hand. Scout pulled his foot away, barked softly, and lay on his side, pawing at the ground. He said, "Yawrrr," as he opened his mouth wide.

She giggled. "He's very pleasant, Father," she called. "Can we feed him?"

"He'll never quit the yard then," her father yelled from the window.

"He's hungry," she pleaded.

Scout spent the next two hours filling himself with all manner of scraps from the butcher. He slept there that night in the shadow of the moon, against the porch. The young girl watched him from her bedroom window, hoping he'd still be there when she woke up. She was sleeping when he wandered away.

Scout was puzzled how to proceed when he came to a dock next to a river. He walked out onto the sturdy wooden platform that reached some distance into the water and stood there. Thunder's scent was strong here at the edge of the dock. Scout looked down, wondering whether he should jump into the water, but he could barely see the other shore, and his instinct kept him from making the plunge. He retreated from the platform and paced back and forth along the river's edge, trying to find the scent again, but there was nothing to indicate that they'd traveled anywhere other than onto the dock. Scout sat there for a long time, watching the moonlight ripple across the water and wondering what to do. Tired and muddled, with no idea how to get across, he crawled into some bushes to rest until daybreak.

✱✱✱✱✱✱✱✱✱

Sunrise and the noise of men came simultaneously. The dog peeked his head above the grass where he was sleeping to see a ferry pressed against the dock. Men, horses, and wagons moved off the ferry as other wagons arrived to wait in line. Scout stepped out of his hiding place to see if Matt and Thunder were among these men, but he could neither see nor smell them. He followed one of the wagons onto the floating platform, trying to hide from the man directing the vehicle onto the boat.

"That your dog?" the man said to the driver of the last wagon.

"Not mine," the driver replied.

"Whose dog?" the ferryman yelled to the people waiting. When he got no answer, he waved an oar in Scout's face and forced him back onto the dock with the waiting wagons. The ferryman pulled the gate up and gave the order for his men to begin moving the large barge to the other side of the river. Scout sat there dejected as the ferry moved slowly away from shore.

CHAPTER 10.

DIRECTION

Matt spent the rest of the day building a fence with three teenage sons of John Boyd. Matt had learned the finer points of fence building two weeks earlier from the Taylors, so he had no problem doing his share of the labor and even instructing the teens on a few occasions. He tried his best to keep a smile on his face, despite his screaming headache. Their mother, Margaret, brought lunch out to the pasture for them, and Matt sat eating with the boys. They talked mostly about girls while Matt listened. It was an entertaining topic that took away some of the pain in his head.

When they had finished for the day, they stopped at the well to wash up for dinner. Matt had to smooth the hair away from his face as he washed; it was long enough now that he could put it in a ponytail. Supper was served on a picnic table behind the farmhouse under large shade trees that separated them from most of the other barns and livestock pens. Matt sat with Margaret and John Boyd, their five sons, the wife of one of the sons, and five hired men.

Matt received no attention at first, and he thought that he might be able to leave the meal without having to explain himself. But he couldn't escape the curiosity of Paul Boyd, twelve, who was the first to inquire.

"What happened to you and your horse, Mr. Miller?"

"I got attacked on the road and my horse was stolen," Matt replied.

"By who?" It was one of the older boys named Adam.

"By people sent to rob me," Matt said. "I insulted a man in Richmond...I was stupid."

"He sent someone to rob you?" the oldest of the hired men asked. He had a critical look in his eye and stroked his full beard as he waited for Matt to answer.

"Yes," Matt replied to the table. "It goes to show you, be careful who you insult."

"What was the insult?" asked Paul.

"He was the town ruffian," Matt replied. "I confronted and teased him. I should have left well enough alone."

"Jason said you *must* confront them or they return again," Paul said. Matt looked over at John Boyd, expecting him to react to his son's statement, but the older man's face remained blank.

Matt nodded. "I never would have guessed the time men are willing to spend on revenge."

"Some are off the hooks." It was Jason, the oldest Boyd son, who was married. "You must hit them before they can understand."

"This isn't our way," his father scolded.

"Still, Father," Jason replied. "There is some chasm between what we say and what we do." The father's silence seemed very much like an acknowledgment.

"Did you know the men who attacked you?" Jason's wife asked, concerned. Georgia was pretty, with dark red hair, and almost too young in Matt's eyes to be married already.

"No," Matt replied. "I'd seen one of them in a pub in Wilmington. One was short, one very tall, and I remember the third like he was right in front of me. He had a blue coat and an old brown leather tricorner, and he spoke in a very deep voice."

"We saw these men!" Charles Boyd exclaimed, looking at Jason. "On the road—they were belligerent and smelled of spirits as they passed."

"Enough!" their father cautioned.

"Which way were they heading?" Matt asked excitedly.

"Mr. Miller!" John Boyd warned.

"I apologize," Matt said. There was an awkward silence until Simon Boyd, the second-youngest son, asked Matt, "What did you do in Richmond?"

"I worked on a horse farm," Matt said. "I helped bring in the hay, tobacco, and corn. I'm an expert at stacking bales."

"Ugh!" Paul said. "I despise the corn."

"Ha!" Matt said. "But do you realize that corn represents the affairs of men?" He was trying to channel the enthusiasm of Thomas Taylor when he'd first explained his theory to Matt as they'd sat around the dinner table on the Taylor farm.

"How so?" John Boyd asked, intrigued.

"Let me tell you!" Matt exclaimed. He put his thumb and forefinger to his chin like he had seen his chemistry professor do whenever he was making a thoughtful explanation. He then went on to introduce Thomas Taylor's whole theory on how growing corn was a metaphor for a man's life and goals.

When Matt was done, Jacob said, "I imagine it could be any crop, though, right?"

"I like to save it for the corn," Matt answered. "There isn't much else redeeming about being in a cornfield." The table broke out in laughter.

✶✶✶✶✶✶✶✶✶✶

After dinner, everyone went to perform evening chores. Matt borrowed a few brushes and went to clean the mud from Thunder's coat. The horse had finished with the mare and was back in his own corral.

"Looks like you got dirty," Matt said to the animal as he decided between the brushes in his hands. The horse turned to the sound of his voice and nudged him with his head. "I didn't mean it like that, you scoundrel," Matt joked. "We're back on the road again tomorrow."

Matt worked a brush through Thunder's coat a few more times before his concern about finances compelled him to pull his remaining money from his pocket: two joes and ten shillings. He probably had enough to forget about the men, avoid trouble, and make his way to Philadelphia. He looked up at the sky.

"Well?" Matt said. "What should I do?"

"Sorry to interrupt your prayer." Matt turned around to see Jason.

"I never get any answers anyway," Matt said.

"I'm no expert, but I don't think it works like that."

"Couldn't it just once?" Matt said to himself.

"Those bravos were on the road yesterday," Jason announced.

"That's what you said," Matt answered. He wanted to shout at the man to tell him more.

"Were they drunk when they robbed you?"

"I don't think so. They probably drank the whiskey in my bag."

"Do you oft carry whiskey?" Jason asked. He seemed disappointed.

"It was a gift from a friend in Richmond. He gave me orders to share it only with important men."

"I imagine those three didn't qualify, then?" Jason said, laughing. He spoke quietly. "My father cannot know what I will confess."

"Your secret's safe with me," Matt replied.

"You kill them, you'll get the noose," he warned.

"Do I look like a killer?" Matt found Jason's noncommittal shrug a little disappointing.

"They were headed into Wilmington." Jason acted like he was going to say something more, but then went silent.

"What else?"

"I heard something about the Treasure Chest."

"My bag was the treasure chest," Matt replied. "There was a lot of money."

"No. There's a pub by the dock that caters to sailors...strangers...visitors. They have gambling and ladies. It's called the Treasure Chest. That's where I'd look."

Matt raised his eyebrows. "Thanks."

"May God be with you, Mr. Miller," Jacob said, then turned and walked away, not looking back.

"Now we have a plan," Matt said to Thunder. He returned to using the brush to sweep the caked mud from the horse's coat.

CHAPTER 11.

SAMUEL, PART I

Samuel lost track of his gang when he returned to Wilmington. When they first arrived, they headed to the river to rent the best rooms they could find. His partners shared while he took one for himself, telling them he needed his own room because they had gross habits and smelled, but the real reason was that he wanted to count the extra money he'd hidden in the saddlebag. After stashing their things, all three went to the first pub they saw and gorged themselves on food and drink. They stumbled home together, too drunk even for whores. Their first day in town ended in a stupor.

The second day was similar. They spent it drinking in a tavern down at the waterfront, then branched out into buying almost every whore they encountered from the brothels that lined the Delaware River. Watching his partners carry on with every manner of toothless trollop at the dock disgusted Samuel, so when his companions came by for him on the third day, he decided not to go. He couldn't look at one more drunken old cat. They went without him, and he took the opportunity to flash some of his gold in the Treasure Chest.

When he returned to his room that night, his companions were missing, and he hadn't seen them since. Samuel was sure they'd find him once their money was gone; they always did. Even though they ran with the same people in Virginia, Myles and Ephraim never seemed to be able to find jobs on their own. *The boys always come back to Sam.* He was starting to miss their company, though, so Samuel decided if they did return with empty pockets, he'd loan them as much as they wanted.

Missing his boys was not enough to weaken Samuel's satisfied grin. He was content in the thought that he had enough gold to enjoy everything he desired and a little more besides. He was on a streak of luck that didn't seem possible. His trumps had started when they'd floored that swell and found all the money in his saddlebag, and now it was all he'd won at the card tables last night. The ride from Richmond was long and hard, but it had paid off. They'd followed the wagons from town to town, waiting for an opportunity to get that bugger alone. There was a moment in Fredericksburg when he was walking through the streets, but there were too many people around. Samuel and his boys had resigned themselves to riding all the way to Philadelphia and grabbing him there.

Samuel didn't know Levi Payne personally, but he felt some kinship toward the man who had hired him to hurt and rob Matthew Miller. Miller was the type of man Samuel had despised all his life: a nib walking around like he was better than everyone else. They'd watched Miller closely in Wilmington the night before they clubbed him. The men that bugger traveled with had spent time during that day unloading their wagons. There were fewer of them around after that, and Samuel knew somehow that they wouldn't be continuing with him on his journey.

Samuel smiled, thinking about how he'd played with Miller the night before. In the pub, that rascal had looked back, bewildered, when Samuel raised his glass in a toast. Samuel saw how uncomfortable Miller was to return the gesture and then how quickly he resumed smiling at his friends. *You should have paid more attention, rascal.* Samuel thought briefly of the man's beautiful horse and wondered where he might have gone. *Under some other swell.*

Samuel wondered again about his boys and doubted that they would be coming back anytime soon. *They're probably lying rough somewhere in their own vomit.* He'd go early to the Treasure Chest, win more money, and see if he could find that same red-haired wench. He'd keep her longer this time, maybe even convince her to come back to his room. He'd show her all his money and she would bow at his feet like he was her king.

Samuel's excitement was almost too much to contain as he reached into the saddlebag for the stolen clothing. He was disappointed to find that the breeches were a little too long, but happy to learn that the waistcoat was an almost perfect fit. A wicked grin filled his face as he looked down at his new suit. He'd be a rank swell tonight and it would be obvious to anyone with eyes that he was a wealthy man. He opened his purse to check the gold coins and then left the shack, making sure to lock the door behind him.

Samuel walked the short distance to the Treasure Chest underneath a cloudy sky. He looked up once or twice, wondering if it would be raining on his walk home. He was in no hurry and had plenty of money, so he could wait the rain out if he had to. He'd show them like he had yesterday. He was better at cards than other men, and to top it off he had more luck.

****

Even this early in the day, the pub was filled with drunken men and wenches scattered in every seat. He walked in and sat at the bar. *I could buy this pub and take whores anytime I wanted.* "Your finest ale," he said, smiling at the barman, "and some stew to fill my stomach."

"You have two shillings?" the man asked.

"I have to flash my purse to get respect?"

"So there's no trouble," the barman answered.

Samuel fished out his purse in a dramatic fashion. "I banged it up in here last night."

"Jist preventin' trouble," the barman repeated. He looked at the money in the purse. "Who'd you crash?"

Samuel tried to act insulted. "My family's wealthy."

"Mine too," the barman retorted. He turned and poured ale from the barrel behind the bar.

Once Samuel had finished two ales and his stew, he paid the barman and handed him an additional shilling. "I'd like to go back to the tables," Samuel said.

"No tables," the barman replied, looking down at the coin in his hand.

Samuel's face filled with irritation. "I stripped 'em last night."

"Don't know nuthin' about no tables," the barman repeated.

Samuel reached into his pocket for two more shillings and handed them to the man. The barman remained silent and his hand stayed open. Samuel had to drop five more shillings there before the barman motioned to his companion, a large blond man standing beside a closed door that led into the back room.

The man walked over. "Lemme see your stakes."

"Already showed him," Samuel replied, nodding to the barman.

"Need to see 'em," the man warned.

Samuel pulled his purse out of his pocket and showed the contents. The blond man motioned he should follow him to the back of the pub.

"I know where it is," Samuel said. He trailed behind him to the door, all the while imagining any number of ways that he and his boys could follow this man from the pub and smash his face. The blond man opened the door and then shut it behind Samuel. There were ten or so tables where men were playing cards. The room was loud with conversation and smelled of old spilled ale and cigar smoke. Samuel searched the room and recognized the men he'd played with the night before.

"I came to give you a chance to win your gold back," he announced, putting his hand on the back of a chair.

"So sit," said an old man he didn't recognize.

"Name's Samuel Kemp," he said proudly to the old man as he sat and pulled out his purse. *Topping men always say their names.* There was some haggling as Samuel made change for the coins he placed on the table, but then he was in the game. He smiled, looking around at their faces, sure he'd be richer in a few hours. Samuel dreamed of a future when he wouldn't have to take things by force and could make his money gambling. *I've more brains than most.*

Samuel lost the first few hands and dismissed it as other men's blind luck. He kept looking toward the door, wondering if the red-haired whore would be there when he went into the bar with his winnings. The game slowed.

"This is church work," he said. "I've somewhere to be."

"Turn up, then," another man said.

"And not win my gold back," Samuel replied. "A capital scheme in your mind."

"I'd turn up before I lost more," the man repeated.

"I've a lot to lose," Samuel quipped.

"Put your stakes on the table, then."

Looking around, Samuel could see that the other men waited for his reaction, so he pulled out his purse and dumped three more joes and other assorted coins on the table. Samuel saw the respect in their eyes. "There's more where that came from," he bragged.

"Deal the cards," another said.

Samuel won the next three next hands and smirked each time as he pulled the coins. He then lost two and shook his head at the fact that some men could play at cards without any skill at all. Finally, the deal gave him three kings. He bet a small amount so as not to scare anyone away, and remained stoic when most at the table followed him in. His next card was an ace. He bet more this time, hoping to scare away the ones who relied only on luck. Three men folded and he knew that his plan was working. He gazed again at the door, wondering what that red-haired doxy would be wearing.

The last card came and it was the second ace. A shiver of excitement went through his body. He opened with a high but conservative bet, hoping to draw someone further into his trap. Three men remained and each matched his money. The last, the old man who was new to the table, raised the bet another joe. Samuel's stomach leapt with anticipation. The play came to him and he matched the old man's bet and raised him an additional gold coin. He'd keep pulling him along until all the man's money was out on the table. Samuel had one more gold coin in his purse. Both other men folded their hands.

The old man pulled out three more gold coins and pushed them along with another into the center of the table. "I raise it three joes," he said.

"I don't have that much gold on me," Samuel replied. "I can get it, though." It was true. Samuel had the other pack of gold coins hidden under the bed in his room. He knew he had a winning hand, but he could easily make up the extra money if, by some miracle, this man won.

"Put it on the table or fold," the old man said. "You can write a marker, but I'd expect it to be paid tonight."

Samuel motioned for one of the squares of parchment that rested on the corner of the table.

The house dealer spoke to Samuel. "Are you sure you have it? Mr. Lloyd don't tolerate fellows who can't pay."

I'll take all this old buzzard's money and make him watch me buy whores and drinks for everyone. Samuel pulled one of the squares of parchment along with the quill and ink. He dipped the quill and wrote a figure. "I double your bet," he said. He pushed the square into the center of the table.

"Good luck, then," Lloyd replied. He pulled three coins from his purse and dropped them onto the pile. Samuel put his cards down on the table as he smiled silently. He wanted everyone to read them for themselves. *A full house, aces and kings, you bastards!* The table went quiet, and Samuel lost track of how much time had passed. Thoughts of the redheaded woman consumed him as he made a motion to collect his winnings.

"I'll expect my gold tonight," Lloyd said, setting his cards down. He had four queens.

CHAPTER 12.

OLD DRUNKEN FELLOW

It was midmorning by the time Matt reached the city. Thick clouds were floating across the sky and intermittently obscuring the sun, causing the temperature to go instantly from comfortable to cold. Matt's shivers made him hope he wouldn't have to go without a jacket for too long. He was following a map drawn by Jacob Boyd to a stable he recommended in Wilmington. Jacob's father had looked on critically as his son made recommendations and drew the map, but he hadn't forbidden it. Matt intended to stay in the city for a few days to stake out the Treasure Chest in the hope that he would spot the three men who stole his things. He'd hang out at the pub and watch people come and go.

As Matt approached Wilmington, he tried to convince himself to forget the thieves and make his way directly to Philadelphia, but his internal debate ended the same way every time; he needed that bottle of ibuprofen. Without the tablets as a reference, it might take him his whole life to confirm that he'd made the drug. It was worth spending a few days to find the men; if they never turned up, he would have made his best attempt. For his self-worth alone, he would need to say that he had been bold enough to try to retrieve his things.

When Matt arrived at the stable, he took the Walther out of the holster, made sure there was nothing in the chamber, tucked it into his belt and covered it with his shirt. He left Thunder, the holster, and his jacket with the stable master and started out on foot for the Delaware River. Jacob's map guided him to the wharf, which was a wooden dock covered with randomly placed and mismatched structures that ran parallel to the river for as long as he could see. The strong smell of fish mixed with a hint of human waste permeated the air enough to make Matt's nose wrinkle.

He stepped up onto the wooden platform to get a better view of the riverbank. Boats, barges, and buildings in assorted shapes and sizes extended along the entire distance of the wharf. The barges either bobbed silently in the water or had men moving onto them as their cargo was transferred between any number of warehouses and shelters. Matt turned back to look where he had come and was pleased to see more than a few vagabonds wandering a short distance from where he was standing. He found an old wooden barrel, pulled it in between some stacked crates on the wharf, and sat there in a hidden roost, waiting for the right person to come along. He wasn't completely concealed, so he made sure to keep his longish hair over his face to keep from being accidentally recognized by the men he hoped to find.

Matt had been there for less than half an hour when he saw an old drunken man of about the right size moving alone through an alley. The man was holding a bottle and wearing a large dirty coat and a worn tricorner hat.

Matt eased himself from his barrel, hopped down from the wharf, and hurried into the alley.

"Excuse me, sir," he called. The old drunkard looked over his shoulder and sped ahead. "Excuse me, sir," Matt repeated as he followed him.

The old drunkard turned to speak even as he picked up his pace. "Hain't got no silver," he hollered over his shoulder.

"I have a proposition," Matt called. "I'll pay you."

"Bottle's mine," the old man announced. "'Taint enough as it is."

"I'm not going to rob you or take your bottle," said Matt. He was gaining on him. "I'm a God-fearing man...I go to church."

"Hain't got nothing to confess," the old man replied. He was walking slower now.

"I'm a Good Samaritan," Matt said.

The man stopped abruptly. Matt was now staring straight into dark eyes that looked worn from years of exposure to wind, sun, and rain. The old drunkard's scraggly grey hair poked out from under his hat and rested on his shoulders. He moved his jaw like he was warming it up to speak, then said through missing teeth, "Better not be tryin' to fleece me."

Matt reached into his pocket and pulled out a shilling. The old drunkard glared suspiciously, but then opened his hand to receive the coin. "There's more," Matt said. "You can walk away or you can listen."

The drunkard gave Matt a toothless grin. "Not sharin' my bottle."

"I want to buy your coat and hat."

"Fer how much?" the old drunkard asked. "Anyways, I need 'em."

"I'll give you enough to buy a new coat and hat, and another bottle," Matt said.

"Why'd you want to do that?"

"My business," Matt replied. He fished six shillings from his pocket and showed them in his outstretched palm.

"For a torn jacket?"

"Hat too," Matt said. He reached into his pocket and added another shilling. "That's eight."

"Seven," the drunkard corrected.

Matt saw another man out of the corner of his eye and pointed. The old drunkard's eyes followed. "Maybe he'll take my deal," Matt said. "I want my first shilling back."

"Aw," the old man yelped as he inspected the coin. "I was going to buy another bottle with that."

Matt snapped his fingers and put his hand out expectantly.

"Hold your horses," the old drunkard said.

Matt had already decided to move on, but without a word, the old man took off his hat and jacket and handed them over. The jacket was surprisingly heavy, almost like it was wet. Matt gave him the rest of the money. "Go buy a new jacket and hat before someone takes that silver."

"I'll do what I want, sonny," the old man replied as he closed his hand around the coins. He handed Matt his bottle. There was a little left swishing at the bottom.

Matt watched the old man walk away before looking at his purchases. The coat and hat were dark with grime and smelled like dead animals. Matt shuddered as he put the hat on his head, hoping there were no lice. He wrapped the jacket around him, buttoned its two remaining buttons, then walked out into the street and headed to the wharf. He saw a fire pit on the way, so he grabbed a handful of ashes and stepped out of view. He rubbed grey on his face and mussed ashes through his hair. He pulled the hat down as far as it would go over his head and then followed the road just off the wharf with the bottle in his hand.

CHAPTER 13.

SCOUT, PART III

Scout picked himself off the ground and paced back and forth behind the rope gate as the ferryman secured the ferry to the dock for another load. The man looked down at him and snarled, "Get, you nasty cur."

Scout cautiously slinked out of sight but peeked out regularly from behind a wagon, looking for an opportunity to sneak onto the ferry. After a while, he heard a whistle from one of the wagons. "Hey, dog," a boy whispered loudly. Scout tilted his head up to look at him. "I can help you get across. You understand. I can tell."

The dog sat there half-listening to the boy while he watched the men loading the ferry. The boy patted the railing of the wagon.

"Can you jump?" He patted the railing again.

Scout looked at him, knowing that most boys were more trouble than they were worth when it came to dogs. Scout suspected the boy had a leash somewhere.

"Come on," the boy said, patting the wagon harder. Another head peered over the edge. It was a little girl. Scout looked up at her and made two odd-sounding half barks like from a rabbit.

"He's funny," she said. "Come on. We can take you across." She waved for Scout to come into the wagon. The presence of the little girl changed the equation in Scout's mind, and he tried to jump up to the back railing of the wagon from where he was standing. He almost made it over the edge, but then fell back onto the ground after trying to scramble his way up with his hind legs.

"He can't jump that high," the little girl observed.

"He needs a running start," the boy replied.

"Get a running start," the girl called.

Scout had already decided to try again, but to her it seemed like he understood her completely and was taking her advice. Scout stepped back, ran, and leaped to the rail, finding himself face-to-face with the boy, bowling him over as he tumbled into the wagon. Scout yelped as his leg twisted against a case at the bottom of the vehicle. Tears began streaming down the boy's face. The girl tapped him and put her finger to her lips.

"What's the commotion back there?" a man's voice asked from the front. Both dog and boy lay crumpled against the side of the wagon.

"Nothing," the girl said. "Tommy fell, but he's fine."

"Settle yourselves," the voice said. "We've still a long way."

"Yes, Father," the girl replied. She put her finger to her lips, motioning to the boy.

Tommy wiped the tears from his eyes and pushed the dog off. "Dumb dog!" he scolded, still half-crying. Scout got to his feet, limped to him, and licked his face.

"He likes you," she said.

"He almost killed me."

"He's trying to say sorry. He's hurt, too." She reached up to rub Scout's fur. The dog stood there for a long time, moving into the children as they scratched him.

"I wonder where he's going?" the boy asked.

"He has a collar," she said. She reached down to his neck and held the metal tag. "Says his name's Scout and he's from Richmond."

"Hi, Scout. I'm Tommy," the boy said. The dog's ears perked up at the sound of his own name, and both children smiled. "I wonder why he's trying to cross the river."

"To find his owner," the girl answered. She reached into the burlap sacks that surrounded their seats in the back of the wagon, pulled out food she thought a dog might like, and handed it to her brother. "You should feed him," she said. They had Scout chewing on jerky and sweet biscuits by the time their wagon moved onto the ferry.

Scout finished his meal drinking water the children poured into a wooden bowl. With his hunger sated and the kids rubbing his back, Scout relaxed and fell asleep, nestled between the crates and sacks of supplies. He had no idea where he was when he was awakened by a man's voice. "The dog has to go. He's someone else's."

"Can't he stay with us for a while longer, Father?" the girl asked.

"The farther we take him in the wagon, the harder 'twill be for him to find his way."

Scout sat up on his hind legs and offered his paw to shake.

"I allow he's a fine animal," the father said, "but he must go." The man snapped his fingers and pointed to the side. Scout looked at the boy, the girl, and the man, then walked dejectedly to the back of the wagon and jumped to the ground. He sat there on the edge of the dirt road, watching the children wave as they rolled away.

Scout looked around, but there was no one in sight. He sniffed the air, hoping to catch the scent of Matt or Thunder, but smelled nothing he could recognize. He walked for a while, watching the wagon turn into a tiny cloud of dust and then disappear completely into the haze that obscured the line where the sky met the earth.

CHAPTER 14.

TREASURE CHEST

True to Jacob's map, the Treasure Chest was located about a hundred yards off the river, in clear view of the docked boats. Matt sauntered drunkenly up to the tavern and lingered as he inspected the front of the weathered grey building. A bouncer sat underneath a wood awning that reached out almost to the street. Nailed to this overhang was a large sign painted with a colorful picture of an open treasure chest filled with shining gold coins and gems. Matt stood outside the door, wondering if he should step inside.

"Move along, old man," the bouncer said after Matt had loitered too long.

"I'm looking for my brother...real tall man," Matt replied. He motioned with his hand to show the man's height. "He in there? He owes me money."

"Move along, you drunken scallywag, before I throw you in the river."

Taking the man at his word, Matt walked away to assume a position in the shadow of a painted green warehouse in view of the Treasure Chest. He sat there on an old crate for most of the day, watching people come and go from the tavern, leaving once to relieve himself and again to get a loaf of fresh bread and some hard-boiled eggs and to fill his bottle with water.

"You're rank," the baker said after Matt had paid.

"Money still spends," Matt replied in the best old-drunken-scallywag voice he could muster. Matt divided the loaf and the boiled eggs among the coat's big pockets, then resumed his position to watch the tavern.

In the late afternoon, Matt was nodding off when he was shocked awake by an extremely tall man and a short one who stopped as they were walking by. He recognized their voices immediately and saw that the tall one was wearing his stolen hat. Matt eased his arm slowly to his side to be able to reach his pistol.

"Whatcha doing, you old badger?" the short one jeered. "Look 'bout ready to drop off the perch."

"Don't have long," Matt replied from under his hat. "Got the fever. People on the river been passing it 'round. Ah think it's the fleas." Matt swatted at his shoulder to emphasize the bugs. "Jump from man to man. Itchy as the devil."

The criminals stepped back. "Go jump in the river, you old cuff," the tall one said. He turned to his partner. "Let's go where we was last night. Them misses sure was civil."

The short one nodded and then said, "Sam's a molly." He reached into his pocket as he spoke, pulled out a shilling, and threw it to Matt. "Talkin' to fine swells, you are," he said. "Buy yourself another bottle."

"Thank ya kindly, sonny," Matt replied, trying his hardest to sound like the previous owner of his jacket.

The men turned away from Matt abruptly. "Be funny if he walked into the Treasure Chest to buy a bottle and gave everyone the fever," the short one said to his tall companion. They laughed as they walked away.

Matt waited until they were a safe distance down the road, then followed them to their destination. The tavern's sign pictured two roosters squaring off in front of a ship's wheel with the words "The Fighting Cocks" painted in yellow under the birds' legs. Aside from the sign, there was very little distinction between this building and the Treasure Chest. Matt found another crate and took up a similar position outside this new pub to watch the entrance. He planned to wait for the criminals to leave, follow them to where they were staying, and figure out a way to take his stuff back. Matt didn't have much hope of recovering the money, considering that they were walking around town bragging about being wealthy and giving coins to town drunks.

Matt sat outside The Fighting Cocks for a long time and dozed briefly as he leaned against the warehouse wall. It was almost four in the morning when he saw the men leave the tavern, staggering drunk. Matt had to focus on not following them too closely. He could hear them singing. The tall one fell over and lay on the dirt road. "Jist let me sleep," he said.

"Ground's too hard," the short one replied. He pulled his tall companion by the arm until he regained his feet. They stumbled in their drunken stupor to a grassy area hidden from the road and both collapsed to the ground.

"Great," Matt said impatiently. "Now what?"

CHAPTER 15.

MORE THAN HALF

Matt pulled the hat lower over his face and walked silently toward the sleeping criminals. He began carefully frisking them under the light of the moon. He would take their money in hopes of forcing them to return to wherever they were staying before they could do more celebrating. Matt found a skeleton key, three gold coins, and fourteen shillings in their pockets. He put the coins in his own pocket, returned the key, and retrieved his stolen hat. Having the hat in his hands was enough of a victory to bring a satisfied smile back to his grey-smudged face.

"Whatcha doing, you old badger?" the short one said unexpectedly from the ground.

Matt lifted an arm to shield his face. The short man had one eye open and was waving his hand violently, but then, as quickly as he'd awoken, he slipped again into unconsciousness. Matt stood up and looked down at his two assailants, fighting the urge to kick the hell out of them as they lay unconscious on the ground, and then contemplated his next move. There wasn't much else he could do besides let this play out.

Matt quietly backed away, making sure neither man opened his eyes to see him moving to his hiding place. When he was far enough, he circled around the clearing where the criminals were sleeping and settled in a patch of thick trees on a hill. He sat against one of the trees. After checking that he could see the men on the ground, he wrapped his tattered jacket around him and curled up to wait until daylight.

****

Matt shuddered awake from the heat of the morning sun as it made one last attempt to peek out from behind the rain clouds that were gathering in the sky. *Crap!* He looked over in a panic, hoping the criminals hadn't already gone, but to his relief, they were still sleeping. He situated himself for a clear view and began to eat his bread and hard-boiled eggs.

The criminals didn't stir until noon. The taller one woke first and shook the other. They talked briefly, and Matt could see them frantically checking their pockets and looking around. He ducked as they scanned the woods. They appeared to make a decision, then moved from the clearing and started walking. Matt got up to follow them, pleased that they were headed away from the river rather than back to the tavern.

Tracking them was easier when they stepped from the road onto a dirt path where the trees thickened. Matt was close enough to hear their conversation. He stayed on the path as they came to a clearing containing ten or so greyish shacks. Some had smoke coming out of their chimneys. The men stopped as if trying to remember which one they'd rented.

Matt quietly shifted on his feet to find a lane between the trees to be able to see. The sun was now totally obscured by dark clouds, making it hard to distinguish the men from the buildings. Matt cupped his hand to his ear to hear.

"He'll give you some," the short one said.

"He always has money," the tall one replied. "He's in his room."

"Even if he ain't," the short one said, "I still got me some."

"Mine's all gone."

"You spent all five joes?"

"Didn't spend. That old drunk stole 'em from me, you said."

"All your gold?"

"Had it in my pocket. Safest place, I thought."

"Sam will lend you some."

It was hard for Matt not to get excited as he listened to them quibble. If these two only had ten coins, there were twenty others somewhere. Had they not found them in the saddlebag? The men finally stepped up onto a porch and pounded on the door. Matt shifted again to get a better view.

"He ain't there," he heard the tall one say.

The shorter one pounded again. "Wake up, Sam," he yelled. They paced around the porch for a while and then walked to the next shack. The tall one pulled out his key and unlocked the door, and both men entered.

Matt stood there for ten minutes waiting for them to emerge, but it remained quiet. He finally stepped out of the woods and walked purposefully to Sam's shack. He stretched to peer into a cloudy glass window to make sure that the room was indeed empty. Satisfied that it was deserted, he walked around the shack looking for an entrance but found no obvious way to break in. He was sure that smashing a window or door would have more than the men he'd been following coming out to check.

Matt then got to his knees, pulled at some slats around the foundation, and found a crawl space. He pulled a few more slats off to make a hole large enough to slide under the structure, and then he got on his hands and knees and crawled in. Matt kept having to brush cobwebs from his face as he moved farther under the house. He stopped when he saw a hint of light coming through cracks in the floor. *Good a place as any.*

Matt rolled over onto his back, put his feet against the baseboards, and pushed. The boards flexed, but didn't give. He pulled his feet back and stomped upward. He felt something break. He stomped again twice, this time harder. Nothing. He rested for a moment and decided that one loud bang might be better than the noise he was making now. Matt pulled his feet back and kicked hard. Three of the baseboards gave way and launched into the room, broken.

He thrust his head through the floor and looked around to make sure he was alone, then pulled himself up through the hole and onto the floor of the one-room shack. Light was streaming through the window, and he could see items strewn about the room. *Yes!* His saddlebag was on the chair. Quietly walking over to it, Matt picked it up and crouched with it on the floor. His hands shook as he undid the buckles and opened the bag. His shaving kit was inside; the medicine bottles were there and so were the bullets. *The phone, too!* There were no clothes or shoes, though, and the money was gone. As he looked around the room, hoping to see a package of gold coins, Matt heard footsteps on the porch. He froze.

"I heard 'im," the short one said.

"I didn't hear nothin'."

The men banged on the door.

"Ain't here," the tall one insisted.

"Come on out, you ignorant Teague," the short one called.

"No one's in there."

"I told you," the short one replied, "I heard his door slam." They knocked again.

Matt slowly reached back for his gun, pulling it from his pants and gently chambering a bullet. *Click.*

"Heard him jist now," the short one said.

"It was me walking. I'll look for 'im in the window."

Matt was in full view of the glass. *Idiot!* The whole room was visible from the window. In a crouch, Matt hurried over to the bed and slid underneath. He held the pistol as he lay there on his back, looking up at the wood frame of the small bed.

"No one's in there," the tall one said, peering through the glass. "I told you. You're hearin' things."

"Where is he, then?" the short one called out.

"Treasure Chest, I reckon," the tall one called back. His voice was moving around the house, toward the front door again.

"You hungry?" Matt heard the short one say.

"Am," the tall one replied.

"Got me enough fer us to get drunk as Davey's sow."

Matt waited under the bed as they shuffled off the porch and their voices trailed away. He was sliding out from under the bed when it caught his eye. There was a package tucked there. *Could it be?* He reached up and pulled it from its cradle. He knew as soon as he touched it that it was one of his two packs of coins. *Half!*

Matt stood, pulled the curtain, and looked around the room again to make sure he'd gotten everything. Sam's stuff was on the table. The only thing of interest was a flintlock pistol. Matt picked it up and considered it for a moment, thinking that it might be a good idea to relieve Sam of his weapon, but then thought better of it. Matt had no idea how to use a flintlock, plus it was heavy. He set it back down on the table, slung his saddlebag over his shoulder, and unlocked the door of the shack. He turned the latch, eased the door open, slipped through, and slowly closed it behind him. He pushed it as far shut as it would go without latching so as not to make any noise.

Matt stepped calmly off the porch and slipped into the forest. He walked purposefully for maybe half a mile before he felt far enough away to be safe. When he finally stopped, he looked up into the sky and let the cool droplets rinse his ash-covered face. It had started to rain.

CHAPTER 16.

SAMUEL, PART II

Samuel stared down at the four queens his opponent had just laid on the table. "Cheat!" he spat.

"You're cleaned out, Mr. Kemp," Lloyd said coldly as he motioned to two thugs who had been sitting in the corner and drinking from large ceramic steins. "I'll ignore your insult provided you pay me my gold by the end of the night. My men will retrieve what you owe."

The two thugs now stood above Samuel. Their impossibly large bodies were stuffed into woolen breeches and stockings. The one with bright yellow hair pulled back into a ponytail placed his hand firmly on Samuel's shoulder.

"I trust these fellows with my life," Lloyd said.

Samuel looked around at the polite smiles of the other players. "You'll have your gold," Samuel rasped as he cleared his throat.

"Tonight," Lloyd repeated.

"I said," Samuel huffed. He could see the men around the table judging him. "What're you looking at?" Two of them stood to face him. Lloyd put his hand up casually and smiled. They returned his gaze with satisfied expressions and retook their seats.

"Retire now, Mr. Kemp," the older man said calmly. He waved to his men and they urged Samuel to his feet. "Tonight," he said a third time. "I would not desire to be both insulted *and* cheated in a single evening."

Samuel didn't reply. He pushed the blond man's hand from his shoulder and turned. He chafed at the eyes he felt on him as he made his way to the front of the Treasure Chest. On his way out, he glared back hard at the barman, who gave him a knowing look.

****

The ground was wet from the rain that fell while Samuel was in the tavern. The sky was clearing now, and the moon was peeking out through clouds and reflecting off the river. "I've grown tired of the Treasure Chest anyway," Samuel said to the two men, who were on each side of him. Their silence was beginning to unnerve him.

"Why?" the blond man asked. "I like it in there."

"Me too," the other said. He was a perfect physical match to his companion, but had a darker complexion and hair that didn't glow as brightly in the moonlight.

It was apparent to Samuel that these were big, dumb brutes, but there was nothing in their voices that said they were going to hurt him. Given no other option, he'd pay them their six joes and that would be the last Wilmington would see of Sam Kemp. He'd go back to Richmond where his money was respected.

"What's Lloyd's business?" he asked, trying to keep them talking.

"Owns ships," the blond one replied.

"Privateer," the darker one offered. "More than a few ships."

"Put him in a tweak, you did," the blond said. "I'd give up the gold and bolt."

They were coming up to the shack Samuel had rented. The bright moon was lighting the house so he could clearly see the porch and the door. He pulled the key out of his pocket, hoping to slip quickly into the room. He didn't want these brutes following him inside.

"Stay here," Samuel instructed as he put his foot on the first step of the porch.

"You got a popper in there?" the blond one asked. He pulled his pistol out of his belt. "There's two of us, don't forget."

"You'll have your gold and then I quit this town," Samuel said. He scanned the other shacks, hoping to see his boys. They'd know to ambush these two, but there was no hint of them inside or out. He'd have to pay.

Samuel knew something was wrong before he reached the door. It was ajar. Someone had been inside. Was it his boys? He stared back at the men, pretending to unlock the door.

"Won't be long," he called to the two men, who were now positioned at the base of the porch.

"We'll be waiting," the darker one replied. He patted the pistol at his belt.

Samuel was disappointed to find that no one was inside. He opened the drapes to let light into the room. The saddlebag was gone. He reached up under the bed frame for the package of coins. His money was gone! His list of options, having been long only minutes before, was now quite short. He picked up his pistol and stood quietly.

The darker man opened the door and peered inside. "You square?" he called.

Samuel shot the flintlock pistol at the sound of the man's voice, and the door splintered with the deafening boom of the gun. Samuel choked on the white smoke that filled the room, his ears ringing. He went for the window, smashed it with a chair, dived through onto the ground, and picked himself up to run. A musket shot rang out, and he was slammed to the ground by the force of a sickening thud in his lower spine. He reached behind. When he pulled his quivering hand from his back, it was coated in bright red.

The large men were now standing over him. "Almost took my nob off," the darker one said. The side of his head was red with blood where the musket ball had grazed his skull. It gave Samuel pleasure to watch the blood stream down the brute's face.

"Where's the gold?" the blond man demanded.

"There is none, you beef-head," Samuel growled as he struggled to breathe. "It was stolen."

"No need for name-calling," the blond man replied. "We want what you owe."

"I told you," Samuel said, grimacing. "There is none." He could feel the blood running freely down his lower back.

Samuel was dead by the time they tossed him into the Delaware River.

CHAPTER 17.

SCOUT, PART IV

Scout trotted along the road until dusk and then crawled into some brush for the night. The countryside was too open for him here and the chatter in the dark made him uneasy. He heard wolves in the distance and was relieved when they finally moved away. Their howls made him aware for the first time since he'd left the farm that he was without the protection of his pack. Scout's sleep was interrupted most of the night and so he was happy when the sun came and he could start down the road again. He searched for the greater part of the morning, trying to catch some scent, but there wasn't a hint of Matt or Thunder.

About the time the sun reached its highest point in the sky, a city became visible in the horizon and Scout increased his pace. As he passed the first homes on the side of the river, he smelled Thunder and became excited. The city was busy and he was forced to dodge wagons and humans as he traveled through the streets. Signs of the horse and the man were strong there, and Scout went from block to block, trying to make sense of their direction. He got frustrated and rested for a while in the shade, then with new energy restarted his search. More than one wagon in the busy commercial district was forced to stop abruptly for a large dog moving frantically through the streets with his nose to the ground. Then Scout found the road where Matt and Thunder had left the city. Their vivid colors in the air told him they were close, so he hurried along the road and out of town.

Scout reached a spot where the road overlooked the river and the horse's colors changed dramatically. The dog put his nose in the air, trying to interpret the layers of clues that surrounded him; they painted a picture of panic. The dog stopped to growl at the place where the road entered the trees. He quieted once he saw that nothing was there and trotted to follow the scent. The man's identity was strong on the ground, mixed with fear and sweat, and then his scent led over the cliff.

Scout struggled to climb down into the valley and onto the dry riverbed. The man and horse had been there on the ground. The smell of blood was there, and the dog knew Matt had been hurt. He followed their trail along the river until he came to a road and then to a farm. Scout stood in front of the farmhouse before wandering to the barn where Matt had slept, and then to the corral that had housed Thunder. The dog returned to the farmhouse and stood there, considering whether Matt could be inside. Scout got impatient and barked. He barked again and a woman came to the door. The dog sat watching her closely, but occasionally looked up at the dark clouds that were starting to fill the sky. Scout knew that his time to track Matt and Thunder was growing short.

"John," she said. "You better come see this."

"Woman," he replied, "there's only so much I can do."

"Set it down and come see," she said. "There's another animal out front."

The man walked onto the porch and saw Scout sitting there. "You don't think that's his dog?" he asked. Scout sat patiently on his hind legs and stared at them.

"Matthew?"

They saw Scout's ears perk.

"I knew it," the man said.

There was a long silence until the man and woman exchanged a smile, realizing they were waiting for the dog to explain his intentions.

"Matthew," the man said. He pointed to the gate at the entrance to the farm. "That way."

Scout looked around to the gate and back again at the couple on the porch. He barked one last time toward the farmhouse, hoping Matt or Thunder would hear him, and waited. After what seemed like an eternity, he realized that neither his horse nor his young man were on the farm. The dog looked one last time at the couple on the porch and then trotted back out the way he had come.

"I knew there was something odd about that boy the first time I laid eyes on him," John Boyd said.

"Good heart, though," Margaret Boyd replied. "Never seen such loyal animals."

"God's creatures following him around like he's Noah or something," her husband mumbled as they watched the dog head down the road and out of sight.

****

Scout ran for a while, following the trail back toward the city. He reached a place where he became confused because the path pointed in both directions, like the man and the horse had traveled back and forth between city and farm. The dog meandered along the many pathways and roads. He knew that Matt and Thunder had recently passed through here. Should he go back into the city?

At last, he found himself on a dirt road he recognized. He'd passed this way before, but the scent hadn't been this strong. He began running again, retracing his earlier steps, knowing he'd just missed his man and horse. He ignored the smell of the predators the second time as he reached the portion of the road that overlooked the river and returned into the woods. The trail was strong now, and he was so close that he could taste them on his tongue. He hastened his pace, excited to meet them.

There was suddenly an overwhelming sense of moisture in the air. Scout stared up at the sky and a splash of water hit him on the nose. Some of the colors that made up his world were already running together. Then the sky let loose in a rainstorm and the dog's senses turned to grey. Scout stopped in his tracks when the last evidence of the young man and his horse washed into the ground. All traces of them were gone, and he knew they would never return.

Scout found an oak tree and sat under its canopy listening to the staccato sound of the raindrops. He became sad like he always did when the rain came and erased his world. He looked around, wondering where he'd go now that his man and horse were lost forever. Without their scent in the air or on the ground, there was no hope. Scout stayed under the tree even after the rain stopped and the full moon moved out from behind the clouds.

He didn't know what else to do, so he got up and began to run. He'd take the road north.

CHAPTER 18.

CAN'T GO ON

Matt rode Thunder for as long as he was able, but the road signs to Philadelphia told him there was no possibility that he'd get within sight of city before dark. The thunderclouds were looking ominous again, and he was relieved when he came to a farm with a sign that read "Rooms to Let." There were a number of farm buildings off the road, situated between tilled fields and pastures.

Douglas Gage, the owner, was leading him past the barn and some sheds to a long building. Gage turned to watch Matt, who was hobbling behind him, trying to avoid the mud. "You hurt?"

"I'll be fine after a meal and some sleep," Matt replied. He'd been on Thunder since he'd recovered his things. He was bow-legged, he hadn't slept properly in two days, and his wet breeches had rubbed his legs raw where they met the saddle. His body was sore, there was a penetrating throb in his skull from being clubbed, and the injury had shaken something loose in his brain. His sight was intermittently clouding over with high-speed flashes. He'd had to stop a number of times as he rode away from Wilmington to wait for his vision to return.

They were standing in front of an elongated one-story building with five equally spaced doors that shared the same porch. "These are the rooms," Gage said. He glanced back at Thunder, who was tied to a hitching rail. "'Tis an extra shilling for the animal."

"For feed and straw?" Matt said with some irritation.

"You could go," Gage replied. "There are rooms farther down the road." He looked at the clouds and continued in a sincere voice, "We're a God-fearing family, but we must profit like everyone else."

Matt dreaded one more second in the saddle. "I'll take the bed, but I expect the horse to get as much as he can eat, and I want him out of the weather." He pointed to an overhang that reached out over the corral.

"We'll do everything except let him sleep in our own beds," the man said, exasperated. "Something singular about him?"

The sarcastic tone of the man's question added to Matt's growing impatience. "He's from champion stock," Matt said. "I'll claim my bride on the back of that horse."

Gage warmed his exasperated gaze and chuckled. "They usually prefer carriages."

"How far to Philadelphia?" Matt asked. He pulled at his breeches to move them away from where they stuck to his raw legs.

"Day's ride. You'll find out soon enough."

"Can I get food?" Matt asked.

"Main house. My Emma's a fine cook."

Matt reached into his pocket for a few of the coins he'd taken from the drunken thugs and handed them to Gage, then accepted the room key.

"You've time to settle your horse," Gage said. "She'll call when she's putting the food away."

Matt stood watching Gage walk to the corral to say something to a teenage boy. Matt's vision started sputtering again and he pressed his temples. When the flashing subsided, he went to Thunder, untied him from his post, and walked him to the corral.

"Here you go, boy," he said, patting the horse's wet neck. Thunder reached his head out and made an affectionate snort. Matt stepped to his side to remove his saddle and then took the bit out of his mouth and replaced it with a halter. Matt inspected the corral again. The overhang wasn't as large as he would have desired, but it was shelter enough against another rainstorm.

The teenage boy was filling up the trough with hay. He wore a tricorner hat and an oiled jacket that seemed to do a pretty good job of repelling the rain that had started to fall again. The boy saw Matt, dropped what he was doing, and walked to the gate.

"I'll take him," he said, scrutinizing Thunder. "He's a giant."

"He's smart and gentle," Matt said. "Use him kindly. He saved my life." He handed the bridle over to the boy.

"Father told me you were partial to your horse," the boy replied in a sincere tone.

Matt wanted to talk more, but a wave of fatigue washed over him. He reached into his pocket, handed the boy a coin, grabbed his saddlebag, and walked to his room. There was a candle already burning on the table when he opened the door. The room looked as good as any he'd slept in, which wasn't saying much, but having recently spent the night on a dock, he was happy with anything with a roof. A wave of melancholy washed over him as he thought of the Taylors' hay barn. His wholesome and clean life on the farm felt very far away.

Matt's stomach growled. He headed over to the main house to eat, deciding there wasn't much he could do about his damp breeches except wait. He carried his saddlebag, not trusting a lock that could be opened with a skeleton key with his every possession, especially with how much he'd just gone through to get everything back. His pack would stay at his side for the remainder of the journey. He patted the gun in the holster at his ribs and made sure his jacket covered it completely, then stepped up onto the porch and knocked.

"Who might you be, handsome?" the woman asked coyly as she opened the door. Matt thought for a moment that she might pinch his cheek.

"My name's Matt Miller."

"The horse lover," she said boisterously.

Her enthusiasm went a long way toward melting his weariness. It was the same enthusiasm Matt had met almost everywhere since he'd arrived in the colonies. Colonial America was excited to be alive. All the people he'd met, whether farmers, merchants, or laborers, seemed ecstatic. It made him jealous at times as he tried to figure out why this was so foreign to his modern sensibilities. He couldn't remember people being so full of life back in his own time. *Why was I such a cynical sod?*

She motioned for him to come in. "Mr. Baker is already eating."

Matt shook the thoughts from his head and stepped inside.

CHAPTER 19.

THE BAKER BROTHERS

Matt followed Emma through a dim hallway to the kitchen in the back of the house. Despite the clouds, there was still some light that streamed through the glass panes. A twenty-something man sat at the table spooning stew onto his plate. When he saw Matt, he stood up, wiped his hand on his side and met him halfway to shake.

Matt was the first to speak. "I'm Matt Miller."

"Your name sings," the man exclaimed with a bright smile. "I'm Benjamin Baker."

Matt returned his grin. "Never thought of it as singing. Rhymes a bit."

Benjamin gave him a mouthful of straight white teeth and pointed Matt to a chair. "My brother James should be along soon. He had some bad pork yesterday."

"You're both welcome to finish the pot," Emma said from behind, "but put aside some for young James." She thought for a moment and added, "The poor thing." She stepped out of the kitchen and left them alone with their meal.

"You've stayed here before?" Matt asked.

Benjamin nodded. "'Tis at the end of our route and they use us well," he said.

"What do you sell?" Matt asked.

"Candles," Benjamin replied.

"Benjamin Baker, the candlestick maker," Matt observed.

"I was blessed to have such a name," Benjamin said.

"Where do you make your candles?"

"Philadelphia," Benjamin replied. "We sell in and around the city."

"You headed back to Philadelphia?" Matt asked.

Benjamin nodded. "Empty wagon."

"You do a good business selling candles?"

Bayberries used in Candle Making

Benjamin nodded again. "Strictly bayberry." He said it like the benefits were obvious. "And even then, ours smell better than most. What's your trade, Mr. Miller?"

"Apothecary. I'm going to Philadelphia to start a business."

"We can help you."

Matt thought quickly about the possibilities. He imagined that Baker saw him as not only a potential customer, but also as a distributor. "I'd appreciate your help."

"We've lodgings for hire," Benjamin offered. "It's clean and you'd be among friends. I suspect that the only place you'll find cheaper will be under a bridge."

Matt's couldn't keep the smirk off his face thinking that Benjamin might be surprised at how much he knew about sleeping under bridges.

Benjamin grabbed the spoon for the stew and motioned to Matt's plate. "More?"

Matt shook his head and patted his belly. He suddenly thought of Thunder. "I need a place to board my horse."

"We've a barn and a pasture," Benjamin replied. "James takes fine care of the animals."

Benjamin leaned down and divided the loaf of bread. He handed half to Matt and said, "Take this for the road." Matt saw him smile. Benjamin handed him three apples. "They have ten trees out back. They'll not miss these."

Matt stuffed the apples into his pockets and held the bread in his hand. They stood up from the table at the same time. "I'm surprised at my brother," Benjamin said as he looked into the hall. "He should have come by now."

"I have medicines that might help his stomach," Matt offered.

He had Alka-Seltzer and Zantac in his bag. It was only a small bottle of Zantac, which in 1762 was the world's supply. If Matt thought hard enough, he could probably remember the structure of ranitidine, the active ingredient. He'd taken a class in graduate school called Pharmaceutical Blockbusters where they'd had to memorize the properties and structures of the top-selling medicines during the "golden age" of the drug industry. He remembered Prozac for depression, Zantac for ulcers, and Lipitor for cholesterol. At their peak, each had been the biggest-selling drug in the history of mankind. Prozac or Lipitor would be hard to sell in 1762 because you couldn't feel them working, but an antacid like Zantac might sell very well, considering how nasty colonial food could be.

Common Name: Ranitidine
Chemical Formula: $C_{13}H_{22}N_4O_3S$
Molecular Weight: 314.4
Natural Source: None

Matt didn't know exactly how to synthesize ranitidine, but he could give it a try. The best way to confirm that you'd made a chemical compound was to compare it to a known sample. He'd need to keep as many of his Zantac tablets as he could for future experiments. Alka-Seltzer, on the other hand, was a lower-hanging fruit than Zantac. It would be easy to make if he could find sources of citric acid, sodium bicarbonate, and aspirin. His first big project once he was in Philadelphia was to make aspirin. It wouldn't be hard then to include it in something like Alka-Seltzer, which he imagined being a big success with the average colonist. The fizzing was fascinating and you could feel it working almost immediately.

"Let me know if he needs something for his stomach," Matt said to Benjamin.

CHAPTER 20.

ALKA-SELTZER

The candle was still burning in Matt's room when he returned. The room moved with the flickers of light that danced from wall to wall. He set his stuff down, picked up the ceramic jug, and walked back outside to visit the privy and fill the jug at the well. It had stopped raining and a full moon lit his way. When he returned, Benjamin was at his door with a young man.

Matt called out, "Hello, gentlemen."

Benjamin waved as Matt got closer but didn't say anything until he'd stepped up onto the porch.

"James would try that medicine," Benjamin explained. "Neither of us will sleep with all his moaning."

The boy nodded. He looked to be in his mid teens. "My stomach hurts."

Matt waved them into his room and patted the boy on the back. "We'll get you fixed up."

Motioning for Benjamin and James to sit at the table, Matt went to the small dresser, where he grabbed a tin cup and filled it with fresh water. He reached into his pack for his shaving kit and grabbed a pack of two Alka-Seltzer tablets and a Zantac.

citric acid

sodium bicarbonate

Acetylsalicylic Acid

Trade Name: Alka Seltzer
Common Name: Citric Acid, Sodium Bicarbonate and Acetylsalicylic Acid
Natural Sources: Citric Acid: Citrus Fruit, Sodium Bicarbonate: None,
Acetylsalicylic Acid: None

"This is good stuff," Matt announced. He dropped the two Alka-Seltzers into the cup and they started fizzing. They all watched with interest.

"Is it magic?" Benjamin asked.

"Not magic," Matt affirmed. "The bubbling helps the medicine go into the water."

James looked at the cup suspiciously as the tablets finished fizzing and Matt swirled the water around to dissolve the last particles. Their focus reinforced Matt's appreciation of how important showmanship was for a colonial apothecary.

"Here you go," Matt said. "It's not going to taste very good, so I'd drink it quickly."

"Ha!" Benjamin said. "Medicine never sits well in my mouth."

Benjamin had spoken another cultural truth. Even in Matt's own time, people often expected medicine to taste bad or to have some other negative effect, and this helped convince them that it was working. Many medicines that Matt could think of had a demonstrated placebo effect. Even for Zantac, more than fifty percent of the people taking placebo had their ulcers cured after six weeks based on the belief that they were getting the medicine.

Of course, the people taking actual Zantac had about a seventy percent cure rate, so the drug was clearly better, but it did make you appreciate the power of the human mind. The placebo effect was even stronger when treating mental diseases. People receiving a placebo would start to feel better based solely on the fact that they were finally seeking treatment; this alone made them less depressed or anxious.

They watched as James gulped down the liquid and then let out a giant burp. "Pardon," he said, covering his mouth.

"I have another pill," Matt said, "if you can keep that down."

James burped again.

Matt chuckled. "That's how you know it's working."

James let out a third belch. "I feel better," he said, surprised.

"Swallow this without chewing," Matt said as he handed the boy a Zantac tablet. He poured another cup of water.

James swallowed the pill on the first try. "It didn't taste like anything. Are you sure it's medicine?"

Matt laughed and the teen put a look of insult on his face. "It's medicine," Matt replied. "You'll feel better tomorrow, though I can't guarantee that you won't be making mad dashes to the privy tonight." The color was already returning to the boy's face.

"What do we owe?" Benjamin asked. "One hopes you aren't as costly as apothecaries in Philadelphia."

"I'm very *costly*," Matt said. "But not among friends." Matt took a moment to think about a fair price, even debating whether he should charge them at all. But after considering what he knew about the importance of trade in Colonial America, he decided he should ask for a reasonable payment. "I'd like a cooked meal and one night's lodgings when I get to Philadelphia, and then for my horse to be housed and fed for one week. I'll need time to get situated in the city."

"Agreed," Benjamin said.

Matt stood up, reaching his hand out to shake, and they said their goodnights. Matt escorted them through the door into the moonlight and watched them walk down to the farthest room in the building and let themselves in. Matt felt a sense of satisfaction when, as their door was shutting, he heard James tell his brother, "I feel better."

Matt closed the door and got ready for bed. He filled a tin basin with the water that remained in the ceramic jug and used this to wash his tired and bruised face. The cold water felt painful. He finished up by brushing his teeth. The toothpaste situation was looking grim; only a third of a tube left. He wondered again how hard it would be to make toothpaste. *There are so many things I can work on.* It was only a matter of finishing something that people would be willing to buy. He already had a working knowledge of many of the great inventions from history. If he managed to act on any one of them properly, he could be as rich as any man in America.

His mind raced with a million questions. *Would my actions change history if I succeeded? What about the people who originally had the ideas? Would it mean they wouldn't have their own success? Is it ethical to steal someone else's idea from the future? Were any of them from the future, too?* The skeptic in him came out when he thought of Thomas Edison. *He invented too many things; he was from the future for sure!*

The scientists from Matt's own time, who had been working on returning him, were worried about Matt changing the future. When Matt decided to stay in Colonial America, he'd narrowly escaped their attempt to bring him home by force. One thing he couldn't say any more was that he was in Colonial America by accident, but he was hoping that the universe wasn't going to be transformed based on the actions of some random twenty-six-year-old. Even if one of his actions did change the course of history, like in so many of the movies, who was to say it wasn't supposed to happen? *Doesn't everyone have the power to change the future with everything they do? Can I do what seems right and then trust the universe? Am I making excuses for my decision to stay?*

****

Matt checked that the door was locked before he got into bed. The bed wasn't too disgusting, considering how many people might have slept in it after traveling on dusty and dirty roads. He thought briefly about starting a fire in the fireplace, but it felt like too much work now that he was in bed. As a compromise, he got up for another blanket. He mind was cloudy with fatigue and he fell asleep almost as soon as his head hit the pillow.

Matt was awakened by someone walking on the porch. He sat up in bed and eased his feet onto the floor. *Did they follow me?* He grabbed his pistol and listened closely, but now he heard only the sound of trees bending and windblown rain tapping at the sides of the building. Then, there it was again, a distinctive clicking or pacing. It went silent for long enough to convince him that it was gone. This calm was broken by scratching noises on the door, loud enough to startle him. Someone or something was trying to get into his room. He stood and watched the doorknob, expecting turns that never came. *An animal?* The bread he took from dinner was wrapped in his oil-cloth. *Maybe a bear can smell the bread?*

Matt was now worried that either a large animal or a man was going to come crashing into his room, but he felt silly standing there, cowering behind a door, holding an automatic weapon. He quietly unlatched the door and slowly turned the knob, ready to confront whoever or whatever was there. He pulled the door open quickly and leaned around to point the gun into the darkness. A large animal was in his sights, silhouetted against the moonlight. *A wolf!*

The wolf backed to the edge of the porch away from the open doorway. Matt could see that it was dark, scraggly, and wet. "Get!" he said. "Go!" With all the violence he had experienced over the last few days, he had no desire to kill anything. The rain soaked animal looked toward him from the shadows. "Leave!" Matt yelled. The wolf, still a silhouette, barked. Matt's mind raced.

The animal walked slowly into view and Matt kept it in his gun sights. Matt stepped from behind the door and set the gun on the ledge. He was shocked at the ghost he was seeing.

"Scout?" he said. The wet, shivering dog walked to his feet, and Matt stooped to wrap his arms around him. Scout licked his face excitedly. Matt's eyes were glassy. "Don't know what you're doing here, but I'm glad to see you."

Matt stood and scanned the moonlit yard, but the dog had come alone. Scout trotted into the room, leaving a trail of water, and hopped up onto the bed.

"You're all wet," Matt exclaimed. Scout lay at the foot of the bed with his head on his front paws. "Fine," Matt proclaimed. He latched the door and crawled under the blankets. As he stretched his legs out, he heard a low growl. He pulled his legs up slightly and the dog grew quiet.

PART II.

PROPHET

CHAPTER 21.

PHILADELPHIA

Matt was riding Thunder through the frozen cloud that formed from the horse's breath in the cold winter air. An icicle beard was steadily growing under the animal's mouth and Matt wondered if he should stop and try to crush it off, but he decided to wait until they were back in the warm confines of the stable. Tugging at the horse's jaw would only irritate him more, and Matt had no desire to take his gloves off and start a struggle on this country road in the middle of a snowstorm. Scout was keeping their pace just off the road, randomly hopping as he kicked up rabbits from their hiding places in the snow. He never caught them, but he gave chase for as long as they were visible, slowing just enough to extend the pursuit.

They'd been riding outside the city for more than an hour and Matt's toes were feeling the frost. It was two days after Christmas, and Philadelphia was paralyzed from the snow that had fallen constantly for almost two weeks. The mood was anything but festive. The drifts made it impossible to move through the city streets, so Matt gave up on going to the laboratory. With nothing happening in the city, he was left with time to exercise the animals. He wore a large wool cloak that covered his body to the tops of his boots. It captured the heat that rose from the horse, keeping Matt mostly warm, but his feet and face were exposed. To complete his discomfort, a headache was coming on. He didn't want to be too far out of town in the event that it became bad enough to lose his vision.

Bastards! Matt reached up with his gloved hand to rub where they'd clubbed him in the head, then retook the reins to slow Thunder. He moved the leather straps across the horse's neck to change direction.

"We gotta head back, boy," he said. "I'm cold." The horse hesitated, but then followed the command. Thunder was smart enough to know that turning in the road signaled the end of their trip. "Tomorrow's another day," Matt said. He patted the horse's neck and searched the woods for the dog. "Scout, let's go!" he yelled into the wind. There was nothing at first, and then shuffling as the dog came bounding through the snow and brush. The horse shook his head and made the *pwafft* sound that was his usual reaction to the dog. "We're going home."

The dog looked down the road toward their destination. They'd lived in Philadelphia for less than four months, but Scout could already recognize most of the people and places by name. Matt had worried that it might be hard for the animal to become accustomed to the city, but Scout took easily to the lifestyle. James Baker, the teenage boy Matt cured of a stomachache on his way to Philadelphia, took care of the dog while Matt tried to get his business off the ground. The teen let Scout follow him around on his daily chores and let him ride atop his wagon during deliveries.

Matt's original timeline had crumbled to the point where he had no idea when he'd be able to return to Richmond. After a promising start, it had proven impossible to make enough aspirin to sell. The first couple of small reactions had worked so well and looked so pure that he chanced taking the drug himself and was happy to learn that the aspirin did what it should. Matt could synthesize it in small quantities, but every time he tried to scale the reaction up, it turned to brown tar. Four months of constant work had yielded only ten doses.

The recent blanket of snow muted the sounds on the country road except for the strong breathing of the horse and the jangling of the buckles on the dog's leather collar. The sun was low on the horizon and the lanterns of the city pubs appeared as they moved closer to town. The pubs were always better lit than the houses and easiest to spot in the distance. Matt's plan was to return to the Bakers' complex, bed Thunder down in the stable, and go back to his room for strong tea and aspirin to push his headache away.

The Bakers didn't condone Matt's bringing the dog into the room he rented, but they looked the other way since the weather had turned harsh. Matt couldn't remember it being as cold in Philadelphia as it was now. He dwelled on this thought for a moment, thinking this might be an entirely incorrect way to think about his experience. It wasn't the past he remembered, was it? His memories were from the future, so technically his experience hadn't happened yet. It wouldn't be as cold in the future, two hundred and fifty years from now. His mind grew tired when he focused on his place in the timeline for too long.

The dog's ears perked up now as they moved into the city. Sometimes stray dogs harassed them, or rats scurried along their path as they passed. Scout would bark or growl when he thought a dog might be threatening, and always at the rats, who didn't capture his imagination like the rabbits in the countryside. The dog took his role as protector very seriously. Today, though, they were alone as they stepped through the large chunks of ice and piles of drifted snow that blocked their path.

****

Thunder was still steaming when Matt finally walked him up to the stable. Matt opened the barn door and led him inside. There was no heat, but the barn was relatively warm from the eight animals housed there. Matt checked the horse's bedding and feed, walked him into his stall and closed the gate. He'd come back later and cover him with a blanket after the perspiration had dried. As Matt situated the horse, the dog wandered over to his sleeping area.

After young James Baker convinced his father that the dog wouldn't bother the horses, the man agreed to let Scout sleep in the stable. As time went on, the elder Baker became downright comfortable with the dog, often spending long moments talking to him, scratching his head, and bringing him bones. Matt heard him saying "good dog" one day in response to Scout's barking at anyone who entered the stable who wasn't a member of the Baker family. The dog had a way with people and gravitated toward those that were solid and sincere. Matt wondered at times how an animal could be so good at judging character.

Matt poked his head into Scout's stall and saw that he was intently chewing on a bone left by the older man. After checking his water, Matt decided to leave the dog in the barn. "I'll see you later," he said. "You may be here all night with the size of that." The animal glanced up but returned quickly to chewing. Matt shut the door of the stable as he walked outside. The ground was brittle with snow that crunched as he walked and made him shiver.

Matt's room was behind the building where they kept surplus equipment for their candlemaking workshop. The room was comfortable by colonial standards but was cold in the winter like most eighteenth-century buildings. It was dark when he entered except for a log that was still glowing in the fireplace. It always smelled strongly of smoke when he entered for the first time. Matt grabbed another log and tossed it onto the smoldering embers. Sparks flashed and traveled up into the chimney. He poked the split wood until it was sitting fully on the red coals and fiddled with it until it burst into flames.

Matt poured water into the kettle and pushed it over the fire, wondering again why the room didn't have some sort of stove. When he was still in Richmond, he had started a list of inventions that had by now grown substantially. His most desired invention, since winter had started, was a Franklin stove. He'd been under the impression that everyone had them in colonial times, but he hadn't seen one yet. The cold Pennsylvania winter was teaching him firsthand that the traditional fireplace wasn't efficient for either cooking or heating.

Matt changed out of his riding boots into thick wool socks and short black shoes. The fire was starting to pop and steam was rising from the kettle. He put three times the usual amount of tea in his metal pot, poured the hot water, and let it steep for a couple of minutes before pouring it into a cup. He walked to the windowsill where he kept the milk and added some to the tea along with a spoon of honey. The tea was strong but tasted as good as any he could've gotten in his own century. He stood there looking out the window, waiting for the caffeine to take effect, hoping it would prevent his headache.

Matt lit a candle and sat back in front of the fire to read. He reached around for his book until remembering he'd left it at the laboratory. He rested there for a while, watching the fire dance, but after he finished his tea, he became bored. There had been too many nights recently, in between the headaches, where he'd obsessed about getting his business off the ground. Tonight he needed human company. Matt replaced the metal screen in front of the fire to prevent embers from popping out into the room. He grabbed his wool cloak that had been warming near the fire, put it on, and walked out again into the cold winter air.

****

Matt felt surprisingly warm as he walked the four blocks to Poor Tom's Tavern. His head and his mood were both better after the tea. There were two other taverns on the way, but he chose to go the extra distance. The taverns he skipped were full of men with thick Cockney accents whose primary purpose, it seemed, was to get drunk and fight in between propositioning whores. Poor Tom's attracted wealthy businessmen and educated people, and the women there were at least subtle in their approach.

A sweltering steam of unwashed humanity confronted Matt as he opened the door to Poor Tom's. Nonetheless, he was grateful for the warmth, and while he noticed the smell, it no longer bothered him as it once had. There was a band playing off in the corner. It sounded like an Irish tune, but most tavern music in the eighteenth century sounded Irish to Matt, so he wasn't sure. He walked to a table next to the bar and sat. Charity, an attractive barmaid who was probably five years younger than him, looked over, and he signaled her to bring him an ale. She smiled flirtatiously through locks of dark brown hair as she set it down.

"Good evening, Mr. Miller," she said. "Haven't seen you in ages."

"I've been busy with work," Matt replied. "The weather hasn't helped." He surveyed the tavern and realized there were more seats open than usual. "Anything exciting?"

"Cold's keeping people home."

"I needed to get out," Matt replied.

Charity was staring over Matt's shoulder in the direction of a table in the corner. Matt turned to see three men sitting there. One was gesturing excitedly to the two others as he spoke. "It may come to blows," Charity said to Matt, rolling her eyes.

"I've never seen them in here," Matt said.

"Dr. Franklin hasn't been for a while," Charity explained. "He's recently returned from England."

"Ben Franklin?"

"Yes," she said simply. "Do you know him?"

CHAPTER 22.

FOUNDING FATHER

Matt felt star-struck as he tried to get a hint of recognition from a face he'd only seen in two-hundred-year-old paintings. He resisted the temptation to pull out the hundred-dollar bill he carried in his pocketbook. He had often joked to himself that meeting one of the founders of the United States of America would be no big deal, but now he was paralyzed.

"Mr. Miller," Charity said, noticing his change in manner. "Have you had some dealings with Dr. Franklin?"

"No," Matt replied, "but I'm aware of his reputation."

"Do you desire an introduction?"

"You know him?"

"He's quite charming," she said, smiling warmly. "Send them ale. Did you wish to speak on some topic in particular?"

Matt was dumbfounded. He was from Philadelphia and had spent his childhood walking through the Franklin Institute, and now he had no idea what to say to Ben Franklin. "I'm a scientist," he mumbled.

"A scientist?"

"Hard to believe?"

"Perhaps," she said.

"Why?"

"The lettered men who come in here are exceedingly proud," Charity said.

"So am I," Matt said, smiling.

She rolled her eyes, but he could tell she was intrigued. "Too proud for a simple barmaid, then?"

"You shouldn't judge me so harshly."

She smiled at him and then, much to his surprise, she leaned down and kissed him on the cheek. The warmth of her lips contrasted with the coolness of her hair as it traveled across his face.

"I guess that works," Matt said. He could still feel the softness of her lips.

"I shouldn't have done that."

"Your secret is safe with me."

She curtsied and walked away with a spring in her step.

Matt sat drinking his ale, still with no idea of what he'd say to Franklin. He felt like he knew everything and nothing about the man. He considered talking about electricity and tried to remember when Franklin did the kite experiment. His train of thought was broken as he watched Charity take three mugs over to the table. Franklin turned and waved him over.

"Thank you for the ale," Franklin said, standing up to shake Matt's hand when he had reached them. The two other men stood hesitantly and gave Matt suspicious stares.

"Matthew Miller. I'm a scientist and have followed your work for some time."

"Dr. Benjamin Franklin," the older man replied, still grasping Matt's hand. "What kind of science?"

Matt decided it would be best to speak the truth. "Apothecary," he said. "I've invented a few different medicines."

Franklin glared at his companions. "Are you going to introduce yourselves?" Both men shook Matt's hand and said their names.

"We can continue the conversation another day," Franklin said to the two men. "The Crown will not forget us anytime soon." The men shook Franklin's hand to leave. One put money down on the table and they both walked away. Neither had touched the drinks Matt bought.

"They're a bunch of old mad toms whenever we talk about the king's taxes," Franklin explained. "There's naught we can do sitting here."

"Nothing is certain but death and taxes," Matt said with a grin.

"Ho! 'Tis true," Franklin cried. "Would it vex you if I were to repeat that?"

"Not at all," Matt said, feeling shameless. He was sure Franklin had been the one to say this, but it was obvious from his reaction that he hadn't said it *yet*. Matt wanted to kick himself. Why hadn't he prepared for meeting someone famous? Coming from Philadelphia, he should have at least thought about meeting Ben Franklin, his childhood hero. It was going to be hard to lie. Franklin was *the* Leonardo da Vinci of the eighteenth century. He was well-traveled and might know enough to spot discrepancies in Matt's story. There was also the problem that Matt could no longer use the elaborate cover story he developed in Virginia, which involved telling everyone that he was from Philadelphia.

"Have a seat, young man," Franklin said, pointing to one of the chairs vacated by his colleagues. "What brings you to Philadelphia?"

"I moved here recently from Richmond," Matt replied. "As I said, I've invented some medicines and I'm trying to establish an apothecary business."

"Where did you take your education?"

Matt thought quickly. "The College of William and Mary." He changed the subject before Franklin could ask any follow-up questions. "Someone said you've recently returned from England. How long is that journey?"

"Six to twelve weeks, depending on whether you're coming or going and how stubborn the captain."

Benjamin Franklin's Chart of the Gulfstream

"Does the wind blow differently in one direction?" In his own time, it took an hour longer to fly west across the United States than east because of the jet stream.

"The currents flow favorably in some parts of the sea," Franklin replied. "It's only a matter of convincing the captain to take a less obvious route."

Matt remembered something about Franklin discovering the Gulf Stream, but he hadn't been aware of the practical use until now. "Do you make the journey often?"

"Only when necessary. What can you cure with these medicines of yours?"

"Headaches, pain, and rheumatism. I'm working on something that will prevent morsel." Franklin's eyebrows went up. Matt wasn't sure whether he was excited or doubtful.

"Do you have a storefront?"

"Grace Apothecary, one street off Market."

"I might come to buy some of this rheumatism medicine."

"I have a few tablets with me now."

"Here?" Franklin asked, surprised.

"You should see them fizz," Matt said as he waved to Charity. She beamed and walked to the table. "We need two cups of clear water."

When she had left the table, Franklin observed, "Seems that young lady fancies you."

"I'm already pledged to a lady in Richmond."

"Anglicans?" There was some disdain in his voice.

Matt nodded.

"Righteous, maddening people," Franklin said. "I've done my penance with them."

"She's beautiful—rides horses."

Franklin grinned and looked like he was going to say more, but Charity returned and they watched her set ceramic cups of water on the table. Matt pulled out two small waxed-parchment packets containing two tablets each. Despite not being able to synthesize aspirin in large enough quantities to support his business, he'd been able to come up with enough to try out a number of prototypes of his version of Alka-Seltzer, which he promptly named Miller Head and Stomach Tablets. Matt pulled the cups close and dropped two tablets into each. The water began fizzing vigorously.

Franklin watched in amazement. "You certainly know how to put on a show."

"Wait for it to stop fizzing," Matt instructed. "It makes you feel better even if you're not in pain." Matt doubted Franklin was listening. He'd been too busy watching the bubbles. Matt swirled his cup and gulped the liquid until it was gone. When he was finished, he said, "It doesn't taste as good as I'd like."

Franklin stared at his glass. It was no longer fizzing. He picked it up, swirled it like Matt had, and drank. "Limes and mint," Franklin said, puckering his mouth. "Now what?"

"It doesn't take long," Matt said confidently. "Your bones will feel loose for the rest of the day."

"That gives us plenty of time to finish these other drinks, then," Franklin said. "Where're you living?"

"South of Market. I'm renting a room from a candle maker by the name of Baker—"

"I can feel the medicine working already," Franklin interrupted. "It's like having brandy, but keeping your wits."

"Now if I can only make enough to sell. I have two years to make my fortune and claim my bride."

"Two years?"

Matt wasn't sure whether that was long or short in Franklin's mind. "Kind of. Her father actually said no," Matt explained. "I agreed with her in secret."

"Business ventures are never guaranteed," Franklin said.

Matt nodded. "I'm already having trouble."

"Beautiful ladies *are* bewitching," Franklin observed. He looked off into the distance, obviously thinking of someone in particular.

Matt smiled as he remembered Franklin's reputation as a womanizer, but also the fact that he had become somewhat less successful at it as he got on in years. Franklin's libido had remained strong throughout his life.

"I'll sleep well tonight," Franklin yawned. He looked over at the large clock in the center of the room. "It's my bedtime."

Matt nodded. "I'd enjoy meeting with you again sometime."

Franklin raised his finger in reply. He stood up, walked to the bar, borrowed a quill that had been sitting there in a jar of ink, and wrote on a piece of parchment. He handed his written address to Matt as he came back to the table. Franklin remained standing as pulled on his jacket, then put money on the table, shook Matt's hand, turned, and walked out the door.

Matt sat there for a while, replaying his conversation with one of the most famous men in American history. He waved for Charity to bring him another ale and she came over smiling to set the drink down.

"You spoke long with Dr. Franklin," she observed.

"And I owe it all to you," Matt replied.

"Remember me, then, when you're famous for your philosophy," she said, giving him a flirty smile. "Or tonight when you go back to your lonely room." She turned with a swish of her dress to resume her place behind the bar. She glanced toward him only once more and then focused on her other customers. Matt sipped slowly at his ale, content to ponder the bubbles as they moved through the liquid.

CHAPTER 23.

THE THAW

It took almost five days for the snow to melt enough to bring traffic back to the Philadelphia streets. Matt had spent the mornings away from the city riding Thunder, and the afternoons helping the Bakers remove candles from drying racks and pack them into slotted wooden crates for delivery. Matt considered the work a fair trade for the three meals they were feeding him and also the fact that they were giving him as many bayberry candles as he could carry. Mr. Baker handed him a box every time he left the factory.

Matt carried one of these boxes with him to the laboratory when he finally was able to go. When he arrived, he pushed snow away from the door with the old shovel he kept on the porch. The laboratory was one block from Market Street and not what he considered a prime location, but for now it was functional and the rent was cheap. Despite being off the main drag, he was selling a number of items each week, which paid for rent and a little more besides. He had painted a large sign with "Grace Apothecary" in white and nailed it high up on the storefront. He thought it was clever. Each time he walked up to the building he was reminded of why he came to work, and everyone else thought it was just a good Christian name for a business.

Matt set up a small retail store in front and used the two other rooms as laboratories. The storefront had an apothecary counter with medicines on the back shelf. He'd stocked the shelves with Benjamin Scott's Richmond apothecary in mind, but only chose medicines he thought had some scientific basis for their healing properties. He kept an empty jar labeled "Leeches" to make everyone comfortable, but all inquiries yielded the same explanation: "I've just run out." Strangely enough, he was making a living as an apothecary, though it wasn't exactly what he considered *Grace Taylor* money. He'd need to be more than a store owner to impress her father.

It took Matt almost two weeks to build a tablet press, and although he wasn't able to synthesize the active ingredient in aspirin in sufficient quantities to sell, he was able to make fizzing antacid tablets, which he labeled "Dyspepsia Medicine."

Matt also sold dental supplies. He contracted with a local brush maker for wooden horsehair toothbrushes, and he concocted a mint-flavored toothpaste that he sold in round tins alongside the brushes. There was also a supply of toothpicks and silk dental floss. Matt thought the silk floss was much too expensive, but it still managed to sell to customers who were in distress from food caught in their teeth. The toothpaste was sweetened with a xylitol syrup extract he obtained by boiling cornhusks. From what he could remember from biochemistry class, the xylitol shouldn't cause tooth decay. Both the antacids and the dental supplies came with instructions he ordered from a local printer.

Common Name: Xylitol

Chemical Formula: $C_5H_{12}O_5$

Molecular Weight: 152.2

Natural Source: Corn husks

A bell on the front door alerted Matt when patrons came in. When there were no customers, he did experiments in the back. He was working on penicillin, the production of which was still a complete mystery. When Matt arrived in Philadelphia, he bought a couple crates of cantaloupes, which he'd allowed to mold in ten covered ceramic crocks. He collected and dried the mold on a weekly basis and used alcohol to extract from it a brown powder. At best, the powder was composed of four different compounds, one or two that he hoped were some form of penicillin. The mixture had antibiotic properties, but he wasn't confident enough to ingest any to test its safety.

Every modern chemist knew the story of penicillin. Its discovery was credited to Sir Alexander Fleming in 1928, but it wasn't until World War II that it could be produced on a large scale. Fleming discovered penicillin when he noticed that bacteria cultures contaminated with mold had areas where the bacteria wouldn't grow. Simple bread mold contained penicillin, but other molds gave a higher yield.

Common Name: Penicillin V

Chemical Formula: $C_{16}H_{18}N_2O_5S$

Molecular Weight: 350.4

Natural Source: Bread and fruit molds

Matt's immediate concern with the "biotech" section of his operation was that the moldy cantaloupes smelled. The door had to remain shut or the odor would travel into the front room and chase customers away. Matt only went into the crock room after the shop was closed, and even then only to collect mold and leave as quickly as possible. He tried to keep it very clean, in part due to his guilt at the concern that he might be doing permanent structural damage to the building.

Matt had been gone for days because of the snow, so he knew his harvest was overdue. The fermenting crocks were warm despite the relatively cold temperature in this back room. He locked the front door, hoping not to be interrupted. He forced himself to be as patient as possible when customers entered his store, even though in most cases it was during some crucial step in his experiments.

Matt went into the back room, opened the door quickly, and shut it behind him. He was confronted by the smell of fifty putrid and rotting cantaloupes. He scraped the mold from the crocks, capped them, and placed the brown spores on a drying tray. Once dry, ethanol would be used to extract the mold, and then the ethanol would be allowed to evaporate. The resulting brown powder was then transferred into a covered collection tin. Matt was always in some state of holding his breath in the cantaloupe room, so when he was finally able to get out, he inhaled deeply.

The aspirin synthesis room was tidy by comparison and much easier on the nose. He was trying to convert a supply of willow bark into aspirin. In his own time, freshman chemistry majors routinely made aspirin in a simple lab experiment, but it was elusive for Matt because he had no eighteenth-century source of acetic anhydride. He had burned through a fortune in willow bark over the last four months trying to get the reaction right.

Common Name: Salicylic Acid
Natural Source: Willow Tree Bark

Common Name: Acetic Anhydride
Natural Source: Unknown

Common Name: Aspirin
Natural Source: None

Matt looked at all the chemistry glassware, thinking maybe he should try again today, but instead he went to the front room and started straightening the store. He was restocking the toothbrush display when a man rushed through the front door.

"You Matthew Miller?"

Matt stepped back, wondering if he was sent by Levi Payne, then quickly decided that this stranger didn't have the persona of an assassin.

"Dr. Franklin said you had medicine that would cure my daughter's blood poisoning," the man said, gazing out the window into the street. "Franklin said you were on Market. It took forever to find you."

"I'd have to see your daughter to know what she has," Matt replied.

The man returned his gaze to Matt. "She has a corruption," he said. "They say she'll be dead in days." His eyes went glassy with tears.

Matt wanted to help this man, but he wasn't sure if he should. He had some untested brown powder that might or might not be penicillin, and that might work if the girl had a bacterial infection. The last thing he wanted to do was try it for the first time on a child. "There's got to be someone else in the city that can help you."

"Are any of you worth your salt?" the man replied, suddenly very angry. He put his hand on the doorknob. "You're all useless lunatics."

Matt found himself unexpectedly angry at the injustice of the man's unfounded pronouncement, but then he remembered Benjamin Scott, who was thoroughly incompetent. The vision of that bumbling apothecary was enough to make Matt want to change this stranger's opinion of science. The words came out before he even had a rational plan. "I already know this is a mistake," he said, more to himself. "You better be prepared for the worst."

The man looked at his hand on the doorknob. "How much worse can it be?" he replied quietly. He took his hand off the door and used his thumb and forefinger to massage his swollen red eyes.

"I'll get my things," Matt said. He hurried into the back room, pulled down the tin of brown powder he'd isolated from the cantaloupe mold, grabbed three doses of home-made Alka-Seltzer, and gathered containers for mixing and stirring. He packed them into a leather case and followed the man out. Matt turned the sign on the front door to "CLOSED" and locked it behind him. He stepped into a carriage that was warm inside.

"I'm Phillip Ricken," the man said. "The others proclaimed there was naught we could do but pray."

"I'd pray as well," Matt replied.

CHAPTER 24.

ISABELLE

It was a ten-minute carriage ride to a large colonial mansion. Phillip Ricken leaped out as he motioned Matt to follow. Matt jumped to the ground and then turned around to pull his case from the carriage floor. Ricken was already waiting for him halfway to the house.

"It's this way," he called, waving Matt forward.

Matt took a deep breath and reminded himself of the man's situation, and then he did his best to demonstrate that he, too, was hurrying.

The mansion's entry was as grand and dramatic as Matt expected from the outside. Two spacious rooms with richly colored furniture to the left and right were split by an elaborate multilevel staircase that led up to the second floor. Ricken motioned Matt to hurry upstairs. Two black servants in livery watched them as they climbed. Matt followed Ricken into the second bedroom on the top floor. The bed, located near an open window, seemed small amid the vast room and the other furniture. A well-dressed middle-aged woman with grey-brown hair stood over her sleeping daughter. It was too cold in the room to be comfortable.

The woman moved to meet them as they entered. Her colorless face contrasted with her red-rimmed eyes. It looked like she'd been crying. "She's slipping away."

Matt nodded. "It's too cold in here."

"She's has a fever and falling sickness," Ricken replied. "The cold prevents the palpitations." Ricken stepped to his daughter's bedside and roused her gently with his hand. "I've brought a doctor who can cure you," he said.

"No more leeches," she whispered hoarsely.

"No more leeches," he replied. "Mr. Miller, this is Isabelle."

"Good day, Mr. Miller," Isabelle whispered. She smiled painfully. "I'm quite ill."

"I can see that," Matt said. She was about fifteen, on the edge of being a young woman. Matt forced himself to put a warm expression on his face and then he turned to speak to her parents. "Tell me what's wrong, exactly."

"She cut herself at the stable," her father explained. "We thought naught of it, but then it became red and the redness grew." He reached down to move the bedcovers and the nightgown away from his daughter's leg. There was a scabbed-over cut surrounded by angry red splotches that traveled to her trunk.

Matt briefly thought of a Hemingway story called "The Snows of Kilimanjaro," about a man who is slowly dying from blood poisoning contracted from an untreated cut.

"It's a bacterial infection," he said. "Small creatures are in the wound and have begun to grow inside her."

"Like worms?" Ricken asked.

"Yes."

"Can you cure this disease?"

"I've a medicine that might work," Matt said, "but it could make her sicker."

"Will she get better without it?" Ricken asked.

"I doubt it," Matt replied. The red rash was moving up into her abdomen. Matt couldn't remember if dying from blood poisoning had anything to do with the infection finally reaching the internal organs or the heart, or if that was just an urban legend. Matt motioned for the man and his wife to follow him out of the room. He shut the door behind them and spoke in a low voice.

"I'm going to give her something that will reduce her fever," he said. "Then I'll give her a second medicine that may cure her disease. It might make her very sick at first and could even kill her. Franklin should never have told you about me."

The father looked at his wife and she nodded. "Give it to her," he said. "I can't—we can't lose her." His voice was cracking. The man crossed himself. "It's in His hands."

"Have others died from this medicine?" the mother asked Matt.

"Yes," Matt lied. "But some have been cured."

"Then give it to her," she said calmly.

Her resolve pushed Matt past his doubts. "I need a cup of water for now, and another cup filled with apple cider as soon as you can get it." He turned away from her and stepped back into the room to see Isabelle sleeping. Looking up, he silently prayed as he questioned both higher intelligence and his own conscience as to whether he was doing the right thing in testing an unknown drug mixture on a teenager.

The mother returned with the glass of water and Isabelle struggled to open her eyes. Matt felt her forehead. She was burning up. He took the glass of water, set it on the side table, and pulled out the same tablets he had shared with Franklin. He dropped them into the water. The sound of fizzing echoed from the glass.

"Is that medicine?" she asked.

Matt nodded. "It's the first one. You get the second one later. Your insides won't feel very good either way. Can you be brave?"

"I think," she replied softly.

Matt found himself starting to make deals with God. He'd even forgive Levi Payne. He realized what he was doing and shut the thoughts down. *Not likely God makes these kind of deals.* Better that he just asked for guidance. He knew the aspirin would work, but the crude brown mixture would probably make her sick, even if it did eventually cure her.

Matt handed her the glass. "Drink this all down. I don't want to hear about how bad it tastes." The girl reached up and started drinking. She sipped it at first and then drank almost all of it on the second try. She paused and then finished what was left.

"Better than leeches," she muttered.

"I'm going to step out for a moment," Matt said. "You can talk to your mother about what you want to do when you're healthy again."

"Fine," she breathed.

Matt turned around, grabbed his bag, went into the hall, and stood above the first step of the staircase. He set the dial on his watch for thirty minutes, which was about enough time for the aspirin to kick in. One of the servants brought a cup of cider, and Matt walked back downstairs with it, balancing it gently in his hand. He set the cup down on the kitchen table, grabbed another from a rack on the wall, and pulled out the can of brown powder he'd extracted from the cantaloupe mold.

From the crude analysis he'd done, he knew it was composed mostly of four molecules, along with whatever made it brown. Pure drug was usually white, which meant that even if this mixture was composed of penicillin and related compounds, there was still some unknown toxic muck in there. He had to be prepared for the girl to have a strong reaction, maybe convulsions or vomiting, and for dealing with the parents when this happened.

Matt measured out about a gram and a half of brown powder and put it in the empty cup. He pulled a bottle of rum from his bag, poured about an ounce over the powder, and swirled it around to dissolve it. Matt then filled the cup about halfway with cider and swirled again. He was relieved to see more of the brown muck dissolve than he had expected. He had thought the girl would be drinking mud, but after some stirring, the antibiotic mixture looked like a cup of strong, cloudy coffee. He became unexpectedly optimistic; maybe it could work.

By the time he finished mixing and stirring, the half hour was almost done and he walked up the steps with the glass, stirring it with a spoon to keep the powder suspended. Isabelle was sitting up when he entered the room. "My chills are gone," she declared.

"The medicine should have brought your fever down," Matt replied. "This next one will be tough." Matt spoke to the mother. "I need you to find a big bowl in case she vomits." They waited for her to return with a large wooden bowl.

Matt handed Isabelle the brown slurry. "Drink it all."

It took a number of gulps to get it down. She gagged and her mother stepped close, ready with the bowl. "Tastes rotten," Isabelle said when she finished.

"I haven't had a chance to work on that," Matt said, smiling. "Sorry." Matt addressed her mother. "Someone should sit with her."

"I will," she replied. She nodded to her husband, who was standing by the door. As if on cue, they all stared at Isabelle with critical faces.

"It's not killed me yet," she announced back at them with a painful but irritated smile. Their laughter was enough to melt the thick tension in the room.

"Be ready for anything," Matt instructed. "It can be vomiting, shakes, falling sickness, anything. She'll need more in twelve hours, or the disease will return." He grinned at Isabelle. "Hang in there."

"Hang where?"

"Get better," Matt said. He turned to walk away, again giving in to making deals with God.

CHAPTER 25.

REGRET

They'd finished the asparagus and servants were bringing bread and roast beef topped with tomato sauce to the table. The meat was delicious and the bread was still steaming. On any other occasion, Matt would've been sitting and enjoying the excellent home-cooked meal. They'd poured him wine, but he dared not touch it. He wanted to be ready for anything. They sat there in relative silence until Ricken spoke.

"Where are your people from, Mr. Miller?"

Matt spent some time telling Ricken his story. The man acted like he was giving his full attention, but Matt suspected he was only partially listening as he snuck glances toward the stairs. When Matt reached a polite place to end his story, he said, "You should go check on her."

"She's all I can think of," Ricken admitted. He pointed. "The library's that way." He stood and walked up the steps to his daughter's room. Matt went down the hall and sat in the library to read. He read and nodded off for a couple of hours until he heard commotion from upstairs.

"Mr. Miller!" the mother said. "Please come!"

"Dammit," Matt said aloud. He rushed up the steps. The girl was convulsing violently over the bowl her mother held for her. The room smelled of vomit and moldy cantaloupe. Both parents gave him venomous looks as he entered.

"We didn't expect her to be so consumed," the mother said harshly. She held the girl's head by her hair. The contents of her stomach were all over the side of the bed where the mother hadn't been able to control her. The father looked at him with fire. Isabelle's eyes had rolled up into her head and her body had grown rigid. Her mother tried to push her abdomen down.

"This is some folly!" the father exclaimed.

"Can't you do something?" the mother demanded of Matt.

Matt looked at her, bewildered. "There isn't anything we can do now except wait."

"You intend on giving her more of this rot?" the father asked.

"Even if she feels better, she has to take the medicine for a whole week," Matt replied. Isabelle convulsed and threw up again.

"We've made a grave error bringing you here," Ricken declared.

The mother was crying and shaking her head. "How did you convince us that you could help?" she asked as she tried to clean her daughter's face.

"Our driver will take you home," Ricken said.

Matt met the young girl's sorrowful eyes and mouthed the words "I'm sorry," then turned to leave. No one accompanied him out into the courtyard. He asked the driver, who had been standing in front of the carriage, to take him home and he stepped inside. Matt regretted deeply that he had ever gotten involved.

CHAPTER 26.

MISERY LOVES COMPANY

Matt stepped from the carriage and walked directly to the stable to check on the horse and dog. He saw Thunder first. "Sorry, boy," he said as he rubbed the horse's head. "Nothing for you today." He had been too preoccupied on the journey home to think about stopping to get the horse a snack. Matt could usually find carrots or apples at the market, although they were getting more expensive as winter progressed. It was surprising how long fruit and vegetables could be preserved in a cellar. He patted Thunder one last time and walked to Scout's stall.

Scout was chewing on a bone. Matt stooped there and ran his hands through the dog's fur, hoping for his mood to change. Usually the animals had a calming effect, but it was different tonight. Matt couldn't get the image of Isabelle out of his head. It was going to take more than petting the dog to forget the girl he could not save, so he contrived a plan to go immediately to the tavern and drink himself into a stupor. Matt gave the dog one last pat and then returned to his room to prepare himself for a night of drinking.

****

Poor Tom's Tavern was crowded with colonials laughing and carrying out boisterous conversations. The sounds of mugs slamming on tables were like explosions in Matt's head. His initial thought was that he had made a mistake in coming and that he should leave, but then he saw a seat at the bar. Charity's father came out from a back room as he sat.

"Good evening, Mr. Miller," he said. "My daughter's at home tonight. Could I still convince you to stay?"

"You have a beautiful daughter, sir," Matt said. "But you know I'm promised to another."

The man smiled knowingly. "What can I get you?"

"A large ale. It's been a terrible day."

The man came back with a stein of frothy dark ale. Matt sat there staring into his drink and thinking of the day's events. He considered how he could have handled things differently and wondered what the consequences of his actions were. There was a selfish part of him that feared retribution from a wealthy man like Ricken. He might blame Matt for killing his daughter.

"Don't you have a sick girl to cure?" Someone put his hand on Matt's shoulder.

"Wha—?" Matt said, surprised as he turned. It was Ben Franklin. Matt frowned.

"You saw Isabelle?" Franklin asked.

"She had blood poisoning."

"I've seen many die from her malady," Franklin said. He scrutinized the bar. "Are you committed to spending your time at this filthy counter, or would you come to a proper table with Alexander and me?"

"I wouldn't be good company. I'm planning to drink myself silly."

"Do it at our table, then," Franklin said. He had a mischievous twinkle in his eye.

"Fine," Matt finally replied. He drained his mug and left it on the bar to follow Franklin back to his table. Franklin's friend had two empty mugs in front of him. "Matt Miller," Matt said, reaching out to shake the man's hand as he stood.

"Alexander Collinson," the man said, pointing to a chair.

Another man in the bar was waving to Franklin. "Alexander was at the Rickens' earlier in the week," Franklin said. The man at the bar was now motioning for Franklin to come over, so Franklin put his finger up and stepped away. While he was gone, Matt and Collinson traded stories about Isabelle Ricken.

"I had leeches all along the poison," Collinson explained with a cracking voice. He went silent, trying to regain his composure, and then took a long drink of ale.

Franklin returned and quietly listened to their conversation. "She's in God's hands now," Franklin said. He looked at Matt. "I thought you were further along with your medicine?"

"Ricken's not too happy with me right now," Matt replied. "Both he and his wife were in a rage."

"Once they've had time to grieve, they'll thank you," Collinson replied.

"Was her death painful?" Franklin asked.

"I don't know," Matt replied. "They made me go."

"You didn't see her die?" Franklin asked, surprised.

"I'm pretty sure she did," Matt said.

"Visit them tomorrow," Franklin suggested. "First thing."

Matt shook his head.

"Parents must be given leniency," Collinson explained.

The men were irritating Matt. There was no way they could understand how upset Ricken was in those last moments. "He made it clear that I wasn't to return."

"You'll go," Franklin commanded, "to either apologize for his daughter's death or join him in celebrating her recovery."

"Fine," Matt said drunkenly. He was intoxicated enough now to agree to anything.

Two hours later, Matt staggered home in the dark. When he crawled into bed, he prayed not to dream about the young girl he could not save.

CHAPTER 27.

TUESDAY, TUESDAY

The pendulum swept back and forth across the sky. Each swing cleared a path through the rubble and made ripples that formed streams that moved away until they disappeared. Matt shuddered with agonizing pain at each crash. The only respite from the suffering came when the pendulum pulled away from the swath it cleared. He looked closely along the track that it made. The rubble took form and he could recognize the pieces as they fell and were destroyed. There were people and places there, some he could recognize, and others that just slipped away.

Matt saw his father standing by his taxi and he watched as the pendulum smashed him into pieces. The fragments fell to the ground and he could feel his father's life force draining away. But Matt realized that not every piece was falling. A few were being pushed into the streams that moved away from the swinging monolith. *Is this how time works? Does it destroy the old and push the rubble to the new?*

Matt looked to the side in time to see the pendulum crash into him. He felt the pain of change as he was broken and slammed into a new alley. When he slowed, his body reassembled and his world reappeared. The pendulum hit him again and there was more agony. He tried to dodge it the next time, but it hit him again. He couldn't regain his footing, and it hit him once more and he couldn't breathe. Incessant, it swung again and again, painfully smashing him every time he re-formed. Then the drumming started, *bam, bam, bam, bam.*

"Mr. Miller?"

Matt opened his eyes. He looked toward the door from his bed. Early morning light streamed into the room. "I'm here," he called out. "Give me a moment." He sat up in bed. His head hurt even more than usual from his hangover. *Time to take those last headache tablets.* He pulled his pants on and went to the door.

"What!" Matt said, opening the door. "It's early—" It was Isabelle's father, Phillip Ricken. "Mr. Ricken!" Matt stepped back, suspecting that the man came to hurt him, but Ricken wasn't angry. Matt gambled on a question. "She feeling better?"

"Franklin told me you planned to visit today," Ricken said, "but I'll pay you a premium to come over now and take care of her."

She's alive! Matt looked up at the sun. He'd slept late.

"Franklin told me where to find you," Ricken said. "You understand? I didn't know what to think."

"A sick child is always upsetting to a parent," Matt said, remembering the coaching he had gotten the night before. Wind blew through the doorway, making Matt shiver. He realized he was standing on bare feet, shirtless in the doorway. "I'll need twenty minutes," he told Ricken. "Isabelle shouldn't be treated by someone who looks like a vagabond. Can I eat at your house?"

"Of course. I'll wait for you," Ricken replied. He smiled and went back to the coach waiting in the driveway. Matt watched him walk away and then looked at the sky, wondering again if he was part of some plan. *I'm still in the game.*

Matt put his shoes and shirt on, walked to the privy behind the building, and finished up as quickly as he could. He hurried back inside and washed. The water was cold, but not as cold as it would have been straight from the well. His head felt horrible. *Serves you right!* There weren't many tablets left in the Advil bottle, so ibuprofen was out of the question. Matt considered that he might have one of his aspirin tablets. He had two adult doses left. Then he thought of Isabelle and decided that they were best saved for her. He could stretch the headache tablets out into four doses for someone her size. He'd have to tolerate his pounding head. Matt brushed his teeth, put clean clothes on, grabbed the leather case that contained the tin of penicillin powder, and walked out the door.

Ricken was a chatterbox as they drove. Matt's head was swimming, but he tried his best to look comfortable. Matt nodded to the man as he put on his jovial façade. "She vomited for a long time after you left," Ricken said. "'Twas a foul-smelling brown tar." He was quiet for a time, then asked, "Is that the poison in her blood?"

It's the nasty stuff I should never have given her. "You could think of it that way," Matt replied.

"She fell asleep and we thought that we'd lost her," Ricken said. "Her mother sat with her into the night cooling her forehead with a damp cloth. Isabelle was the first to wake this morning. She commanded her mother to repair to her chamber that she might rest. She said, 'Mother, go to bed!' Just like that, she said it."

"I have to give her more medicine," Matt said. "You know that, right?"

"Now we know what to expect," Ricken replied.

****

Matt was surprised to find Isabelle sitting at the dining room table eating. "How do you feel?"

"Not very well," she replied. "My stomach hurts badly, but the worms have been chased away."

Matt reached out and felt her forehead. "Your fever's gone."

"No more chills," she added.

"Get something to eat, and then we'll talk about what's next," Matt said. "I want you to drink a full cup of water, right now."

"A full cup?" she asked. Her mother was already pouring water from a pitcher.

"Drink," her mother said. There was more resolve in her than before.

"Can I see the rash while she eats?" Matt said to her mother. She nodded yes, reached down, and pulled the girl's gown up. Her leg still had red splotches that traveled up to her trunk, but they somehow seemed less angry. She had survived the first dose and it looked to have worked. Matt would need to dose her every day for a week. He thought to warn her of this, but decided she should be allowed to finish her meal. The soup she was drinking was the perfect food to be absorbed quickly before he shocked her system again.

The servant brought him a breakfast of cornmeal cakes, eggs, and bacon, and he sat there with Isabelle, eating and asking questions about her life.

"Are you going to make me drink more of that medicine?" she said unexpectedly.

"Yes."

"I'm not going to die now, am I?"

"No, you're not," Matt replied. He was struck by how confident and powerful he felt.

"I heard the others whispering."

"They were wrong."

"Then I'm ready for more medicine."

"Take a break," Matt said. "You need food." They talked for a long time as her mother moved in and out of the dining room to steal glances at her daughter, to judge her recovery and to listen. The mother interrupted them only once to set down steaming biscuits, peach preserves, and butter, which they both gladly accepted while discussing life in Philadelphia.

Matt dosed her again before noon and waited with her until she had finished vomiting. It wasn't nearly as bad this time. He cut the dose in half after that and found that she only complained of an upset stomach for a couple of hours. She was cured of her infection after seven days, with only a few bouts of vomiting on the last two.

CHAPTER 28.

PROGRESS

Three weeks had passed since he'd treated Isabelle Ricken. Matt was now selling so many sundries that he hardly had time to go into the laboratory. He'd only managed to harvest the mold from his cantaloupe cultures, and even then had to force himself. He was mostly selling personal care products, which included a number of toothbrushes and toothpaste. He had different kinds of soap and the candles from Baker and Sons. He'd sold every free candle they gave him and was now buying crates of them to keep up with demand. With the combined sales of all the items, he'd already made thirty pounds profit.

There were customers in his store constantly during the day and he was becoming a recognized member of the community. He'd close the store about three o'clock and take Thunder and Scout riding outside the city. He felt he wasn't spending near enough time with either the dog or the horse, but he had no idea how else he could find the time with his busy schedule. He'd spend his nights reading Grace's letters and writing his replies. The letter writing had gotten more difficult since treating Isabelle. He'd been able to write Grace a detailed account of his colorful adventure while curing the young girl, but lately there seemed to be nothing of consequence. *I do the same thing every day.* He was opening another box of candles when two familiar faces appeared.

"My dear Mr. Miller!" Isabelle exclaimed. The girl rushed to give him a hug, squeezing him tightly as her father looked on.

The hug was long enough to make Matt uncomfortable, so he stepped back when it was convenient. "Very good to see you, Isabelle!" She had ribbons on her dress and in her hair. Matt got the distinct impression that some of them were for him. "In my professional opinion, you're healed," he proclaimed.

"I feel wonderful," she replied. "I came with Father to thank you." She turned to her father. "Can we invite Mr. Miller for dinner?"

"Maybe, darling," he said. "Mr. Miller has his own life and ladies his own age he'd like to entertain." Matt winked at him surreptitiously. "Say your thanks," her father said. "I must talk to Mr. Miller in private."

She stepped in to Matt and gave him another tight hug. "Thank you again, Mr. Miller." She curtsied and walked out to stand on the front porch.

"Sorry," Matt said to her father. "I'm not doing anything to encourage that."

"She's starting to notice men," he said. "Unfortunately they're all a decade too old."

Matt smiled. "She looks great. How's her leg?"

"Healed. She's singing in front of the church this Sunday."

"I'm glad I could help."

"I never received your bill," Ricken said.

"The experience was worth more than money. I was glad to help." It was true. Matt had learned that he did, indeed, have a working form of penicillin. He still felt somewhat guilty for testing it on a young girl, though, and considered himself fortunate to have escaped unscathed.

"I know what it's like to build a business," Ricken declared, "but you should make every effort to collect your debts. You never know when an opportunity will present itself. What if you have no capital?" Ricken pulled a large purse from his pocket. "I'll not attempt to put a price on my daughter's life. You saved her and managed to capture my imagination. I don't want to hear that you've spent this on wine and ladies."

Matt accepted the purse. The weight of it surprised him. "Thank you."

Ricken reached out and shook his hand. "The best of luck to you, Mr. Miller. If I can help, please visit."

Matt nodded and watched the man leave. He put the purse in a drawer behind the counter without looking inside. He thought back to his conversation with David Taylor. When he left Richmond, it was important to David that Matt understand that his success and acceptance in the Taylor family wasn't dependent on money. Matt was making a living now in Philadelphia, and he was doing it all on his own.

Matt was sure that being a shopkeeper wasn't worthy of Grace Taylor. He'd promised her a large farm with horses where they could raise a family. Selling soap and toothpaste was nowhere near his vision. It might be different if he planned on having a soap empire that stretched across the colonies.

Just then, another customer walked in and Matt sold him four bars of lye soap. He looked up at the ceiling afterwards. "Very funny."

He pulled a slate and some chalk out of a drawer and wrote "Help Wanted" in large letters, and then hung it in the window. It felt like a giant weight had been lifted from his shoulders. He locked the door, went into the back laboratory, and set up another chemical reaction to synthesize aspirin.

It was still light when he got home. A letter from Grace was waiting for him in the box at his door, and it made him smile. "Got another letter," he said to the dog. He still had an hour or so until he was supposed to meet Franklin for dinner, so he went inside to read the latest news from Richmond. Graine and Will had set a wedding date for late August, right before harvest. A smaller card from Will was enclosed, inviting Matt to join the wedding party. He would need to travel down to Virginia in two months. A wide smile filled Matt's face at the thought of seeing Grace and her family. Unexpectedly, though, his happy daydreams were interrupted by a vision of Levi Payne.

The migraines had been a regular occurrence since he was clubbed by Levi's thugs. When the headaches came, his vision clouded over with indistinguishable snapshots of the future. Most times he could consciously force the visions out of his head, but it was impossible during a migraine. Matt had often suffered for hours as unfiltered images of the future assaulted him. There were certain scenes that were clearer than others, and those almost always came to pass. One of his most lucid visions was of fighting Levi Payne, then lying bleeding on the ground.

Thus far, for lack of a solution, Matt had avoided thinking about how he'd deal with Levi when he returned to

Richmond. He hadn't mentioned the mugging in his letters to Grace, but Matt had told her about the Paynes being a threat and that her family should be careful. She had written back that they were taking precautions. Levi hadn't come up again. *I'll have to confront him.*

Matt stooped down to the dog, ran his hands through his fur, and felt a little despair. "They'll probably want you to stay," he said, "though I don't know how they'd prevent you from running away again."

When Matt finished reading Grace's letter, he pulled Ricken's purse from his bag. He opened it and shook it out onto the bed. The coins added up to about three hundred pounds. *More money than I know what to do with...again.* Large sums of money now made him uneasy. He gathered the money and pried up the loose floorboard under the bed, then dropped the purse next to the hundred or so pounds he'd already saved.

CHAPTER 29.

COME CLEAN

Franklin was already seated with a mug of ale in front of him. He stood momentarily when Matt entered the tavern and waved to get his attention. Matt smiled, then looked over at Charity standing behind the bar and motioned for her to bring him his own mug. She arrived with his ale as he removed his coat and sat down.

"How's business?" Franklin asked once Matt was seated and had taken a drink.

"I've decided to hire someone to mind my store," Matt said. "It'll help me spend more time in the lab." He was interested in whether Franklin believed the additional expense made good business sense.

"Still no progress, then?" Franklin asked.

Matt shook his head. "I need to find a better supply of willow bark—"

"You think that will help?" Franklin replied, cutting him off. He gazed intently at Matt from under a furrowed brow.

"Something will work...eventually," Matt said, trying to interpret the older man's hard line.

"Have you thought about speaking to your old instructors?"

Matt hesitated to compose himself, as he always did when Franklin asked about his past. He stretched the moment out by taking a drink. "I already asked them," Matt replied carefully. "They don't know any more than I do."

"I'm going to William and Mary to lecture in two weeks," Franklin declared. "I can ask them for you."

"They wouldn't be able to help. I'm beyond what they were able to teach." Matt strained to find a new topic. He wanted to kick himself for using William and Mary as a cover story. He scrutinized the mug in front of him, wondering if taking another drink would make him seem more or less confident. He involuntarily moved his hand toward the ale and saw Franklin's eyes follow his fingers. Matt covered his movement by reaching up to push the hair off his forehead.

"At least tell me their names," Franklin demanded. "I'll wish them well and inform them that their prize student has become a prosperous businessman."

"I'd rather they weren't involved," Matt said. "We didn't always agree."

"I'm sure they'd be happy to help."

"No need," Matt insisted. He laughed, trying to sound collected. His head was starting to swim.

Franklin stood up and reached for his coat. "I don't know what your ruse is," he said threateningly. "You can be sure that I'll be contacting the authorities." Matt watched as Franklin buttoned his coat.

"Authorities? For what?"

"They've never heard of you at William and Mary." Franklin turned abruptly to leave.

"There's an explanation," Matt said. He could feel his hands trembling from the adrenaline of a confrontation that had come much more quickly than he had expected.

Franklin stopped in the middle of his first stride toward the door, turned back, and stared down at Matt like a bird of prey. "The explanation," he replied, "is that you're a liar, a swindler, and probably a thief."

"I'm not a swindler and I'm not a thief!"

"My first stop will be the sheriff," Franklin declared.

"If you're resigned to that," Matt said, "will it hurt to sit for a few minutes and let me plead my case?"

"I care not," Franklin replied.

"I lied for a reason," Matt exclaimed.

Franklin faced him again. "A man lies about his past for only two reasons," he declared. "He's committed a crime or he's planning one. Either way, he's a criminal." Franklin put his hands out in a gesture of obviousness.

"There's a third reason you haven't considered."

Franklin scoffed. "Nonsense."

Matt motioned to the chair. "Please, sir, you're considered one of the greatest intellects of your day. Aren't you curious how I managed to fool you?"

To Matt's satisfaction and relief, Franklin stepped back to the table, pulled out a chair, and sat down with his coat still on. "Ten minutes," he scowled.

Matt reached into his jacket pocket, pulled out his wristwatch, and handed it to Franklin. "What do you think this is?"

"A bracelet?" Franklin quipped. "Stolen?" He put his glasses on and looked more closely. "It's an intricate likeness of a clock."

"Not a likeness," Matt said. "Put it to your ear."

Franklin put the Rolex to the side his head. "It chirps," he proclaimed.

"It's called a wristwatch."

"It's small," Franklin observed, inspecting it again. "I've never seen you wear this."

"Because I didn't want to lie about it."

Franklin looked down again at the watch and then to the large pendulum clock at the front wall of the tavern. "Where'd you get this?"

"Philadelphia," Matt said. "It cost me five thousand dollars."

Franklin gave him a questioning look.

"I'd planned on showing you money from my country sometime," Matt explained. "Not this soon, though."

"Until you were caught in your lies," Franklin said with venom in his voice. He was reading the face of the watch. "You've used up three of your minutes."

"I'm going to show you the money I used to buy this watch," Matt said. "It should help with my story." He pulled out the wallet that contained the one-hundred-dollar bill he carried. "Promise me that you'll sit until I've made my case."

"Through your entire ruse?" Franklin said with scorn.

Matt was suddenly pissed and it was his turn to scowl. "You're holding a miracle in your hand," Matt said coldly, "and you're not curious enough to ask questions?" He thrust the wallet back into his pocket and then reached out for the watch in an exaggerated motion. "Give it back." Matt stood as soon as his fingers closed around the watch. "I'm not a criminal. You know where I live. Send the authorities if you want." Matt fished into his pocket and put some coins down on the table. "Good day, sir." He grabbed his coat and walked out of the pub, wondering if he'd taken too much of a gamble.

CHAPTER 30.

QUANTUM LEAP

Matt walked the six city blocks back to his house. He'd pick up Scout and sneak him into his room. It puzzled him how he could be in the most crowded city in the colonies and still feel so alone.

"Can you slow down?" It was Franklin, calling from behind.

Matt felt a twinge of satisfaction that he had aroused the man's curiosity. "I expected more from a man of science," Matt said over his shoulder.

"I should sit quietly and listen to your lies?" Franklin called.

"Not lies," Matt said. "It's a cover story."

"Slow down," Franklin called. "I'm an old man with one foot in the grave."

"You're going to live for another thirty years," Matt said, still walking.

"Only the Lord knows the time and place of a man's death!" Franklin had sincere concern in his voice.

"I read your biography."

Franklin had finally caught up and was walking alongside, breathing hard. "Whose biography?"

"You heard me," Matt replied. He opened the gate to the Bakers' complex and Franklin followed him in. They stepped off the main driveway to the barn where he kept Scout, and Matt slid the door open. He heard some shuffling, and the dog came trotting from one of the stalls and greeted them happily. Matt stooped over and rubbed the dog on both sides of his head. "Hey, buddy," he said. Matt stood and walked to Thunder's stall as Franklin followed. "Hi, boy," Matt said when the horse stuck his head out to greet him. Matt scratched until his hands got tired and then offered him the green apple he had in his pocket. "They're getting a little soft." Thunder chomped happily on the fruit.

Both men stood there in silence, hypnotized by the motions of the horse's jaw. Scout was already leaning into Franklin as the man ran his hand through his fur. Matt looked over at the dog and rolled his eyes. "I'm surprised you came," Matt said as he lifted his head to look into Franklin's eyes.

"I apologize for my initial reaction," Franklin replied sincerely. "Nonetheless, I expect to be treated with the respect my station deserves."

Matt acknowledged him with a nod and made a conscious effort to relax his face and shake off the pretense that had built up inside him. "I'll tell you my story, but you must swear your secrecy."

"Only if you've committed no crime," Franklin declared.

"No crime," Matt replied.

"You have my word, then. I'll take your secret to my grave."

"That's thirty years." Matt smiled.

"How do you believe you can predict the future?" Concern spread again across Franklin's face.

Matt gave Thunder some strong pats on his neck, then turned to Franklin and motioned for him to follow. The dog stepped away from Franklin and joined Matt at his side, looking up at him. "Come on, dog," he said. "Let's go make Dr. Franklin some tea and let him sit down."

"You're trying my patience, young man," Franklin warned.

Matt waited for Franklin to step out of the barn and then shut the door behind them as Franklin watched and waited. "I'm from the future," Matt said simply. "There was an accident with electricity, and I ended up in another century." Matt waved for Franklin to follow him to his room, but Franklin stood for a second to think.

"'Tis all clear now," Franklin called. "You're crazy as a loon." He stutter-stepped quickly to catch up to Matt.

"Either way, here I am in 1763," Matt replied. He reached down to rest his hand on the dog's head as they walked.

"You expect me to believe you're from the future based on your jewelry?"

"It's a wristwatch," Matt said. "Why do they even call it that? Shouldn't it be a wrist clock?"

"Men need to know the time when they stand watch," Franklin explained. "It makes sense, actually. Where did you get your education? Someplace on the Continent?"

"Philadelphia College of Science."

"There's no such place."

"There will be," Matt said. "I received my doctorate from the University of Kansas. Kansas won't even exist for another seventy years. The French own that territory now."

"You're quite mad," Franklin exclaimed.

They were almost at Matt's door. Matt reached into his jacket and pulled out his pocketbook. He unfolded the hundred-dollar bill and handed it to Franklin. "This is money from the United States of America," he said. "I bought the watch with US dollars."

Franklin fumbled with the green paper. "I need my glasses."

Matt waited for Franklin to inspect the bill. "Better if you see it in the daylight."

Franklin put his glasses on and spread the bill open between his two hands. "Why is my likeness on this paper?"

"Look at the year," Matt said, pointing to the bottom of the bill.

"It's a number," Franklin replied.

"It's a year," Matt corrected. "Two thousand sixteen."

"You're from the year two thousand and sixteen?" Franklin repeated. His eyes were still glued to the bill. "This is surely a work of art by some master. Only royalty could afford this."

"Everyone has them where I come from," Matt said. "Many places have stopped taking paper money. The printing technology that's available makes it too easy to counterfeit."

Franklin followed Matt into his room. Scout went to his dog bed in the corner and settled in. Franklin sat while still looking at the bill and asked, "Why would my face be on money?"

"You have some role in the formation of my country," Matt replied. "You want tea?"

Franklin nodded, still inspecting the treasure in his hands. "United States of America," he read aloud. "Are you trying to ensnare me for treason?" He stared suspiciously at Matt. "Some of the things I've said in the past may be misconstrued as against the Crown, but I'm a strong loyalist." He seemed surprised by his own conviction. He looked into Matt's face. "You're an agent of the king."

"Hardly," Matt answered. "I've one other thing to show you. It'll knock your socks off." Matt went to his pack in the corner. "This is probably the most advanced invention in my time. Even a king isn't capable of making something like this." Franklin, still holding the bill, now stared intently at the object Matt had pulled from his backpack. "It's a communication device that plays music and displays pictures," Matt said. He had already pressed the on button and the phone was now glowing. Matt touched icons to get to his music files and pressed play. The small speakers were amazingly effective in filling the room with classical music.

Franklin stood up. "Bach! How is this possible?"

"Electricity."

"Electricity doesn't make music."

"It makes noise," Matt said. "You've heard it crackle and pop. You adjust the strength for different sounds."

"This is wizardry," Franklin exclaimed.

"There's God," Matt said, "and there's the science I think he wants us to discover, but there's no wizardry." He fumbled with the phone again. "I've Mozart in here too. I used it to practice the minuet down in Richmond." Matt stopped the Bach and started the Mozart.

Franklin was now leaning over Matt like a perched owl. "The men are contained in there?" he asked. "No, that's ridiculous! Are there small instruments?"

"There isn't anything inside but electrical memory of the music," Matt replied. "Humans play the instruments and it captures the sound as an electrical impulse and repeats it. It's like an echo. There isn't another man shouting back at you from the canyon when you hear your echo." Matt shut the music off. "Whistle something," he said as he pressed the record button.

Franklin whistled "Yankee Doodle." When he was done, Matt played it back as the older man stood shocked. "This is some magic," Franklin said.

"If I could do magic, would I be struggling every day to make medicine?"

"I'm not sure what you'd do," Franklin replied. "Could you not use this device for profit?"

"How?" Matt said. "Eventually it would be taken from me by someone more powerful."

"It uses electricity?" Franklin asked.

"There's a small battery inside," Matt said. "You can see how much electricity is in the battery there on the right corner."

Franklin looked at the screen. "Thirty-five percent."

"It needs to be charged," Matt explained. "I have a portable device that uses a hand crank to generate more electricity."

"You make electricity with mechanical devices?" Franklin asked.

"Not always. Most people in my time have electricity brought into their homes using copper wires. They use it to power machines and lights. I usually connect this device to those wires and it absorbs the power."

"I knew electricity could be harnessed!"

"It's routine in my time," Matt said. "The average person has no idea how electricity gets to his home. I'm the same. If I lost this charger, I'd be out of luck."

"I might be able to help you put electricity back into this device," Franklin observed.

Matt felt a twinge of satisfaction at the disorientation he saw on the man's face. "Let me show you some pictures."

Franklin stared back in disbelief.

Matt fumbled with the phone again. "I have some of Philadelphia from my time." He had about a thousand photographs from the last couple of years. Matt handed the phone to Franklin. "Recognize that?"

"The State House."

"We call it Independence Hall now." Matt dragged his finger across the screen while Franklin cradled the device in his hands. "You can swipe across to see others."

Franklin's eyes were glued to the phone as Matt showed him pictures. When he could finally tear his gaze from the screen, he said, "Independence from what?"

"Figure it out," Matt replied. He eased the phone from Franklin's hands and pressed the off button. It shut down with a beep.

"I'd have thought a man from the future would know enough to make himself a king."

"Doesn't seem to be that easy," Matt explained. "Take this device. I have no idea how to make one. I do know how to make medicine, but only with the ingredients available in my own time. It's driving me crazy."

"I think I may believe you," Franklin said sincerely, though there was still a puzzled look on his face.

"May?"

The dog had wandered over to Franklin, and the man stooped to scratch him with both hands. "Of course, your story is ludicrous," Franklin said, "but I find it difficult not to trust a man with a dog such as this." He was speaking more to Scout than Matt.

"You're making fun."

"No. Noble animals like this don't tolerate disreputable men. Scoundrels always have some nasty cur at their side."

"Did you hear that, Scout?" Matt said. "Dr. Franklin said you're a noble animal."

"Now *you're* joking," Franklin proclaimed.

"Nothing of the sort. Whose face is on the money?"

"Mine, it seems. I can't imagine why."

"You can decide how much to ask. We should both decide how to proceed."

"You could change the world if what you're saying is true," Franklin proclaimed.

"No, Ben," Matt said. "You'll be the one to do that. I've less than two years to marry the woman of my dreams."

"So I guess naught has changed after, what, two hundred and fifty years?"

Matt looked back at him, puzzled.

Franklin shook his head in disappointment. "Young men have the world at their command and they can only think as far ahead as their wedding night."

CHAPTER 31.

JACOB SMITH

The next day, a young man, probably in his late teens, was sitting on the porch of Grace Apothecary when Matt showed up for work. He greeted Matt with a handshake before Matt could reach the steps.

"I'm Jacob Smith," he said nervously. "I heard about the job and I rushed over this morning, first thing."

"Let's go inside," Matt replied. He unlocked the door and motioned Jacob into the building. Matt set his box of candles on the main counter and pointed to a rack for the young man to hang his coat. Matt pulled out two chairs.

"I need someone to mind the store and sell to customers," Matt said. "What makes you qualified to work here?"

"I'm good with people, hardworking, and God-fearing."

"Do other people say that about you?"

Jacob nodded, then thought for a moment. "Except my father. He's short on compliments."

"Any schooling?"

"I can read and write, add and subtract. My father says 'tis not enough, though."

"Your father must be a hard man," Matt replied, chuckling.

"I'd own the world before he'd say he was proud."

"You give me your word that you'll do your best?"

"Yes sir."

"We'll try you out for the week, and then I'll decide if I want you back."

"Can I start today?"

Matt nodded. "Five shillings a week, plus ten percent of the price of everything you sell. The better you treat the customers, the more you make."

The young man smiled.

"It can be hard when they're complaining," Matt said.

"Customer is always right, my gramps used to say," said Jacob.

Matt spent the morning explaining how he operated. There were more customers than usual, so he was able to show Jacob a fairly representative sample of his patrons. Matt had his customers' names on a list behind the counter, so he could greet them when they came into the store. Jacob watched intently as Matt sold them the sundries that now lined many of his shelves.

After lunch, Ben Franklin entered the store. "Ben," Matt said, surprised. "What can I do for you?"

Jacob, who had been organizing shelves, stopped to watch their conversation.

Franklin went silent upon seeing the young man. "I have questions," Franklin said. "Can we meet for dinner tonight?"

"You all right with everything?" Franklin looked ruffled.

"Just some things I'd like to discuss."

"Six o'clock at Poor Tom's," Matt said.

Franklin reached out and patted him on the shoulder. As quickly as he'd come, he turned and was gone. Jacob watched him walk out the front door.

"That wasn't Ben Franklin, was it? The scientist?"

Matt nodded.

"He's rich," Jacob said.

"I'm not sure if he's rich or not." Thus far, Matt had not gotten a clear picture of how Franklin made money or even how he spent his days. Franklin had demonstrated a knowledge of business, politics, and even things as pedestrian as blacksmithing and baking, but he had never talked about going to a job during the day. The man was an enigma.

Jacob nodded and smiled, like he had some doubt that Matt knew so little about Franklin, and returned to organizing shelves. At three o'clock, Matt left him to mind the store while he went back to harvest the cantaloupe mold. When he was finished, Matt went through a few more details with his new employee and then told him that he could go. Jacob had made almost a pound with his daily salary and commissions. He smiled as Matt paid. "Days aren't always this good," Matt warned.

"Not if I can help it, Mr. Miller," Jacob replied.

Matt watched Jacob walk away with a spring in his step. He briefly regretted the ten percent commission as too large, but shook it off. He knew that if he wanted Jacob to take on more responsibilities, including procuring supplies and stocking shelves, he'd need to keep him motivated.

Matt closed the store and hurried home to exercise the horse and the dog. They spent almost two hours that day riding in the country. The mild February weather had dried the roads, so they could run and gallop at will.

By the time they were done, man, horse, and dog were tired. When Matt got home, he cleaned up for dinner with Franklin, wondering the whole time what the man had on his mind. He wasn't sure how much of the future he should disclose.

CHAPTER 32.

PRESSING QUESTIONS

Matt arrived at Poor Tom's Tavern a little after six o'clock to see Franklin already drinking ale and speaking with Charity. She had a shy smile on her face. The girl greeted Matt with a kiss on the cheek as he walked up to the table. Matt looked around for her father. "He's not here," she said.

"He'd chase me out of here with a musket."

"He would not," Charity said. "What will you have?"

"Some of that darker ale."

Franklin sighed when she walked away. "To be twenty again."

"I'm an expert. Twenty's not as easy as you think."

"Don't ruin an old man's fantasy," Franklin huffed. "I imagine myself having the face and body of a twenty-year-old and the wisdom and means of my own age. That young beauty would be kissing my baby face instead of yours."

"I'm sure we're not here to discuss beautiful women."

"I was up all night thinking about your story," Franklin replied. "I don't believe you in the slightest."

"Still think I'm making it up?" Matt said doubtfully.

Franklin shrugged. "Hypothetically, if a man from the future did appear here in Philadelphia, it might be prudent to ask him a question or two."

"You should worry that—"

"I already know your fear," Franklin interrupted.

"You might change the future based on your knowledge of it."

"Do people in your own time speak often of time travel?"

"Quite a lot, actually," Matt said. "They write whole books about changing the future." Matt waited for Franklin to consider it.

"If you were to go back and somehow cause the death of your mother before you were born," Franklin said, "would you disappear?"

"That concept's almost a cliché in my time," Matt replied, laughing. "Anyway, you'd need to find a very horrible and stupid man to do your experiment."

Franklin looked at him, puzzled.

Matt stared directly into Franklin's questioning eyes with a clever grin. "He'd have to be willing to kill his own mother and be fine with bringing about his own demise."

"Obviously, I haven't given this much thought," Franklin admitted with a perplexed look on his face. "I trust, though, that the Lord designed this world to last an eternity. I can't imagine two random scallywags could undo what He's done."

"So all questions and answers are fair game?"

"I've decided only one thing should remain unspoken," Franklin declared. "A man shouldn't know when he'll die."

"Which is something I've already told you," Matt exclaimed. "I thought you'd appreciate knowing you'll live a long and happy life."

"I've had problems with my industry since learning that my life will last almost forever," Franklin replied. "I can't get anything done!"

"I should have told you that you were going to die in a few weeks. You'd be working on your own statue of David right now."

Franklin purposely ignored him. "I didn't sleep a wink. I've spent the night writing questions."

CHAPTER 33.

SHINING CITY ON A HILL

Franklin pulled a folded piece of paper from his pocket and put his glasses on to read the first question. "Tell me about this place you call the United States of America."

"Hard to know where to start," Matt replied. "It's probably the most prosperous country the world has ever seen. People come from all over the world to seek a new life and economic opportunity."

"Zounds. You must miss it immensely."

"Sometimes," Matt replied. His sudden lack of enthusiasm caused Franklin's expression to change, so Matt followed with, "It's a long story." Franklin was placated enough to drop his surprised expression, though Matt knew him well enough now to know he'd want a more detailed explanation at some point.

"What kind of government do these United States have?"

"Constitutional republic."

"I knew it!" Franklin exclaimed. "Any trouble?"

"People find a million reasons to be angry."

"So even these United States aren't the utopia man has sought for so long."

Matt recognized the cynical look in the older man's eyes. "You don't believe in utopia?" Matt asked jokingly.

Franklin frowned. "Utopia implies a perfect society, but man is imperfect and he makes up society."

"People in my time believe that the United States can become this utopia with a little tweaking."

Franklin waved his hand and scoffed like this didn't deserve a reply. "Speaking of, what mechanisms are there in these United States to help the poor and downtrodden? Do they still believe that if you transfer wealth to the poor, they'll benefit?"

"You are a cynical sod," Matt declared. "They call it welfare. It helps poor people get on their feet."

"Certainly the ranks of the poor are very small, then," Franklin said sarcastically.

"I already knew this about you."

"Then I don't need to explain myself." Franklin looked down at his notes. "What's the status of the fairer sex?"

"When I disappeared, women my age were making higher starting salaries than men, and more women were graduating from university."

"I've always believed ladies were capable," Franklin said, "but I'm surprised that they would achieve more education. Ladies control these United States?"

"Not yet. Eventually the United States will have a woman president."

Franklin contemplated the concept for longer than a moment. He looked again at his list of questions and eventually asked, "What about slaves?"

"Slavery ends about one hundred years from now. There's a bitter civil war. Six hundred thousand men die."

Franklin gasped. "Where do the freed slaves go?"

"They stay," Matt replied.

"As equal citizens?"

"That takes another hundred years. When I left, a black man was president of the United States. He's considered the most powerful man on the planet."

"Your society must truly be without prejudice."

"I'm in science, so I'm probably not the best to judge. I work with men and women of all races. If I started caring about color or sex, my day would get very complicated."

"It's always a complicated interaction between the races," Franklin affirmed. He stopped, then added, "And the sexes." He chuckled to himself, then returned to his list. "Are these United States a free market?"

"More than most places," Matt replied. "Some think the government should control more and make sure the wealth gets spread around."

"The control of capital should never be taken from the people," Franklin declared.

"People in the future will try that too. Some countries will become socialist or communist. Their citizens work for the government and they distribute wealth according to need. There's no private property."

"Are those countries powerful?"

Matt shook his head. "Most didn't last longer than a few generations. Their people were dirt poor and tens of millions were killed, usually by their own governments."

"Any good student of history would predict this."

"Many people in the United States think differently. They believe that the United States would be better at socialism."

"Give all the coin to the government and you'll see that change," Franklin proclaimed. He checked his paper.

"What about religion?"

"Christmas is a national holiday in the United States."

"Everyone is required to be Christian?" Franklin asked, surprised.

Matt shook his head. "There's a strict separation of church and state. The government can't make any laws concerning religion."

"Render unto Caesar the things which are Caesar's and unto God the things that are God's," Franklin recited. "A republic with Judeo-Christian laws!"

"That's about it, I think."

"The Republic of the United States of America," Franklin said. "It has great possibility!"

Matt waved Charity over to the table, pointing to the glasses of ale that were now empty. She brought two more over with a smile on her face. Franklin met her gaze and handed her two shillings. "That's for you, my dear."

"Thank you, Dr. Franklin," she replied. She smiled and walked away.

"I may not have a baby face, but I can still outspend you," Franklin said. He traced the folded paper in front of him with his finger and read another question. "Disease. Has man conquered disease?"

"Smallpox is gone," Matt said.

"Variolation?"

Matt nodded. "Not with smallpox, though. Tell your friends and family to variolate with cowpox."

"Cows?"

"Ask any milkmaid who has gotten cowpox whether she's had smallpox. All will say no."

"And you?" Franklin asked.

Matt shook his head. "I can't get it. I've been vaccinated, which is similar."

Franklin looked down again. "What about hunger? Does everyone in these United States have enough to eat?"

"More than enough, I think," Matt replied, chuckling. "They're always talking about Americans getting fat and especially poor people who don't have access to good food."

"Doesn't the fact that you're poor preclude you from eating too many victuals?"

"Poor people eat more victuals that make you fat," Matt explained.

"Those victuals are cheaper?" Franklin asked, surprised.

"Well, no," Matt replied. "You can get a vegetable salad fairly cheap."

"By definition, poor people can't buy enough victuals or else they're not poor."

"I can't explain why people don't eat healthy food," Matt admitted.

"Does the European continent enjoy this free market society where even the poor are fat?"

"They're considered a free market, but they tend toward socialism."

"So not as successful," Franklin affirmed.

"Some successful and some not," Matt said. "They've organized into a big cooperative called the European Union. It's supposed to be like the United States in the way it trades. It was good for a while, but once the economy got bad, the differences between countries were emphasized."

"Wars?"

"Small ones," Matt explained. "There were two world wars in the twentieth century where almost every country was involved. About sixty million people died."

"Sixty million?" Franklin exclaimed. His expression became almost scolding. "With all you have?"

"I didn't start them," Matt replied. "They say the next world war will be the last."

"Seems there will always be wars," Franklin said disappointedly.

"Not big ones," Matt said. "The last world war ended with a single bomb that can destroy an entire city."

"Do many nations have these bombs?"

"There are enough bombs to destroy the whole face of the planet," Matt replied. "The thinking is that if everyone has them, no one will use them."

"Very trusting," Franklin quipped.

"I always wonder what the chain of events would be that convinces a nation to use one of these bombs again."

"Who used it the last time?"

"The United States," Matt said.

A shocked expression covered Franklin's face.

"Smart people came from all over the world to help the United States be the first to develop this weapon."

"Did they use it to conquer the whole world?"

"They didn't conquer any of it. Americans want to be left alone."

"Does your military rival that of the British Empire?"

"The United States is more powerful militarily than Great Britain by many times, but they're close allies."

"A common culture," Franklin said matter-of-factly.

They both went silent to drink their ale. Franklin was deep in thought, so Matt resisted the urge to say more. Franklin eventually asked, "Why would you not miss this great country? Was it this powerful weapon?"

Matt shook his head. "I never even thought about the bomb. I had a chance to go back to my own time and said no."

Franklin gave Matt a look of disbelief.

"I'm still trying to justify it in my own mind," Matt said. "I left my country and my family for this." He glanced around at the people in the tavern.

"Was it your love for this Virginia lady?" Franklin asked.

"Maybe," Matt admitted, "but it was more than that. There was corruption in my time. People were constantly squabbling. Sometimes I couldn't hear myself think. It was twenty-four-seven name-calling." Matt paused to do some introspection. "Maybe it's as simple as that. I got tired of all the name-calling."

"You're in sore trouble if the only reason you stayed in this time was to escape the loons."

"At least you can walk away from them here," Matt replied. "You can't in the future. They're on your phone, your computer, and your television." Matt tried to think of a better explanation but really couldn't. "There's no science-based justification," he said eventually. "I made the decision to stay, and so here I am."

Franklin shrugged his shoulders like he was fine with Matt's explanation.

"Now I have a question for you," Matt said. "I'm going to Richmond at the end of September to attend a wedding. He's the brother of the woman I intend to marry. The bride's from a wealthy family. I've been to their parties. They're elaborate affairs with many beautiful women."

"You're obviously trying stoke my envy," Franklin said.

"You want to come? I can bring one guest."

"Richmond's a long way, and September is very hot."

"You said you needed to inspect the postal routes."

Franklin nodded and thought for a moment. "Many handsome ladies?"

Matt smiled.

"Let me see if it fits my schedule." Franklin had no commitment in his voice, but his expression told Matt that he already had his traveling companion.

CHAPTER 34.

ASPIRIN

About ten minutes after Matt mixed the new willow bark into the reaction, he knew the aspirin synthesis would be a success. The new bark was lighter than normal and was bone dry. The brown tar never appeared, and when it came time to purify the mixture, Matt knew the yield would be high. He was able to dissolve the product in hot alcohol and form a supersaturated solution that had the consistency of syrup. He let the solution cool and then dropped in a few crystals of the aspirin he'd already made in smaller batches. The new aspirin fell out of the solution as clear white crystals. Matt dried the crystals and filled a quart container with almost five hundred grams of white aspirin powder. It was enough to make a thousand doses of his version of Alka-Seltzer.

Matt started pressing tablets the next day and began selling the fizzing medicine in the store. He already had a regular customer base and it was a natural addition to his stock. He built a display box and set it up in Poor Tom's Tavern. After a few weeks, Charity was selling more Miller Head and Stomach Tablets than Grace Apothecary. Charity was a natural salesperson, having worked

MILLER HEAD and
STOMACH TABLETS

For the relief of headache, ſtomach upſet, body pain, ſwelling, rheumatiſm and fever.

Inſtructions:

1. Unwrap two tablets and drop in a half-pint cup of clean cold water. Allow bubbling to finiſh and tablet to diſappear.
2. Stir for ten ſeconds by ſwirling the cup or uſing a ſpoon.
3. Drink entire contents of the cup including any tablet pieces that may not have diſſolved.
4. For ſuſtained relief, two more tablets can be ſafely diſſolved and eaten four hours after the firſt have been conſumed.
5. Children under five years old ſhould conſume only one half of one tablet. Children between five and ten years ſhould conſume only one tablet.

Cautions:

1. Uſe in moderation. No more than two tablets ſhould be taken every four hours. No more than eight tablets ſhould be conſumed in twenty-four hours.
2. Tablets ſhould not be uſed more than ſeven days in a row.
3. Overuſe may cauſe ſtomachache rather than cure it.
4. If ſtomachache ſhould occur after overuſe, ſtop taking Miller Head and Stomach Tablets until your ſtomach feels better. Treatment may reſume within a few days.

the bar since she was a young girl. Matt made sure she had a supply of free samples. She kept small cups and water behind the bar so she could demonstrate the fizzing tablets and let people feel their effect. Matt loved the way she giggled like a schoolgirl when the tablets hit the water and started fizzing.

Charity's father came to Matt soon after with an offer to sell the tablets around town. The man had a network of Philadelphia tavern owners and was willing to act as a distributor for a cut of the profits. Matt had never imagined taverns as the main distribution channel for his medicine, but they were rapidly increasing his customer base across the city. Matt was already working through one of Franklin's friends in the Philadelphia government to patent the tablets.

Matt charged a half shilling for a two-tablet packet, which seemed a reasonable price. After manufacturing and distribution expenses to the tavern owners, with an additional payment to Charity's father, Matt was making over thirty pounds per week on head and stomach tablets alone. In addition, the traffic in his store had grown substantially, and he was now making twenty more pounds per week selling soap and personal care products.

Because of the demand, Matt was spending most of his time synthesizing aspirin in the laboratory while Jacob took care of the shop. Jacob had assumed responsibility for purchasing the sundries and was making substantially more than Matt had expected after only two months. The young man was contacting new suppliers on his own and arrived in the morning with a wagon full of all manner of items. Jacob recorded everything in a ledger that he kept in the front desk. He seemed to have a natural ability to maximize profits. Truthfully, Matt sometimes had no idea what Jacob was doing aside from selling things and putting money in the strongbox.

One Monday, Matt walked out to the shop carrying a box of ingredients for pressing tablets. There was a young boy there busily stocking shelves. "Good morning, Mr. Miller," the boy said. He stopped what he was doing, walked over, waited for Matt to set his box of supplies down and shook his hand.

"Who're you?" Matt asked.

"Ward Smith," he said. "Quite pleased to meet you, sir!"

"What're you doing here, Ward?"

"Restacking," Ward replied. "These toothbrushes keep falling."

"You know offhand where Jacob is?"

"Picking up the perfumed ladies' soap."

"When did we start selling that?"

"Mr. Chester imports it from England."

A customer stepped through the door. "Pardon me, Mr. Miller," Ward said. He walked up to a man Matt had never seen in the store and handed him a box, then accepted his money and thanked him. "At your service, Mr. Douglas," Ward said as the man left. Matt watched Ward walk behind the counter, write in the ledger, and put the money in the metal strongbox.

"Ward," Matt said, "how long have you worked here?"

"Two weeks. Before and after my lessons."

"How come we've never met?"

"You've been too busy," Ward said. He returned to his task. "I gotta get this done before my brother comes back."

"Oh, okay," Matt replied. Matt pondered Ward while he walked to his tablet press, set it up, and began pressing tablets. Matt realized he'd been in the lab almost constantly, making batches of aspirin. The rule he'd learned as a graduate student was that when an experiment started working and you didn't know exactly why, you kept at it because you never knew when it would stop. The synthesis hadn't stopped working, though, so Matt had stockpiled almost four kilograms of aspirin. The last couple of weeks had been a blur. Matt would arrive immediately after sunrise and would hear Jacob arrive a few hours later. Matt left by three o'clock to exercise the horse and dog, and tried to practice tae kwon do for at least an hour a day, expecting he'd face Levi Payne eventually in Richmond.

It was the first time Matt had used the tablet press in two weeks. He'd pull the lever down to squeeze the tablets together and then pop them from the mold with a pick. He could press two tablets per stroke. "That would be better with two people," Ward said as he watched from the shelf he was organizing. "I could fill those holes and then wait for you to work the handle."

"You think you could measure the same every time?"

"That little spoon doesn't look too hard to use."

"Show me," Matt replied. He pushed the extra molds across the bench to the boy along with the bowl of powder and the measuring spoon. They were soon pressing tablets at three times the speed Matt could alone. "Every two tablets is like making a half shilling," Matt said.

By the time Jacob pulled up in his wagon, they'd filled the bowl next to the press. "Almost two hundred shillings," Ward said, looking at the bowl.

Jacob came in as they were finishing. He inspected the measuring scoop in Ward's hand very closely.

"I didn't know you hired someone," Matt announced.

"Could we talk in back, Mr. Miller?" Jacob replied. There was urgency in his voice and he gave his brother a dirty look. "The shelves should be restocked before the afternoon customers arrive, and the wagon needs unloading." He looked at his brother with a frown and motioned to him with his head to get moving, then walked with Matt into the aspirin synthesis room to talk. "I hired Ward to stock the shelves," Jacob said.

"Fine with me," Matt replied.

"How often will he be required to work the press?" Jacob asked, irritated.

"He was helping."

"He should be stocking and selling."

"Hire another employee, then," Matt said.

Jacob stood in thoughtful silence. "We'd need a bigger space." His grin was obvious.

"You already have a building somewhere?" Matt asked.

"Market Street," Jacob replied. "We could triple our stock and you could use this all for your experiments. Even the ladies' soap can't mask the smell from that cantaloupe room."

"But if I'm here and you're in another store," Matt said, "I won't be able to help out with apothecary questions."

"Most come to the store to purchase supplies," Jacob said. "I mean no disrespect, Mr. Miller, but Ward has been here for two weeks and today is the first day you noticed him."

"I'm busy in back making aspirin," Matt explained, irritated.

"While we're selling them out front," Jacob said. "They're not our only profit. Have you seen the ladies' supplies?"

"Selling ladies' supplies is not what I had in mind for this apothecary."

"You don't want to sell ladies' supplies?"

"If you're making money," Matt said, "I'll stay out of your way."

"I propose a new storefront, then," Jacob replied, "and that my salary be all commission."

Matt took a moment to think, but it was obvious that Jacob had been responsible for growing Grace's Apothecary into something Matt had never imagined. Foot traffic was what sold headache tablets, and Jacob's growing selection was bringing more and more people into the store.

"Fine," Matt said simply.

They spent the next hour working through the details of the growing business and writing their agreement on a piece of paper. They stopped as the evening rush began and Jacob had to return to the front, leaving Matt in back to package headache tablets. Stock was getting low, and he'd have to work all week to replenish the supply.

CHAPTER 35.

FIGHTING LESSONS

Matt was falling into a vertical pit surrounded by a wall of grey rippling paint. He bounced from side to side, and each time he collided with the wall, a jolt of electricity shot through his body and pushed him back. There was a flash, and he was suspended above an enormous frame of rectangular moving portraits. They vibrated and he became overwhelmed with the magnitude and complexity of the frames that stretched beyond the horizon.

Matt dropped toward the ground and his stomach leapt into his throat. He had experienced these prescient dreams enough to know that falling had nothing to do with dying, but nonetheless, he prepared himself for the pain he knew he'd feel as he broke through the moving pictures. As he breached their surface, it surprised him when his energy didn't fade and the pain never came. He looked around to find that he was enclosed in a room of moving stories. Unlike his past dreams, the narrations were slow enough for him to see actions and faces. He looked down and saw the boundary approaching. He braced himself again, but still felt nothing as he smashed through the floor. Cubes came, one after another, until he had destroyed too many to count.

His journey ended with the familiar drumbeats...fifteen, sixteen, and seventeen. His world flashed white and his visions were over. Matt opened his eyes. He could barely make out the ceiling in the dim light of early morning. Countless smashed cubes remained vivid in his mind. *How much did I see?* He sat up, grabbed the pad of paper that he kept beside his bed and wrote as fast as he could. He'd seen his fight with Levi Payne. It would be in Richmond in some place where horses walked all around. The fight ended with Matt's dead body lying face down in the dirt.

Matt took a deep breath to calm himself. He'd worked hard to obtain the success he needed to return to Richmond and ask for the hand of Grace Taylor. The only thing keeping him from his future, it seemed, was a man who had vowed to kill him. This was the same man who was responsible for Matt being beaten, robbed, and left for dead. Matt thought of his visions again, but now the specifics were becoming muddled. Multiple futures now stacked on top of each other, some in which he and Grace were very old, and others where Matt didn't survive his confrontation with Levi.

Matt's loathing for Levi knew no bounds, but he despised him most for this. He would rather wake up in the morning and think only of Grace, but instead, most mornings he rehearsed confrontation scenarios. Some of these included members of the Taylor or Payne family, and others imagined Matt meeting Levi in the street as before. Sometimes Matt questioned whether he was delusional. Sometimes he suspected he might be going insane.

Crazy or no, both his dreams and his reality told him that there was no way to avoid a fight. Levi had already tried to kill him twice, so there was little room left for negotiation. The last time he faced Levi in the street, Matt barely survived, hampered by his inability to execute kicks that should have been routine for a black belt. He'd practiced tae kwon do four times per week since coming to Philadelphia, but he still had the overwhelming feeling that he wasn't good enough to beat Levi Payne, a man who had spent his life fighting.

"Screw it," Matt said aloud as he stood up to get ready for work.

****

Matt spent a couple of hours setting up a new aspirin synthesis and then wandered over to a large storefront on Market Street that advertised "Fighting and Swordplay." An uneasy feeling washed over him as he stepped onto the porch and reached for the door. A dream had warned him about this place, but there was also something pulling him forward. He expected to find both adversaries and friends here.

Matt calmed himself and pushed the door open. He *had* seen this place before in a vision. There were about a dozen men inside working at various stations. Two were circling each other with wooden swords and others were wrestling in a large ring on a worn leather mat. Off in a corner, he saw a man with practically no neck, built like a bull, repeatedly lifting a crude iron block over his head. Another man beside the ring looked up and yelled from across the room, "Good day, sir!"

"I'm interested in fighting," Matt yelled back. He stood there for a moment waiting for a reply, but none came, so he stepped closer and said loudly, "Can you tell me where the owner is?"

"I'm the owner," the man said. He bowed. "At your service."

"Can you tell me what you teach?" Matt asked. The room went quiet. He saw the stranger right before he tried to sweep Matt's feet out from under him. *What the?* Matt hopped to avoid the sweeping legs and stepped back and away. He swore at himself for letting his guard down; he had known something was amiss as soon as he stepped onto the porch. The stranger spun again, this time toppling him to the ground, and Matt found himself in a headlock that was choking him to death. Matt could only struggle and gasp for air.

The owner now stood over him. "Let him go, Seamus," he said. Seamus loosened his arms and it was enough for Matt to force them from his body. Matt popped immediately to his feet, backed away from both men, and put his hands up.

"It's all right, lad," the owner said, motioning. "No permanent damage." Matt looked around, confused, as the motion and noise in the gym resumed like nothing had happened. "No permanent damage, right?" the owner repeated. "I'm Solomon McCalla and this is my brother Seamus." Solomon shook his hand. "You've had training."

Now Seamus approached with his hand extended. Matt adjusted his body to keep both opponents in his line of sight and stepped back again to emphasize that both should keep their distance.

"Nothing personal," Seamus said, putting his hands up. "It's either me or my brother makes first contact."

Not knowing what else to do, Matt reached his hand out cautiously and shook Seamus's hand.

"Seamus could've killed you," Solomon said. "You didn't see the threat when you entered?"

"I felt it on the porch," Matt replied indignantly, "and chose to ignore it."

Solomon considered this for a moment, then gave an "oh well" gesture and said, "Next time, pay attention to your instinct." He spent a moment looking Matt up and down while Matt held the casual defensive stance his Korean master taught him for when he was unsure whether he was facing a friend or foe.

"It must have been embarrassing to let Seamus get the better of you."

"I know how to fight," Matt replied.

"Show me, then," Solomon said as he stepped back.

Matt nodded and scanned the room. He settled on a leather bag hanging from a wooden beam. He walked purposefully to the bag and spun his body into a sidekick that tore the bag from its hinges. Next, he moved around toward a slatted wooden divider that separated two areas of the gym and drove his fist through one of the inch-thick slats. One piece of the broken slat was pulled from the wall and went crashing to the ground while the other remained swinging like a pendulum on a single nail. Matt turned back toward Seamus, stepping into a spinning roundhouse kick. He stopped his foot inches from the man's head. Seamus already had his hand up and was laughing. Matt lowered his leg slowly to emphasize his physical control.

"He's a dancer, like in the theater," Seamus said, glancing knowingly at Solomon.

Irritated, Solomon focused on the leather bag and boards lying on the floor. "You've defended yourself against my building."

"Dancer in the theater?" Matt said, looking at Seamus.

Seamus gave him a good-humored smile. It was the grin of a man who wasn't afraid of anything.

"I fought the toughest man in Richmond," Matt said.

"Then why come here?" Solomon asked.

"He's an ox," Matt explained. "He wants me dead."

"How do you know he wants you dead?"

"He hired men to kill me."

"Richmond is far away," Seamus said. "Why not avoid this man?"

"I'm betrothed to a woman there."

"Is there money between you and this man, or maybe this lady you will marry?"

"The man's family and the woman's compete for the same business," Matt admitted. "He'd hoped to marry her."

"Seems he has many reasons to kill you," Solomon said, laughing heartily.

"I won't be able to avoid the fight."

Solomon motioned for Matt to follow him. Matt checked first to make sure Seamus was keeping his distance. Seamus gave him a satisfied smile when their eyes met. "At your service," he said, bowing slightly, and then peeled away to help two men who were wrestling on the other side of the gym. Matt followed Solomon into a back room and sat down.

"You're sitting with your back to the door," Solomon said. "How do you know Seamus won't return to hit you on your head?"

I would have felt it from my dreams. Matt looked over his shoulder into the gym, then shifted his chair to the side.

"Always on guard," Solomon explained. "They'll not dress in fighters' costumes or wave flags before they stick a knife in your belly."

"I refuse to live in fear that someone is always about to attack me, though."

"Do you wear shoes?"

"Yes," Matt admitted reluctantly. The man's line of logic was already clear.

"Do you live in fear of stepping on a stone?"

"No."

"And so it should be as you walk among men. You've skills, but you don't wear them."

"Are you going to teach me or not?"

****

Matt started at the McCallas' gym the next afternoon. When he arrived, he was waved over by Seamus to an elevated boxing ring.

"You've returned?" Seamus said jokingly. Matt thought of one or two snide remarks, but he chose to remain silent, thinking that Seamus would have no qualms about teaching him a painful lesson. Seamus waved to another man, pointed at Matt, then walked to a shelf and pulled down a leather helmet and body armor. He transferred them to Matt's outstretched arms. "Put it on," he said, "and then you're up." Seamus tilted his head at the boxing ring.

Matt struggled with the equipment until Seamus got impatient enough to step down and help him fit the chest protector and lace the gloves and helmet. Seamus then led him into the ring and called over another man, who had been punching a bag with padded hands. The man was about half a head shorter than Matt. His gloves didn't look nearly padded enough to Matt.

"William is the best fist-fighter we have," Seamus said. "Nothing better in close quarters than fists." Seamus pulled William to the side to talk and then pointed him to the center of the ring. "Punches above the waist," Seamus said to Matt. "No kicking or dancing."

Matt acknowledged him with a simple nod, again struggling against the urge to answer with a smart remark. Seamus signaled them to begin. Matt faced William, put his hands up, and adopted a traditional upright tae kwon do stance. It was much like a boxer's stance and gave no hint that it would let Matt strike with his legs. He held the pose as he slowly circled his opponent while William turned to follow him in his orbit.

"You ever going to hit each other?" Seamus jeered.

Matt ignored Seamus as he circled the shorter man, then snapped his right hand into William's face. To Matt's surprise, William's head disappeared halfway through the motion and Matt's hand collided with air. Matt followed immediately with a left to the man's body but missed again. William had dodged his punches with uncanny speed. On Matt's third attempt, William sidestepped the punch and countered hard into Matt's face. Matt felt the familiar scrambling in his head, but he shook off the blow. He saw Seamus motion to William to ease up. Easing up consisted of Matt being hit ten more times over the next five minutes. Matt was breathing hard and sparks were firing indiscriminately in his head, mildly disrupting his vision.

"Enough!" Seamus shouted. Both men stopped. "Fine job, William."

William reached out and patted Matt on the shoulder before he left the ring. Matt hadn't landed one punch.

Still trying to catch his breath, Matt said, "I've never seen anyone react so quickly."

Seamus laughed. "You were announcing your punches before you threw them. Punch me in the face."

"You don't have any equipment."

"You won't be able to hit me."

Matt was indignant. He had a black belt and these men were acting like it was nothing. He stepped up to Seamus with every intention of knocking him out. Matt knew after he threw his first punch that he would have to wait for another day to put him to sleep. He couldn't connect.

"Frustrated?" Seamus asked. He reached out and slapped Matt on the face.

Matt countered, but he missed again.

"Give up?"

"I don't ever give up."

Seamus smiled. "There's hope, then."

Matt still had his hands up. "Are you going to tell me what I'm doing?"

Seamus gave him a sly smile. "Build your strength." He pointed to the bag Matt had kicked off the wall, which had been repaired. "Five hundred hard punches into that bag and then you can go."

Seamus walked away leaving Matt frustrated. His head was hinting at a migraine, but the flashes had stopped. He made it through two weeks of fighting before he was hit hard enough to go completely blind.

CHAPTER 36.

SECOND SIGHT

The building Jacob selected as their second location was almost new construction. It was originally built as a tobacco warehouse and retail store, but the owner took on debt during a downturn in the market and sold the building as an alternative to debtors' prison. It had been empty since, but still had a rich and pleasant smell of tobacco mixed with fresh lumber, like a humidor filled with fine cigars. Matt was immediately drawn to the building since the smell reminded him of harvesting tobacco on the Taylor farm. The building had a central location on Market Street, the main Philadelphia thoroughfare, which almost guaranteed high foot traffic. The owner stood on the porch while Matt and Jacob wandered through the structure.

"It's almost too big," Matt said quietly.

"We could triple our sales."

"The rent's high."

"We should buy it," Jacob said. "It's been sitting idle for months."

"Grace Apothecary doesn't make enough. I don't want to stick my neck out for something like this."

Jacob answered him with a look that was somewhere between irritated and befuddled. "Of course we make enough."

"We can buy it once we're sure," Matt said.

"Mr. Pollock deals with my father. He'll watch our business grow and then have no scruples charging a higher price."

"You're that confident?"

"Business has increased every week. We'll be adding items that are guaranteed to sell."

Matt shook his head. "You can't predict."

"My father owns the Atlantic Trading Company," Jacob said. "I know what'll sell."

Matt inspected Jacob's face for some indication that he was joking. Matt had often speculated about Jacob's background but had avoided asking serious questions. Based on Jacob's short and uncomfortable descriptions of his father, Matt was under the impression that Jacob's family was either very poor or somehow abusive. Now Jacob's involvement in Grace Apothecary made even less sense. Matt exclaimed, "Why are you and your brother working for me?"

"We need to do it on our own," Jacob replied.

Matt waited for more of an explanation, but Jacob had already returned to examining a wooden counter that could serve as a natural divider for items displayed in the front and those stored in the back. "My father's store is nearly this large," Jacob said. He raised both his arms to point at the front and back rooms of the tobacco warehouse. "He does one hundred twenty pounds per week and doesn't have the headache tablets, toothpaste, and whatever else you'll invent."

"I'd think if you wanted to prove something, you'd start your own business," Matt said. "What keeps me from buying this building and you deciding to leave?"

"Even my father started in a partnership."

"There's no partnership. You work for me."

"I wanted to speak about that."

"We just wrote a contract," Matt said, incredulous.

"This building changes that."

Matt was trying his hardest to keep an open mind. Jacob had increased profits substantially, and he paid attention to the kinds of details that bored Matt to tears.

"We split profits from the store by half," Jacob explained. "We agree on some fair value for Grace Apothecary and I pay you until I own half."

"Half?" Matt said. He was thinking aloud rather than questioning the fairness of the deal. "You'll have to start paying half on this building too if we buy it."

"I can pay over time."

"Headache tablets are off the table."

"Why should they be singular?" Jacob said, surprised.

"My invention. I'll sell them to Grace Apothecary at a discount. It's a business within the business."

"I expected half the profit on the headache tablets," Jacob exclaimed.

"At some point I'm moving out of town, and I'm taking the tablet manufacturing with me."

"Then everyone will be selling them," Jacob said, distraught.

"We can negotiate a discount and maybe some exclusive rights, but that's it."

"I want this in writing."

"You're demanding a lot, considering it's still my business," Matt said, smiling.

Jacob ignored him. "We should decide on the building today."

"I'm not ready to take the risk on buying the building," Matt declared.

"Do you have enough money?"

Matt glared at the young man long and hard, waiting for him to flinch, but only saw confidence and resolve. "Fine," he finally said, against every careful bone in his body. "I have someone who could probably lend it to us."

After some haggling with Pollock, they reached an agreement and Matt gave him a deposit. Matt was soon in a carriage, business records in hand, on his way to speak to Phillip Ricken.

****

Matt searched for a glimpse of Isabelle as they walked through the long hall that led to the back of the Ricken mansion. He smiled when he thought of her since she was hard evidence of a real contribution he had made to the world. He considered saving Isabelle's life one of the pivotal experiences of his own life, not only because of the great satisfaction it gave him, but also for the series of strange coincidences that had aligned him with seemingly random people and events. It fed his need to believe that there was a plan for the world and that he had some role to play. Quite simply, saving Isabelle was one more piece of anecdotal evidence to support his very scientific hypothesis that God was real.

Matt's musings about his place in God's plan were interrupted as he was shown into Phillip Ricken's office. It was a grand room, adorned in shades of light grey and hung with tapestries. Eight panes of glass filled a large window that overlooked a lush green garden of trees, flowers, and well-trimmed hedges that surrounded a series of connected marble fountains. The evolution of Matt's psyche had made him less impressed with the trappings of wealth, but the view from Ricken's office filled him with envy. He imagined it was a great place to sit and think.

Ricken stood as Matt entered the room, walked around his desk, and met him with an outstretched hand. "How can I be of service, Mr. Miller?"

"I need a business loan," Matt replied. A twinge of fear went up his spine. He felt like he had stepped off a cliff and was falling into a financial abyss.

"Let's see what you have," Ricken said simply. He motioned for Matt to sit while he moved back to his chair behind the large Victorian-looking desk. He held his hand out to accept the folder of documents.

Ricken nodded a lot and didn't say much as Matt explained his need for a new building. He inspected Matt's balance sheet, and after some time he said, "I'll have my man draw up the papers by the end of the week. He'll pay the sum to Pollock directly, and the building will serve as collateral for your loan. You agree to pay one third of the cost of the building in advance, and we'll furnish the remainder. Not making the agreed payments constitutes a default and the property would revert entirely to my ownership after three months of nonpayment."

Matt walked fearlessly out of the mansion when the deal was complete, and he managed to resist the urge to pump his fist into the air until his carriage cleared the driveway.

****

Jacob was with a customer and had two others waiting when Matt walked through the door. "We got the money,"

Matt announced. Jacob smiled happily, then returned to his customers. Matt went into the back and spent two hours finishing up a large batch of aspirin. He'd had trouble drying all the batches recently because of their size and was already thinking about how the process could be improved in order to deal with the high yields he was producing. Even with the expected sales growth, he figured he had almost a six-month supply of aspirin for headache tablets. He'd need to get more package inserts printed.

When Matt was done for the day, he said goodbye to Jacob and Ward and walked to the McCallas' gym. The first week had been a struggle, but he was learning to read his opponents and hide his own intentions. The twisting motion he'd used to cock his hands and broadcast his punches was gone.

Seamus nodded to him when he came in. He was working with a new man in the ring. They were practicing some sort of grappling that looked like Greco-Roman wrestling.

"Get your leather on," Seamus called. "We're going hard today."

I thought we were going hard already. Matt nodded and moved over to the shelf to put on the leather armor. Seamus waved him impatiently up to the ring. Matt moved a set of block steps against the elevated platform and climbed up.

"You're going to be fighting with Jamison," Seamus said. He motioned to the man he had just been teaching. Jamison was almost as tall as Matt and had a head of closely cropped red hair. He wore loose grey pants that went nearly to his ankles and a tight white tunic. Jamison's clothing could not hide a physique composed of large, well-defined muscles. He put his gloved hand out to tap Matt's gloves and smiled with a wide toothless grin. "Good day, mate," he said. "I heard you're a kicker."

"I am," Matt replied, wondering what Seamus had in mind by pairing him with Jamison.

"Need to learn to fight against kickers," Jamison said.

"Hopefully you're a brawler, then," Matt replied, smiling back.

Jamison looked at him strangely.

"Good at fighting with your hands, close in."

"That's me, mate."

Seamus looked at Matt. "You can go full out against Jamison, kicks and all."

"He doesn't have any equipment," Matt said. Jamison looked naked standing there with just padded gloves.

"Don't need it," Jamison replied.

"I could kill him with the right kick."

A look of insult filled Jamison's face.

"I didn't mean anything by it," Matt said. "It's hard to go easy on the kicks."

"Don't expect you to go easy."

Matt looked over at Seamus and got his confirmation. "Okay," Matt said. He was still uncomfortable. Having a black belt meant something, despite the way these men discounted his skills.

"Your best effort," Seamus said to Matt. "I'll stop it before anyone gets hurt." Seamus stepped to the side and both men were left circling each other in the center of the ring. "Begin!" Seamus called.

Matt took a defensive stance. Jamison went after him with a flurry of punches, landing two on Matt's face and body. Matt countered, hitting Jamison hard in the face and then moving away like he had been taught. "Good," he heard Seamus say.

Matt took his stance again. This time, Jamison waited rather than moving close. He was standing at the right distance for a kick to the head. Matt's kick was well executed, and Jamison reeled back to recover for a moment.

"He'll hit you with that leg every time if you stand there," Seamus instructed.

Jamison closed in to hit Matt with a barrage of punches hard enough to shift the leather mouth guard Matt had between his teeth. Matt blocked, countered, pushed Jamison away, and then hit him in the chest with a sidekick. Jamison stumbled violently back into the ropes.

"We haven't seen that one," Seamus said. "The power comes from the back leg. Keep him from setting it."

Jamison nodded again, returned to the center of the ring to face Matt and stood at exactly the right distance for Matt to land another kick. Matt spun into a sidekick aimed at Jamison's head, but this time Jamison ducked to let Matt's foot pass over his head, then closed on Matt with a barrage of fists. Matt had to retreat but still managed to land a few solid punches. He faked a backward motion, then stepped forward into a spinning roundhouse kick that hit Jamison squarely in the face. Jamison shook it off and regained his stance.

"Watch the feet rather than the body," Seamus instructed. "Mr. Miller can fight."

A compliment from Seamus?

"Respected him from the beginning, I did," Jamison replied. "I only ever fought that one kicker."

"And lost," Seamus reminded.

"No accident I'm here," Jamison replied.

Matt was curious to see if the man had learned anything, so he went into another spinning roundhouse kick, this time leading with his left leg. Jamison ducked and punched Matt firmly in the face.

Uh-oh!

Sparks flashed in Matt's brain, and grey flashes began to take pieces of his sight. It was like someone was flicking silver paint on the window to his world and this paint was piling up. Jamison hit him in the face again and Matt panicked. On instinct, he dropped into an attack pattern he'd practiced with his Korean master. Jamison could only back away and managed to hit Matt in the face only once during the attack.

"Ease up, Mr. Miller!" Seamus yelled. "He's not supposed to be fighting for his life."

Matt turned to Seamus's voice, nodded, and murmured, "Sorry." He turned back to where he thought Jamison was, straining to see him through the grey cloud. Then Jamison flashed in front of him as if the paint had completely disappeared. "Sorry," Matt repeated to the man he saw standing in front of him. The grey suddenly returned and then was gone.

What's happening?

In vivid colors, Matt saw Jamison raise his hands and give an "ease up" motion, then watched as he swung in slow motion at his face. Matt waited for the impact, but there was none. He saw Jamison swing a second time. Matt put his glove up and felt the blow impact his hand and then again as he blocked in succession, his face, his body, his face, and his face again. The vivid colors faded again to grey, but Matt still knew in his mind when to expect a swing. Trying to sort out what was real and what was imagined confused him, and he lost track of the punches. In the confusion, a hard punch hit Matt in the face and he went crashing to the platform.

"Step out," Seamus said to Jamison, who was now standing over Matt, confused. Seamus pushed the steps to the side and motioned at them. He waited for Jamison to clear the ring before climbing up and stooping under the rope.

Seamus stared down at Matt. "Why did you stop defending yourself?"

Matt looked up into the grey. "I'm blind."

"Get out of the ring," Seamus said.

Matt picked himself up, walked to the steps, and stooped down to slide between the ropes. He stepped carefully onto the block steps that led down to the floor.

"You can see," Seamus insisted.

"I can't," Matt replied to the flashing grey mist.

"Then how'd you know where I put the steps?" Seamus asked.

I could see them in my mind! "I remembered them from before," Matt lied.

"They're in a different place," Seamus said.

"I must have heard you slide them." Matt motioned around in front of his eyes with his gloved hand. "I'm starting to see shadows again."

Seamus removed Matt's gloves, led him to a back office, and sat him down. "Has this happened before?"

"Mostly from the cold," Matt explained. "It was that punch Jamison threw right before I went crazy and started kicking. I was blind after that."

"You knew where he was going to move before he did."

"It's a series of kicks I've practiced," Matt explained.

"Jamison's lost one fight his whole life."

Matt rubbed his eyes. He could see the outline of Seamus's face beginning to clear. "My sight's already coming back."

Matt did his best to describe what brought on the blindness. At the end of Matt's story, Seamus said, "You better be such a fighter that no one can strike your head."

"What's the chance of that?"

Seamus shrugged.

CHAPTER 37.

RED DOT

It was late afternoon and Franklin had stopped by Matt's room at the Bakers' to see if he was interested in a trip to the tavern. Matt had grown used to the man visiting at random times to discuss whatever topic was bouncing around in his head. Today, they began a passionate discussion of the pros and cons of government checks and balances, which had somehow morphed into a discussion of upcoming cultural events in Philadelphia. They were talking about the Philadelphia symphony when Franklin asked, "Can I hear that machine that plays music?"

"It's a smartphone," Matt replied.

"Why would you call a machine smart?"

"It started out being called a telephone. They turned into smartphones when they could do things like play music. Telephones were once used only to talk. You would pick one up, speak into it, and hear the other person."

"Like I can hear you now?"

"Except they could be in another state or country."

"Across the sea?"

"One tap on this screen with your finger and you could reach anyone in the world."

"The world must seem like a small place in your time."

"For better or worse."

Franklin looked back at Matt, confused.

Matt went on to explain. "Just because we have smartphones doesn't mean we all like each other. I told you there are still wars. There's also something called terrorism, where people blow up buildings using airplanes."

"Such trouble can always be explained by people's want of a useful enterprise," Franklin lectured.

"The devil will find work for idle hands to do," Matt said, smiling. He had always liked the Puritan simplicity of that expression.

"Bah! Men use the devil to excuse their want of initiative! They say things like, 'I didn't get up early today because that damnable devil is controlling my life again. It has naught to do with the fact that I was in the pub last night until it closed.' What's an airplane?"

"A machine that carries men in the sky," Matt said. He imitated a flying plane by moving his hand in the air. "You can travel to England from here in about three hours on the fastest airplanes."

"Ah! It's a future that I'll never see," Franklin exclaimed, distraught. "To be able to fly to London for breakfast on the Thames and then be back in time to have dinner on the Schuylkill."

"Even in my time, it's expensive to fly all over the world. And it's still a lot of work."

"You mean like spending weeks being tossed in the rat-infested hold of a frigate, unable to keep the rotting victuals down?"

"I guess when you put it that way," Matt admitted. "Understand, though, that now that it's possible to fly, people are expected to go to Europe, complete their business, and then return to work in the United States the next day."

Franklin frowned. "Are you going to let me hear that smart machine again, or must I wait until I meet someone else from another century?"

Rolling his eyes, Matt walked into the bedroom and pulled up the plank in the floor where he now kept the phone. He returned to Franklin with it and pressed the power button. The phone started with its signature beeps.

"An electric bird," Franklin observed with a smile.

"An expensive bird," Matt said. "This was the newest model."

"Not many people had these?"

"Most at least had the basic version. This one was very expensive because it does more. I was able to put thirty movies on here, all my music, and a bunch of pictures."

"Movies?"

"Talking pictures…like a play."

Matt took Franklin on a tour of his movie collection for most of an hour. He resisted the temptation to show him anything with zombies, vampires, or space creatures, so as not to shock the man. Matt commented whenever he thought he should to help Franklin interpret American life based on the images that moved across the screen.

"Can I control it myself?" Franklin asked. He reached his hand out. "I've seen how you touch the symbols."

Matt handed Franklin the phone. "Touch lightly."

"It moves," Franklin exclaimed when all the symbols followed his finger as he dragged it across the screen. He pressed the camera icon, so Matt took the opportunity to show him how to take a selfie.

"Ha!" Franklin exclaimed, looking at his photo. "I'm immortalized in this machine. What's this?" Franklin pressed a button before Matt could answer.

"The walkie-talkie function," Matt said, glancing over briefly to check the screen. "If there's another person within range, you can talk to them directly."

Franklin tilted the phone while he looked at the screen. "What's this dot?"

"That shows the position of your phone, and then it will cast a signal around to pinpoint phones that are within talking range."

"It says 'YOU' here under the blue. What's this red one?"

"There's no red one," Matt said, laughing. "That would mean there's another phone somewhere."

Franklin stood up and turned in a circle while holding the phone out at arm's length. "It moves with me."

"Probably a glitch," Matt replied, reaching to take the device and inspect it. Franklin hadn't been mistaken—there was a red dot.

"Glitch?" Franklin asked.

"Electric noise."

"So you're sure there isn't another one of these smart machines nearby?"

"Smartphone," Matt corrected.

Franklin gave him a frustrated stare.

"When the scientists from my own time were trying to rescue me, they asked if I had any contact with three others who were in the same accident." It was as much as Matt knew. The scientists hadn't been able to find these others over the month that Matt had been texting them through a small wormhole they formed with their reactor. Matt had not seen or heard anything since he had arrived in the colonies to make him believe that the three other time travelers had joined him. In truth, he hadn't really given them much consideration, thinking that it was highly improbable that he would stumble on them. Even if they had arrived at exactly the same time and place, they would likely also be trying to keep their true identities secret and melt into society.

Franklin interrupted his thoughts. "Do you know these men?"

"It's one man and two women. I never met them."

"I want to know what their business is in my city."

"It's a glitch," Matt repeated.

Franklin stared back hard.

Matt selected the red dot on the screen and spoke into the phone. "Anyone out there?"

They waited, but there was nothing.

Matt pressed the red dot again. "Hello, anyone out there."

He set the phone on the table between them. "Glitch," Matt repeated knowingly.

"Mother! Shut it off!" said a voice from the phone.

Both men looked down in surprise.

"Are these *glitches* often the fairer sex?" Franklin said with a satisfied smile.

"Funny man," Matt replied. In unison, they returned their attention to the phone. Matt grabbed it from the table and touched the red dot again. "Who is this? Can we talk?" By the time he finished his sentence, the red dot had disappeared.

Franklin was rubbing the stubble on his chin. He leaned back with a smug grin. "My fine city is being overrun by people from the future," he quipped. "Have you some scheme?" Franklin looked at him expectantly.

"What exactly do you want me to say?"

"How about, 'Praise God, another of my kind has been sent to join me'?" The colonial man smiled.

"I had forgotten the possibility that someone else is here from my time," Matt replied. "What are the chances?"

"I'm no longer surprised that there are time travelers in my city, but it makes me no less curious when new ones are discovered."

"Should we try to find them?"

"The daughter doesn't want to be found. I wonder, though, what the mother's ambitions are. She may be seeking a Philadelphia gentleman to comfort her in her new century." Franklin winked.

"You scoundrel. I'm serious."

"Well, so am I. I turned this walkie thing on by accident, but she may have already been searching." He addressed the concerned look on Matt's face. "I'm hardly a scoundrel, in any case."

"You think I should find them?"

"Do it on the sly. Nothing of your story."

"It'll take forever to search the city."

"You said that this red dot showed where they are."

"I only know they're to the northeast. The distance doesn't work without the satellites."

"Satellites?"

"Some other time," Matt replied. "That red dot could be ten or twenty miles away."

"It's two miles to the river," Franklin said. "Most live on this side. I believe the dog needs a good walk tomorrow afternoon."

CHAPTER 38.

SARAH MORRIS

Matt left work early the next day. He picked up Scout and met Franklin at his home, and they set out to look for the "ladies from the future," as Franklin now called them. The older man had brought a compass to guide them on a straight path northeast until they reached the river. They were searching for some hint of the future that would give these women away, although Matt had no idea what it might be. He assumed he'd know when he saw it—maybe an odd window decoration, a strangely painted house, or even a novel business. He would scan every storefront for a modern-looking sign. Matt smiled in anticipation of doing a little undercover detective work with his companions.

Matt regretted taking the other "detectives" on his journey after about the first half mile. This was a new area of town for Scout, so he was interested in smelling every bush, hole, or potential animal hiding place. Matt was constantly coaxing the dog forward or begging him to catch up. Franklin, on the other hand, walked too slowly in between those times the dog wasn't smelling things. The combined effect was that they moved at a snail's pace.

To complicate the journey, they had to work their way across the city blocks in a diagonal fashion, which made it impossible to follow a straight northeastern path.

They came up on Second Street and were in the middle of a bustling merchant area. Scout perked up at the smell of cooked meat coming from one of the shops.

"Mission be damned," Franklin said, smelling the air. "I'm hungry."

"I could go for some food," Matt admitted. "You buying?"

"If that's what it takes," Franklin replied. "The ladies from the future will still be there an hour hence."

"I'm curious to see how they're making a living."

"I'm curious if the mother is educated and beautiful."

"Scoundrel."

"You should be thanking me for coming. You'll give yourself away the first time you open your mouth."

"You'll be doing all the talking, then?"

"Yes, until we can vouch for their character."

"How bad could they be?"

"All ladies have good intentions in your own time?" Franklin asked, looking at Matt out of the corner of his eye.

"Of course not."

"Then I'll do the talking."

Matt hadn't heard Franklin's reply. He was looking at a freshly painted sign posted in the window of a bakery across the street. "Do you know what a cupcake is?" he asked Franklin.

Franklin stared back, confused.

"I didn't think so," Matt said. He pointed across the street to a wooden building under a large sign that read "Morris Bakery." Matt thought for a moment and put his hand up as Franklin began to cross the street. "They're likely to recognize you," he said. "You're not the local blacksmith. I'd be ready for that."

"The currency was hardly an accurate likeness."

"Still," Matt replied.

Franklin, Matt, and Scout crossed the street and stepped onto the grey-painted porch of the bakery. The smell of freshly baked pastries made them stop to breathe in the sweet air. Matt attached the leash he had been carrying in his pocket to Scout's collar, tugged him to the far side of the porch, and tied him to a pole. It was far enough from the bakery doorway. "Stay," Matt commanded.

The dog looked up at him with disappointed eyes.

"I'll get you a biscuit or something," Matt promised. He pointed the dog to the ground. Scout tugged at his leash one last time and then lay down with a defeated groan.

Both men turned in unison, and Franklin pushed open the door causing a bell to ring. They entered what looked mostly like a conventional colonial bakery. Café tables were set up in front of a large wooden display counter. The singular feature that set it apart was that the counter and display case were wooden replicas of those from a modern donut store, with baked goods behind protective glass. They watched curiously as a tall, attractive middle-aged woman walked from a door behind the counter. Her brown hair was peppered in the front with wisps of grey.

She gave them a bright white smile. "What may I get for you fine gentlemen?"

Franklin scanned the rows of pastries and said, "My friend and I desire one or two of these cakes in cups. White ones, I think." He looked at Matt to say something, entirely disregarding their previous plan for Matt to remain silent.

Matt spoke slowly trying to sound as colonial as possible. "I'll have one of these cakes in cups and a piece of pumpkin nut bread."

"The same for me, then, and something to drink," Franklin said.

"We've coffee, tea, milk, or ale."

"Two ales, then," Franklin replied.

"Ale with cupcakes?" Matt said, smirking. Franklin ignored him and motioned to Anne to continue with their order.

"Have a seat, then," she said as she motioned to the tables.

"Is it only you that makes these fine pastries?" Franklin asked.

"My daughter and I," she replied.

Franklin nodded to her and pointed Matt over to a table near the window.

"Sarah," the woman called to the back. "Two ales, please." She was placing cupcakes and pieces of pumpkin bread on pewter plates. She walked around the counter and brought them to their table.

Franklin looked down at the decorated cupcake. "I've never seen anything like this. I did rather expect to eat this from a cup."

"They're made in cups," the woman explained. "We take them out before they're decorated."

Matt looked around at the empty tables. "You do a good business selling these?" he asked. Franklin gave him a cautious look.

"We sell out each day," she said. "It'll be crowded soon with people buying fresh cakes for supper." Sarah, a teenage girl, interrupted them as she came from the back. She set the ales down on the table.

"Thank you so much, young lady," Franklin said.

"You're welcome," Sarah replied. She inspected Franklin suspiciously. "You been here before?"

"I can't remember exactly," Franklin said. "How long have you had this shop?"

Her mother interrupted. "Quite a while."

Franklin took a sip of his ale. Matt did the same as he looked at Franklin, wondering what he had in mind. Scout barked outside.

"Is there a dog on the porch?" the teen asked. She stood high on her toes to peer out the window.

"That's Scout," Matt explained. "He hates being away from the action."

"Does he bite?" she asked Matt. Sarah was staring intently again at Franklin.

"Who?" Matt joked.

Sarah pulled her gaze from Franklin to face Matt again. "Your dog," she said impatiently.

"He's friendly enough," Matt replied. "I promised him a biscuit or something." He looked first to Sarah and then to her mother for some suggestion.

"We have bones from last night's meal," Sarah replied.

"I'll buy some," Matt said slowly, trying to sound colonial.

"I couldn't charge you for scraps," the mother replied. She looked at her daughter. "You can go see the dog with Mister—"

"Miller," Matt said.

"Don't leave the porch," her mother warned. The girl nodded, disappeared into the back room and returned with rib bones and some other meat scraps on a pewter plate.

"Those should make him happy," Matt said. Sarah gave him a tentative smile. Matt stood up, trying to gauge what had suddenly made the mother so uncomfortable. She warned him again with a stern glance.

Franklin had noticed her manner change as well and spoke up. "I vouch for the integrity of Mr. Miller," he said. The woman nodded.

Matt accompanied Sarah outside and the dog looked up excitedly. "This is Scout," he said. "Sometimes it takes him a while to warm up to people."

The girl walked tentatively to the dog, holding the scraps at arm's length, set them down cautiously, and slid them along the floor. Scout reached up with his paw.

"You shake?" Sarah said as she moved close enough to accept his paw in one of her hands. She handled it slowly and then stroked it with her other hand. Tears were crawling down her face. She used one hand to wipe them from her eyes, but they were replaced by others as she cupped the dog's paw again. Letting go, she moved her face cautiously to Scout and kissed him on his head, then reached down, pushed the scraps forward slightly and stood. "I stopped going near dogs," she said softly. Her eyes were wet. Sarah stepped to the porch railing to stare into the street and wave to a number of people as they walked by. She was obviously focusing hard on regaining her composure.

"You're popular," Matt said after she waved to a family passing by in a wagon.

"People in 1763 like cupcakes," she said. "Go figure."

"So you make a good living?" Matt asked.

"We do all right. How long have you been here?"

"I've been in Philadelphia since September."

"Do you have the dreams?"

"What dreams?"

"That is Ben Franklin in there, right? Does he know that you're from the future?"

Matt stared back silently, still not willing to give himself up, but he was curious to learn how she had been able to identify them so quickly. Sarah turned her attention back to the dog. "Dogs don't like me or Mom," she said. "I can't explain it. They hated Patrick."

"Who's Patrick?"

"Another traveler."

"Traveler?"

Sarah laughed. "Don't smile at me with a mouth full of white teeth and expect me to believe that you're from the eighteenth century. I've seen you in my dreams." She moved back to Scout and ran her hands through his fur. "I miss dogs."

"What happened to Patrick?" Matt asked.

"We woke up one day and he was gone."

"Gone where?"

"Probably back to England. That's where he was from in his own time. He made enemies gambling and couldn't control the dreams. He talked about going back to someplace familiar. You were the person on the Quantum yesterday?"

"I've no idea what you're talking about," Matt said.

She ignored him. "Did you wait in those long lines?"

"My rich girlfriend had connections," Matt answered. His sudden candidness surprised him.

"Patrick found us using his phone, too," she said. "I told her not to turn it on again, but she was curious if there was anyone else."

"You don't want to be found?"

"We learned our lesson. We could wake up and more things would be stolen."

"You think I showed up here with Ben Franklin to steal? You must have missed the section on the Founding Fathers in history class."

"I didn't miss anything."

Seeing her stern face, Matt reconsidered his perspective. "I'll admit, I might be a little wary of men in this century."

"Mom trusts people as soon as she meets them. It drives me crazy." Sarah turned her complete attention to Scout, scratching him behind his ears with both hands. "Dogs wouldn't come near us, and when they did, they would growl. People were always apologizing. Kind of spooky, really."

"Scout growled at me for almost a week," Matt said. "Now I can't get rid of him."

"Why would you want to?" she exclaimed. "He's wonderful."

"My fiancée's family in Virginia owns him."

"You took their dog?"

"He followed me from Richmond. Showed up at my door."

Sarah stood up and looked straight into Matt's eyes. "Why did you come to our store?"

"Franklin wanted to make sure you weren't up to some mischief. I don't want anything from you." He smiled at her. "It never occurred to me to make cupcakes, though. I might be your next competitor."

"You're not the cupcake type," she said simply. "How do you make your living?"

"You ever seen Miller Head and Stomach Tablets?"

"Mom says they're Alka-Seltzer."

"We sell them in pubs all over the city."

"Do you hang out with George Washington, too?"

"Even Franklin doesn't know Washington that well."

"Do you think we're here for good?"

"They never contacted you?" Matt asked.

"Who?"

"Scientists were trying to get me back through a wormhole," Matt explained. "They texted me through the phone."

"No one texted us," Sarah said. "What happened?"

"They couldn't guarantee it was safe. I told them I'd take my chances here."

"Do you think they'll try for me and Mom?"

"They said something about having one opportunity. They tried and failed. I'm not going back."

"We like it here," Sarah said.

"How's your mom handling all this?"

"She left a lot of friends behind, but my dad treated her like shit."

"Dr. Franklin's a charmer," Matt said. "He can probably make up for that."

"Fine by me," Sarah replied. "Isn't he like the eighteenth-century George Clooney?"

"A balding George Clooney with glasses," Matt said, laughing. "I think he spends his whole day visiting."

"He can visit my mother if he wants," she offered.

"I imagine he'll be back," Matt replied. "He'll want to talk about the future. This may be the last time for me, though."

"We need friends we can trust, especially men. When do you get married?"

"Hopefully in another year."

"Why so long?"

"Her father won't let me marry her until I have money."

"That's harsh."

"It's a different time."

"You really have bought into this."

Matt nodded. "Where'd your family live in our time?"

"Tennessee," she said. "My father was a big financial guy. Mom, her name's Anne, attended every charity event in the city. I went to private school."

"How did you support yourself when you got here?"

"Mom had her purse, jewelry, and a fur coat," she said. "I had my backpack from school and my diamond earrings. We woke up in a field outside of Philadelphia, sold some stuff, and bought this store."

"Were you in the cupcake business in Tennessee?"

She shook her head. "Mom was always home watching those baking shows on television and making stuff for her friends. My dad was gone all the time."

"Away on business?"

"If you call sleeping with every slut in town business, then yes."

She said this loud enough for Matt to worry that a passerby had overheard. He looked out into the street. "You can't talk like that," he scolded.

"My dad was spending his time with promiscuous young ladies who were impressed by his money."

"Better."

"Will I be invited to your wedding?"

"Maybe," Matt said, "if you promise to keep our secret."

"No one would believe it anyway."

"You can even sell your cupcakes in my store if you can arrange delivery."

"What store?"

"Grace Apothecary."

"We buy our soap there."

"The soap wasn't my idea. I only wanted to sell medicine."

"Hair care! That's what I miss. My mom's going grey."

"I'll tell my store manager. I'll see if he can find shampoo. Not sure about hair color. We'd have to mix it and sell our own brand."

"I'll see what Mom says about the cupcakes. We're selling out most days. We've saved a lot of money since Patrick left."

"Tell me more about Patrick."

"Patrick Ferguson, Englishman," she said. "Tall. Handsome. He had the accent. It makes them all attractive. He'd get the dreams during the day and have to sit down. You have them, right?"

"Flashes where I lose my vision," Matt said. "I usually can't tell what they mean until later."

"Patrick could do it in real time. At first, it was simple things, like he'd say, 'knock, knock,' and a minute later someone would walk through the door, or 'oops,' and Mom would drop something in the kitchen. He'd glaze over right in front of you."

"You said he found you with the phone?"

"Like you did."

"Franklin pressed the button accidentally."

"You showed your phone to Franklin? Aren't you worried about changing the future?"

"Nah," Matt replied. "I even showed him his picture on a hundred-dollar bill."

"Doesn't even look like him."

"It does." He went to pull his wallet from his pocket. Grace's engagement ring dropped onto the porch floor. Sarah picked it up.

"You carry this in your pocket?" she asked. She opened the door and went inside with the ring.

CHAPTER 39.

AP AMERICAN HISTORY

"Mr. Miller asked me to marry him!" Sarah said as she entered the bakery. She held her hand up, showing her mother the ring on her finger.

"I dropped it," Matt explained as he followed her through the door. He was unexpectedly flustered.

"Not true," the girl said. She put a disappointed look on her face.

"Mr. Miller's too old for you, honey," her mother proclaimed.

"He made me promise to keep his secret."

Franklin threw Matt a critical look.

"Is this ring intended for some lady, Mr. Miller?" Anne asked.

"My future wife," Matt explained. "She lives in Richmond."

"I wish you good luck." As she said it, customers entered the store and she stood up. "I must ask you gentlemen to excuse me. The afternoon rush is about to begin."

"We should be going anyway," Franklin said. He looked at Anne. "Same time next Thursday?"

"If it pleases you, Dr. Franklin."

Sarah put her hand up to examine the ring on her finger. "I may keep it."

Matt held his hand out silently until she gave it up. "I'm ready to go," he said to Franklin after he had safely tucked the ring back into his wallet. He opened the door and motioned for the older man to walk through.

Unexpectedly, Sarah followed them outside, and they had to turn back to talk with her on the porch. "Mr. Miller, something else you should know," she said. "Patrick said that a man with knowledge of the future could be a king."

Matt brushed her off. "It's exactly what I used to think," he scoffed. "It doesn't work that way."

Sarah glared back at him impatiently. "Don't be so sure," she insisted. "He couldn't stop talking about how he could change things."

"One person can't do much," Matt said knowingly. "Knowledge of the future only gets you so far."

Sarah's impatience turned to irritation. "What did you come here with? Besides your phone."

"I was hiking. I had my pack."

"I had my school backpack with all my books."

"Textbooks?" Matt said excitedly. "Which ones?"

"AP American history, chemistry, biology, and calculus."

"You were taking all AP classes?" Matt asked, impressed.

"I was applying to Princeton."

"If you're ever interested in selling the chemistry book, it could help me," Matt proclaimed. "Either way, keep them safe."

"That's just it. That asshole took them when he left."

"Does he know how valuable they are?"

"He had a degree in mechanical engineering. I expect he does. He'd sit in our bakery and write pages of plans like some evil movie villain."

"All four books?"

"Five. My copy of Twilight was in there."

"He has information on modern chemistry and biology," Matt said, "and he's a Brit who knows the entire future of the United States."

"And vampires," she added.

"I'm not joking," Matt scolded.

She shrugged. "If I had it to do again, I'd have been more careful."

"He might be on his way to becoming a king."

"Anyway, I thought you should know." She looked over at Franklin and stuck out her hand. "Dr. Franklin, it was an honor to meet you, but you're in big trouble if you break my mother's heart."

"Somehow, young lady, I believe you," Franklin replied. "I promise to use her with great respect."

Sarah reached out her hand to Matt and said, "Good day, Mr. Miller."

"Good day, Ms. Morris," Matt said, kissing it lightly.

"It's Miss," she said. She turned and walked back into the store.

Franklin waited as Matt untied the dog and then they walked together onto the street. When they were finally out of earshot of the bakery, Franklin spoke. "You could have waited a day before spilling the beans."

"My white teeth gave me away."

"How much of the future is in these books that were stolen?"

"A lot. I'm not sure which could cause more trouble, the knowledge of chemistry and biology or knowing American history. Your name's in that book as a signer of the Declaration of Independence."

"Declaration of Independence?"

"It's the document that you write with Thomas Jefferson and John Adams proclaiming that the American colonies are a sovereign nation independent of Great Britain."

"I commit treason?" Franklin exclaimed.

"'We must, indeed, all hang together, or most assuredly we shall all hang separately.'"

Franklin gave him a puzzled look.

"It's what you said after you put your signature on the document."

Franklin glared at him, still in shock. "How many men do you think signed this declaration?"

"I don't have to think; it's a matter of historical record. Fifty-six."

"All these men are listed in this girl's book?"

Matt nodded. "She wasn't such a young girl, unfortunately."

"What does that have to do with anything? Did you ask her to marry you?"

"Nothing will put me off my path."

"Ah!" Franklin huffed. "Better for you to marry someone closer to home."

"The point is that Sarah was taking university-level classes," Matt explained. "Her schoolbooks will be very detailed."

"So, not only will the fifty-six signers of this treasonous document be listed," Franklin proclaimed, "but also their families, vocations, and possibly their addresses?"

Matt nodded his agreement.

The dog stopped to sniff a storefront, so both men stood waiting. Franklin was looking off in the distance down the street. "How would a British subject use such intelligence?" he said, thinking aloud.

"He could cause a lot of trouble," Matt replied. "There's no doubt in my mind."

Franklin shrugged. "It would be hard to convince anyone that this book is real."

"The print quality would be like nothing like you've ever seen."

"Still, a commoner can't get an audience with a man of consequence in Great Britain," Franklin said, "let alone have an opportunity to convince him that he has knowledge of the future."

"You were convinced."

"How did this Patrick find these ladies?"

"Same way we did," Matt said. "He used his phone."

"So he could find you too?"

"They think he went to England."

Franklin threw up his hands. "I'm too tired to worry about this. Let God sort it out."

"Sounds good for now. But I can't help thinking of something I once heard."

"What's that?"

"Trust in God, but lock your doors."

CHAPTER 40.

VIRGINIA

Nothing was going right, and Matt was on the verge of canceling his plans to travel to Virginia to attend Will's wedding. Matt lost his supplier for sodium bicarbonate, and so he had to travel halfway to New York to find someone who even knew what it was. The new sodium bicarbonate wasn't as dry, so the tablets were sticking in the mold and taking twice as long to make. He was caught in an endless loop of not having time to recruit more help to make tablets because he was too busy making tablets. Ward had been helping with the press, but only after Matt begged Jacob. This meant Jacob had to come in an hour early every day to stock shelves, so he wasn't happy.

The good thing was that demand for the tablets was high, especially in the taverns. They'd moved Grace Apothecary into the new building. Customers filled the store for the entire time it was open. They were on pace to make sixty pounds this week in a store that was only partially stocked. Jacob was pumping most of his salary back into purchasing one half of the business. He had hired an additional man to work the store, which was fortunate because otherwise Ward wouldn't have had time to help press tablets. They were barely meeting demand, sales were growing, and it felt like exactly the wrong time to leave for Virginia.

When Matt met Franklin for dinner that night, he said, "Ben, I don't feel like I can go. I've too much to do."

"You're going to miss an important wedding in your future family so you can sell more mouth brushes and tooth soap?"

"They're called toothbrushes and toothpaste, and that's not all I sell."

"Ladies' toiletries are all the same."

"Tooth care isn't only for ladies. Tell me you've been taking care of your teeth."

"Ah! I've more important things."

"You won't impress ladies with breath that smells like rot."

"I know," Franklin admitted. "I told you." He waved Matt off in that way he did when he had no argument and wanted to change the subject. "Get your affairs in order," Franklin ordered. "We repair soon to meet this lady of yours and all the other Anglican ninnies."

"You really don't like the English Church."

"They all think they know the Creator better than everyone else."

"You're going to like them," Matt replied. "If I can find the time to go."

"I've already contacted John Foxcroft. He and another postmaster have plans to meet me in Richmond after the wedding. We're going."

"I can't leave my store for a month."

"Every time I've been there, you're somewhere else, and Jacob has no idea where."

"Making headache tablets," Matt explained. "I'm not drunk on a park bench."

"You'll never be wealthy if you can't delegate," Franklin exclaimed. "Do you trust Jacob?"

"It doesn't feel right to leave him while I go on a month-long holiday."

"Don't call it a holiday," Franklin said.

"It is."

"Take your bubbling tablets and give them to apothecaries and taverns along our route."

Matt thought for a moment as the possibilities streamed through his head. "Hugh Mercer."

Franklin waited for an explanation.

"A war hero and doctor down in Fredericksburg," Matt replied. "I told him about the tablets."

Franklin smiled knowingly. "Play your cards properly and you'll have orders from here to Richmond," he proclaimed. "Now you have every reason to travel to Virginia."

"I'm taking the horse and the dog too. You'll still have your walking buddy on the farm."

Franklin had been taking Scout on long walks through the hills that overlooked Philadelphia. He'd worked out a schedule with James Baker so the dog could be back in time to ride on the wagon during deliveries. Between Matt, Franklin, and James, the dog didn't have a moment's rest, but based on his happy demeanor when any one of them showed up, Scout was perfectly fine with the schedule.

Later that day, Matt informed Jacob of his trip. The young man seemed relieved that Matt would be gone and was happy to learn that there were enough headache tablets to keep them stocked for the next couple of months. They watched their newest employee, Michael, as they talked. He was a good salesman, always polite and impeccably dressed. As Matt watched Michael greet new customers, he became satisfied that the business would run fine without him, and he grew more excited about going on his trip and developing a distribution network that extended all the way to Richmond.

Matt spent the rest of the day cleaning his synthesis laboratory and shutting it down. Unfortunately, even the front room had now taken on the state of controlled chaos that was the hallmark of most synthetic chemistry laboratories. Supplies and manufacturing equipment were stacked in almost every free space along the walls. The messy back room was no less than tragic in scope and smell. The current batch of cantaloupes had yielded about as much mold as they were able and would need to be replaced. Matt cleaned the nasty-smelling crocks and set them outside to dry in the sun. He washed the chemistry glassware and then stacked the boxes of headache tablets in the front room so Jacob could find them easily when the Market Street store needed to be restocked. Matt finished up by setting aside seven display boxes to put in Franklin's wagon.

****

Three days later, Franklin pulled up in his wagon to meet Matt, Thunder, and Scout in front of the lab. Matt loaded the boxes and his bag in the back and hopped up alongside Franklin. They began their journey with Thunder untied, walking behind the carriage with the dog. Matt saw early that Franklin was disturbed by the antics of the dog and horse trotting behind them and wasn't surprised when he eventually asked, "Are you sure you don't want him tied to the wagon?"

"Nah," Matt replied. "Scout will be fine."

Franklin frowned. "I wasn't speaking about the dog."

"We can tie them both when we get close to the cities. I usually worry more about Scout in the towns than Thunder."

"How did they fare on your journey here?"

"The horse was fine. Scout didn't arrive until the last day of the trip. He followed me all the way from Richmond."

"You have a singular relationship with these animals," Franklin observed.

"I never told you how Thunder saved my life," Matt said. "I was attacked on my way to Philadelphia."

"By savages?"

"No. A man from Richmond wants me dead. He sent someone to kill me."

"This is why you've been visiting Solomon McCalla?"

"How'd you know about that?"

"I have friends," Franklin said.

Matt took the next few hours of travel to tell his story and discuss options with Franklin. It was mostly uninterrupted except for the times when Matt would stop to call to the animals to keep closer to the wagon. At the end of the story, Matt said, "We'll need to be on the lookout when we get to Richmond. I probably should've told you this before."

"Nonsense," Franklin replied. "Virginia laws are the strongest in the colonies, and anyway, if the sheriff isn't available, I have Bessie."

"Bessie?"

Franklin took one hand from the reins, reached down across Matt's legs to a ledge on the side of the wagon and moved a tarp, uncovering the tip of a large musket along with two pistols. Franklin replaced the tarp and gave Matt a satisfied grin. Both men sat in silence as the road moved through a stretch of open valley that dropped off into the Delaware River. The grasses and wildflowers moved in unison as they picked up a cool breeze. The plants flowed in hypnotic waves of color across the valley floor.

Their conversation began again as they traveled up and out of the basin to reach the edge of Wilmington. "I should stop to speak to the postmaster here," said Franklin.

"I have friends outside of town, right off the road," Matt said. "Will you be okay without me for the night?"

"There are more than a few reputable beds for hire here."

They arranged to meet on the other side of Wilmington in the morning. Matt saddled Thunder, and he and the dog went to visit the Boyds.

****

Margaret Boyd came out of the house to watch them as they rode up. "Look who's here!" she said.

"You remember," Matt replied.

"You, your horse, and your dog." Margaret smiled down at Scout and he gave a short bark in response. "I wagered he'd find you eventually."

"You know Scout?"

"Didn't know his name, but he's been here before. John and I knew he was yours." She stared for a moment at Matt. "You're a handsome fellow when you're not all scraped up, Mr. Miller. What can we do for you?"

"Just a social visit," Matt said.

"Unsaddle your horse, then. Dinner's in an hour. John's over in the barn with the new foal."

"Thunder's foal?"

"Go see," she said. "He'll enjoy the surprise."

****

It was a wonderful night. Thunder met his son and Scout played with the new foal until they were both exhausted. Matt took the opportunity to relay his sincere thanks to the people who had helped him when he'd needed it most. The next morning, Matt hugged Margaret and shook the hands of John and all the Boyd sons and hired hands before he left.

Franklin was waiting for him in front of a tavern on the edge of town. "Have a good evening?"

"The best." Matt told Franklin about the Boyds for the next hour.

Eventually Franklin said, "If there's anything worse than Anglicans, it's Quakers."

"I beg to differ, Ben," Matt said. "Both are wonderful as far as I can see."

Franklin gave Matt a warm smile. "It's no wonder that you decided to leave your own time."

CHAPTER 41.

HOMECOMING

They made good time as they moved through Baltimore, Alexandria, and Fredericksburg. They were able to dine one night with Hugh Mercer. Franklin and Mercer became instant friends as Matt sat there in relative silence and listened to them talk politics. They would look over at him on occasion, making Matt wonder if the sensitive nature of their discussion was making them paranoid. Some of the topics raised by Mercer might indeed have been on the edge of treason. Franklin, Matt observed, was a pragmatic loyalist, while Mercer had no problem talking about how much he despised the English.

They spent the night as Mercer's guest. In the morning, as had been his plan, Matt left Mercer with a display box of Miller Head and Stomach Tablets after a demonstration which included dissolving tablets in cups of water and having Mercer and Franklin drink them together. Franklin was silent for a time after they left Mercer's home, but eventually he said, "Capital fellow."

"Challenging fellow, I think," Matt replied.

"Doesn't like the Crown. Too much history."

"Isn't that why people come to the colonies? Aren't they all trying to get away from England or wherever?"

"I can't help thinking constantly of this new country you describe. Every conversation with my fellows is tainted with the suspicion that they will have a part in this treason."

"I can imagine Mercer already has a plan." Matt said.

Franklin wrinkled his face in an exaggerated motion and mouthed "uh-huh."

Matt laughed. "I see more subtle signs in others."

"Subtle signs?"

"Pride. The man I bought my shoes from in Richmond; I asked him if he imported his stuff and he was insulted. He told me his shoes were better than anything you could buy from across the sea."

"They probably were," Franklin affirmed.

"One of the first things Grace Taylor told me was that they did without English luxuries," Matt said. "It didn't mean anything to me at first, but I realize now that it speaks volumes about people wanting to build a culture. It's not treason at all."

"You're not going to speak incessantly again about how perfect these Taylors are, are you?"

Matt ignored him. "Americans won't consider independence as treason. It'll feel like an obvious next step."

"Like a son breaking away from his father," Franklin observed. "He doesn't exactly hate the old man, he just wants to do it by himself." He looked up to see the outline of buildings where the road disappeared into the horizon. "We're getting close to Richmond."

"This is all looking very familiar," Matt said.

"Anxious?"

"Of course," Matt replied. He was silent while he pondered his situation. "What if there's really nothing there?"

"Then we'll skip this silly wedding and you can come to Williamsburg with me."

Matt scolded him. "What I needed to hear was, 'Don't worry, Matthew, she probably misses you more than you can imagine.'"

"Then I'm not supposed to mention the rich and handsome tobacco farmer she's courting?"

Matt could see how Franklin relished watching him cringe. He glared back.

"If nothing else," Franklin went on, "I'm sure that there are a number of beautiful Richmond ladies who've always dreamed of marrying a Northerner who sells ladies' soap."

Matt gave him a dirty look. Grace had become larger than life in Matt's mind. He wanted to think of something else, so he changed the subject to the only other topic that consumed him. "I've had dreams that I'll meet Levi Payne. We'll fight."

"I'll keep him away with Bessie," Franklin said simply. "It's like I told you."

"You're taking Bessie with you when you go see John Foxcroft."

"She's *my* protection."

"There're no guns in my dreams. It's a physical fight."

"Unless you're convinced he'll meet you here on the edge of town, there isn't anything you can do about it now," Franklin said impatiently. "I think I prefer it when you are obsessing about your farm girl." Franklin turned his head around as they passed by a cornfield. "Corn looks high this year. Are we getting close?"

"It's about a mile down the road." Matt's mind was racing. Had he built Grace up into something she wasn't? Some Southern goddess? Maybe he'd see her again and decide that he wasn't that attracted. Maybe she would see him and decide the same thing.

"You're sure they know I'm coming?" Franklin asked.

"They expect you," Matt replied.

"Are you sure they know you're coming?" Franklin looked over at Matt and laughed uncontrollably.

Matt grimaced. The anticipation of meeting Grace after so long made him feel ready to explode.

Franklin could see his discomfort. "I'm only jealous," the older man confided. "I'd give anything to be anxious again over meeting a lady. Age has taken that from me. The flame of passion is only an ember."

****

They were coming around a corner, and the main gate of the Taylor farm could be seen about one hundred yards ahead on the right side of the road. The largest fenced-in pasture and the main stable were now visible as they neared the entrance. There were a few horses who were already looking to them as they approached.

"It's big," Franklin observed.

Scout and Thunder knew where they were. Scout, who had been trotting out ahead of the wagon, sprinted forward and then disappeared from the road as he entered the gate. They could hear him barking loudly. "Gone in early to wake everyone," Franklin said.

Excitement and nervousness built in Matt's stomach. Franklin reached over and patted him on the back. "She'll be there and she'll be delighted." Matt nodded in silence. It wasn't only meeting Grace again after all this time that was overwhelming; it was everything he'd experienced in between. He'd lived and died. He was a very different man from the one they peeled from the riverbank.

As they turned to enter the gate, Thunder, who was tied to the wagon, whinnied loudly, upset that he couldn't join the dog, who was already on the porch of the big white farmhouse.

"You know better," Matt said to the horse.

The farmhouse door opened and Grace's mother came outside. She waved as she stepped off the porch and came to them as they climbed down from the wagon. "Welcome back to Richmond, Mr. Miller," she said, reaching out her hand out to shake. Matt closed the distance purposefully and gave her a hug.

"And this must be Dr. Franklin," she said when Matt let her go. She extended her hand. "I'm Mary Taylor."

Franklin took her hand and kissed it lightly. "Call me Benjamin, please, madam. I should say I'm very pleased to meet you."

"How was your trip?" Mary asked.

"Faster coming than going, and less eventful," Matt said. He couldn't keep himself from looking from barn to barn, trying to catch a glimpse of the young woman who had occupied his mind for so long.

"She's around here somewhere, I think," Mary said knowingly.

"Mr. Miller!" a man called.

Matt turned to see Grace's father, Thomas, walking toward him from the main stable. There was a puppy trotting clumsily at his side. The puppy stopped and barked at the strangers every few steps and then happily scrambled to catch up to his master. Scout trotted over to scrutinize this smaller and much cuter version of himself with cautious nudges and sniffs and then greeted

Thomas. When Scout went to Thomas, the man stooped down and scratched him vigorously with both hands.

"Good to see you again, boy," he said with an excited smile. Scout turned back to the puppy, who was now growling as ferociously as a puppy could at this threat to his master. "That's Duke," Thomas announced. The puppy barked at Scout, ran a short distance, and then looked back to see if he was being chased. He barked again, taunting the older animal. Scout jumped to him, nipping at his legs as he let the puppy run just out of his reach. Thomas turned away from watching the animals play, walked to Matt, and extended his hand. "Welcome back," Thomas said with a warm smile.

Matt turned to Franklin. "This is Dr. Benjamin Franklin of Philadelphia, Postmaster General of the American colonies."

"Very pleased to meet you, sir," Thomas said. "I've followed your work for some time." He reached out and shook Franklin's hand.

"Mr. Miller has spoken often of the beauty of your farm," Franklin said, motioning with his arms. "Words don't describe what you have here. I'm overwhelmed."

"I appreciate the compliment," Thomas replied. "I hope you plan to stay long enough to see what we've built."

Matt saw the barn door open, and there she was, smoothing her dress. Grace waved, took a moment to watch the dogs playing and then walked slowly but intentionally toward them. Everyone stopped to measure her approach and then Matt's as he walked to meet her. She was wearing a faded and tattered blue country dress, and her hair was pulled back as was her fashion when she worked with the horses. Even from a distance, her movement and her smile began to paralyze him. She was more beautiful than Matt had remembered.

"Mr. Miller," she said. "You've returned." It suddenly became very awkward as they stood in front of each other, neither one knowing what came next.

He looked into her ice-blue eyes. "Didn't you think I'd come?" he said. His voice was shaking. Matt made a motion toward her, and that was all it took for the apples to spill from the cart. She closed the distance quickly, almost knocking him down, and smothered him with a passionate kiss.

CHAPTER 42.

THE FUTURE IS NOW

He was traveling through the time blocks again, moving slowly enough to look around. Some events could only be seen; others he felt, and then a few were like he was living them completely. Many times the blocks contained nothing he recognized and he had trouble concentrating. It was like driving a car in traffic through an unknown town where there are no recognizable landmarks; you stare straight ahead, trusting that the road will lead you to your destination. Suddenly, though, he'd find himself recognizing people and places and would wonder about the information he had missed by staring straight ahead.

In one block, he saw the Taylor farm, Grace, and the barn where he slept. He recognized Will and Graine's wedding at the Martins' estate. Everyone was in formal dress, including Franklin, who was dancing in the pavilion. Matt caught a glimpse of Grace in a blue velvet gown as she talked with one of the Martin sisters, and he registered its color in his mind. He always liked simple proof of the ability of the dreams to tell the future. When he finally looked up from making plans and taking mental notes, he realized that he was already in the place with many horses and his body was on the ground. He'd missed the beginning...again! He still had no idea how Levi Payne defeated him after all he had done to prepare.

The block began vibrating rhythmically, and Matt heard the familiar drumbeats, *boom, boom, boom,* fourteen, fifteen, sixteen—

Bam, Bam, Bam. "Mr. Miller, are you awake?"

Matt looked up at the ceiling. *Am I still dreaming?* At first there was no evidence that the things around him were real. There was no reference point to help him establish whether he was in the past or the present, but slowly, reality returned. He was on the Taylor farm, with Scout still lying at his feet. The dog had both eyes open, staring at the door.

Bam, Bam, Bam. "Mr. Miller, are you awake?"

Matt recognized Jonathan's voice. "I'm awake," he called. He smiled, remembering the first time he met the youngest Taylor son and how they'd become friends. The kid was a wise old sage when it came to eighteenth-century family and culture.

"Can I come in?" Jonathan said through the door.

"Of course."

Jonathan slid the door open and peeked into the barn. "Mother said you've almost missed breakfast."

Matt looked down at his watch. It was after nine o'clock. He and the dog had slept almost four hours after sunrise. Bright light filled the barn. Matt couldn't remember the last time he'd slept so long. Scout was obviously tired too, having made no attempt to get up after Jonathan pulled the door open.

"Duke, get back here," Jonathan said as the puppy pushed past him and galloped over to Scout. The puppy's feet were four times too big for his body. He stopped almost two yards from the bench they were sleeping on and tumbled to the ground as he slid on the loose hay. He bounded to his feet and barked at Scout. Scout lay there for a moment, seemingly unimpressed by the puppy's antics, but then he popped to his feet, jumped off the bed, and ran out the door as the puppy gave chase.

Jonathan turned to watch them rumble noisily out into the yard. "They like each other."

"I imagine they do," Matt said. "I hear they're brothers."

"Same parents. You can't have him."

"I never wanted *Scout*. He showed up at my door."

"You could've brought him back."

"No, I couldn't. And anyway, why'd you let him follow me? Do you know how much trouble it was trying to find him a place to live in the city?" Matt climbed off the bed.

"He just went," Jonathan said. "He'd been sitting outside every day, waiting for you and Thunder."

"He traveled almost all the way to Philadelphia before he found us. Those animals were sure happy to see each other."

Jonathan smiled. "They probably were."

"Ah hell, I was happy too," Matt admitted. "Scout's kept me company."

"What took you so long?"

"I can't ask for Grace's hand if I can't support her."

"Can you? You know, like you promised."

"Almost."

"She's had other offers," Jonathan said. "We talk about it often at supper."

"I've been working my butt off for your sister."

Jonathan looked back at him, puzzled.

"You know," Matt said. "Your rear end." He pointed.

"That would look pretty funny," Jonathan said. "Is that why you slept late?"

"I've been working nonstop for eleven months. I deserved to sleep late."

"I reckon that's true, but if you want something to eat, you should hurry. Dr. Franklin is already in the cornfield with Father."

"How long has Dr. Franklin been up?"

"Since sunrise. He said, 'early to bed, early to rise—'"

"'Makes a man healthy, wealthy, and wise.' I know."

"Father never heard that," Jonathan said.

"Are Dr. Franklin and your father getting on?"

"They were talking like mad at breakfast. He'll be bored when Father takes him to the cornfield."

Matt shrugged. "It's hard to figure out what old guys think is interesting."

"Jeb didn't get any breakfast last week when he slept late."

"I'm coming," Matt said. "Quit bugging me so I can get dressed."

"Grace is already working in the barn, so you needn't worry about her seeing you all mussed up."

"Why would I be worried?"

"Didn't you travel a thousand miles to see her?"

"Everyone's a comedian. It was only like two hundred fifty miles, anyway."

"Better get breakfast." Jonathan slipped outside and was gone, leaving Matt alone in the barn.

"I *am* hungry," Matt said to the wall. He looked around at the place that had been his home for almost a month and still felt lost. Some days he was Matt in 1763, and other days he was living a waking dream. He quickly washed his face and brushed his teeth, ran his hands through his hair, and left the hay barn. He walked by Scout, who was still playing with the puppy, and then to Thunder's pasture, but the horse was nowhere to be seen. He was surprised to find him in a stall with Grace, who was stroking him with a brush. She looked up and watched him approach.

"You've ruined the surprise," she said. "Did you get breakfast?" He stood there to take her all in. She hadn't changed much from the barn girl he'd first met. She was still a refreshing mix of common sense, hard work, practicality, and drop-dead beauty. It made him marvel again at a Creator that had conceived of such a creature. Lost in his thoughts, it took him a moment to respond.

"I'm going over now," he said as he watched her long hands move the comb through Thunder's mane.

"It looked like he hadn't been brushed for an eternity," she said. "He loves the attention."

"We were on the road for like a month," Matt said. "No time."

"It was ten days," she said, smiling.

"I'm not as good at making him shine," Matt said. "We both get impatient."

"I imagine you do," she replied. "Better go eat."

There was still awkwardness between them, like each was looking for a sign of the other's commitment. Matt was past playing hard to get. He had traveled two hundred and fifty miles to see her. This was what he wanted and he was going to reach for it. He walked forward, opened the stall door, grabbed her around the waist and kissed her passionately next to the horse. She pushed into him hard, still holding the brushes in her hands. He lingered there for a while, kissing her lips, and then backed out of the stall.

"I need breakfast," he said.

She looked at him with a flushed face and a flirty smile and then returned to brushing.

Matt walked through the courtyard in time to see Franklin and Thomas drive through the gate. Thomas slowed the wagon as they came alongside. "You finally awake?" Franklin called.

"Hope you get up earlier than this in Philadelphia," Thomas chided.

Matt gave both a critical stare. *A fraternity of old guys!* "Go ahead and have your fun," Matt said. "I've been working for a month trying to get here. I deserve the sleep."

"It's only a jest," Franklin said, hearing his irritation. They followed alongside him in the wagon as he walked toward the house.

"You get breakfast?" Thomas asked.

"Can't seem to get there," Matt replied.

"We leave for Richmond in an hour for wedding clothes," Franklin said, "Suspect you'll be ready by then?"

The enthusiasm of both these men was almost too much to bear. "Maybe. Don't rush me."

"I hope you'll be in better humor by then," Franklin said.

"We can't dillydally," Thomas announced. "We've a wedding to prepare for." His voice was thick with excitement.

Matt resigned himself to ignoring their maddening positivity. He dismissed them with a wave and headed to find his breakfast. When he was at the porch, he knocked on the door. It was quiet as he stood and then he heard a faint "Come in." He entered and saw Mary working at the hearth down in the kitchen. "You needn't knock, Mr. Miller," she called. "I've saved breakfast." She pointed to the bowls at the end of the large family dining table. The smell of bacon permeated the air. Matt heard his empty stomach rumble.

He sat down expecting to eat alone but was surprised when Mary sat across from him as he spooned scrambled eggs onto a pewter plate. "You shouldn't eat by yourself," she said.

"I wouldn't want to keep you from anything," Matt replied. He realized that he had no idea what Mary did during the day when they didn't have harvest.

"We should speak, yes?" she asked. Her German accent made it sound like a command rather than a question.

"That would be great, Mrs. Taylor," Matt said tentatively.

"May I be frank?"

Matt almost said no to see what her reaction would be, or simply to break the tension, but he bit his lip and nodded respectfully.

"I know my daughter has made some secret pact with you."

"We made some promises," Matt affirmed.

"Have you had your success?"

"Some."

"Enough to support a wife?"

"I need another year."

"Then it's not enough," she declared.

"I told her she'd have her horses and stables."

"I don't agree to this uncertainty."

"I've written to her almost every day."

"And yet nothing is resolute."

"Is this Grace's concern?"

"Yes," Mary said. She was silent for a moment, then a look of resignation filled her face. "No."

"It's her parents'."

"You must allow," she replied.

"I've been working day and night to win the hand of your daughter," Matt explained. "Less than a year from now, I should be in a position to run my business from anywhere in the colonies."

"Grace is not getting any younger."

"She's twenty-one," Matt said, laughing.

"The marriageable men in Richmond are disappearing."

Matt felt the exasperation grow and then it came out harder than he expected. "I don't care if all the marriageable men in the colonies are gone," he exclaimed. "The only man she should consider is me."

"There's no proof of your commitment," she declared.

"I've traveled hundreds of miles to see all of you."

"Two friends on an adventure. Dr. Franklin already has my husband convinced he should accompany him on a tour through the colonies."

"I've had enough adventures," Matt said.

"Dr. Franklin is a charming man." She smiled and stood up from the table. "You can bring those dishes down to the kitchen. The clothes Will selected should make you look quite handsome. Grace's blue gown brings out the color of her eyes."

It is blue. Matt nodded and watched her walk out the front door.

Matt finished eating in peaceful silence, cleaned up his dishes, and walked back to the hay barn. He saw Franklin and Thomas standing outside a ring, watching Jeb, the middle Taylor son, train a new horse. Thomas would tap Franklin on the shoulder intermittently and point, and both men would nod.

"Ready to go to town?" Matt called. He waved to Jeb, who was guiding the young stallion around the ring. "He's a beauty," Matt said to the young man.

"Homegrown," Jeb called back proudly. He was six inches taller than the last time Matt was on the farm, and his voice was deeper. He looked and sounded like a man.

"Ready, gentlemen?" Matt repeated.

"I was enjoying watching this beautiful animal," Franklin proclaimed.

"I don't want to hold you two up," Matt said. "You seemed more excited than ladies about your new clothes this morning."

"Young fellow," Thomas said, smiling. "We'll see how eager you are the day your firstborn is married to the prettiest lady in Virginia."

Matt smiled.

"I'll get the wagon," Thomas said.

Franklin waited until Thomas was out of earshot. "A real gentleman," he said.

"Looks like you two hit it off," Matt replied.

Franklin gave him a puzzled expression.

"It means you've become quick friends."

"We've a lot in common."

"I thought you had naught in common with Anglicans."

"Harsh judgment of a grumpy old man," Franklin admitted.

"Ya think?"

"Sometimes you're very hard to understand," Franklin declared.

Matt rolled his eyes. "What do you think about the farm?"

"I've always wondered how you were able to afford your thoroughbred," Franklin said. "He looks as if he belongs in King George's stables. I come here to find a whole farm filled with such animals. Do they realize what they have?"

"Their horses have to be better," Matt explained. "They don't keep slaves."

"No slaves?" Franklin asked, surprised.

Matt motioned around at the farm. "See any?"

"The slave quarters are out back."

"They use those shacks for seasonal labor from town."

"A curious dynamic."

"And another thing I find attractive about this family."

Franklin laughed.

"What?" Matt asked.

"Her pretty blue eyes have nothing to do with slaves."

"I'll grant that she's beautiful," Matt replied. "But, you gotta admit that the lifestyle looks pretty good."

"Maybe," Franklin admitted. "They're incredibly gracious people. They were up at sunrise to work this beautiful farm."

"I told you."

"I have one nagging question, then."

Matt waited for the razz he knew was coming.

"Seeing how hard they work, how will you ever fit in?" The older man almost chuckled himself off his feet.

CHAPTER 43.

SWORDSMAN

They rode the few miles to Richmond under the late-morning sun, protected by the canvas canopy of their square wooden wagon that was drawn by two brown thoroughbred mares. Matt sat silently behind Thomas and Franklin, happy just to eavesdrop on their conversation. It satisfied Matt to learn that Thomas could hold his own in a political discussion with Franklin, a man who would someday be placed among the greatest political thinkers in history. Matt hoped Thomas's abilities would be more proof to Franklin that Matt's motivation to join the Taylor family was well founded.

Henry Duncan's store was in a grey-painted wood building with white shutters in the center of the Richmond business district. The clothier shared a single porch with a small shoemaker and a bookseller located on either side. Happy memories bombarded Matt as he looked up at the elaborately painted sign reading "Duncan's Clothier" posted above an awning that jutted out over a large multipaned window that looked into the store.

Matt had come to know Henry Duncan while working on the Taylors' horse farm during his first month in 1762 and had kept in touch with him through regular correspondence. Henry was Richmond's most prominent fashion plate, its finest dancer and most skilled swordsman. To Matt he was also a friend and a mentor.

"Matthew Miller!" Henry Duncan exclaimed as Matt led Thomas and Franklin into Henry's store. The man rushed to Matt and shook his hand vigorously. Henry was about three inches shorter than Matt, with light brown hair that was receding at his temples. Though Matt had never asked his age, Henry looked younger than Thomas and Franklin, who were hovering near their fifties.

"And this must be the esteemed Dr. Franklin," Henry said, stepping past Matt to meet the older man.

Franklin reached out his hand to shake. "Mr. Duncan. I've heard so much about you it's like we've already met."

"All good, I hope," Henry proclaimed.

"We often discuss your letters at our weekly dinners," Franklin said. "I keenly remember that you are an aficionado of all things London."

Henry nodded. "A wonderful city," he said, and gave Franklin a bright smile. He turned to Thomas. "And how goes it with you, my friend?" he said with a sly grin. "Does it vex you to give your son away?"

"Absolutely not," Thomas replied. He turned toward Franklin. "She's a beautiful lady from a good family."

Henry motioned for them to move into a tailoring area with two elevated platforms and a full-length mirror. There were four chairs around the perimeter for people to sit and observe when they weren't being fitted. Henry handed them suits wrapped in coarse paper and pointed them to a dressing room. Matt's suit fit almost perfectly based on the measurements he had sent and required only small adjustments, while Franklin, who had been overly stingy in the assessment of his own dimensions, had to spend some time while Henry let the waist out on his breeches. Once the clothier had worked his magic, though, Franklin looked handsome in his new suit. The Founding Father gazed at himself in the full-length mirror.

"Capital," he proclaimed.

"Made of the finest cloth," Henry replied.

Franklin glanced over at Matt, who was sitting in a chair dressed in his new clothing. "I'll take care of this young man's debt, Mr. Duncan. It's worth the gold to finally see him out of those rags."

Thomas, who was sitting next to Matt, waved his hand. "Cost isn't their concern, Henry. It's been a good year."

"Are you certain, sir?" Franklin asked.

"Most honored," Thomas replied.

Franklin bowed and then looked again into the mirror. "I don't think I could've gotten a finer suit in London." Henry beamed with pride.

The conversation turned from clothing as Henry made the last adjustments to Matt's suit. "Mr. Duncan," Franklin said, "I heard you know the sword."

"I learned in England as a young man," Henry replied with his eyes on Matt's breeches. He cut a dangling thread, motioned that he was finished and signaled to Matt to step down from the platform.

"Might we see a demonstration of your skills?" Franklin asked.

Henry nodded and motioned toward the hallway that led to his studio. They changed out of their suits and Henry rewrapped them tightly. He locked the front door, turned the sign to "CLOSED," and led them to his studio.

This was where Matt practiced the minuet with Henry during one of his last visits to Richmond.

Henry walked to a rack and grabbed a sword. He stepped to a wool-padded figure at one end of the room and narrated while he demonstrated various attacks, each one ending in the sword making contact with the human-shaped dummy. Afterwards, he pulled blunt-edged practice swords from a shelf and worked first with Franklin and then with Thomas. Despite being a fan of sword fighting, Franklin had little experience, but it was obvious that Thomas had some training.

"I learned as a young man," Thomas explained proudly after one successful parry.

Matt had expected he'd be next to try the sword, but when his turn came, Henry said, "Why not demonstrate your fighting style? I remember that you've been practicing."

"I could show a move or two," Matt said, smiling. The three older men watched as Matt kicked off his shoes, removed his waistcoat, and undid a few buttons to loosen his breeches. They grew increasingly curious as Matt gathered props from around the studio. There were pieces of lumber stacked in the corner, so Matt grabbed a thick board and brought it over. "Do you care if this gets broken?" he asked. Henry shook his head.

Franklin looked on with great interest. Matt returned his grin with a satisfied smile, handed him the board, and waved Thomas over. "You too, Mr. Taylor," Matt said. He showed them how to support the wood with straight arms, then walked over and pulled the head section off the man-shaped target Henry had been using. It was a ball on the end of a thick wooden dowel. He handed it to Henry. "Hold this with both hands and move it up and down like a man's head."

"How high?"

"Make him tall," Matt said, "like Levi Payne."

Thomas shot Matt a look of disapproval.

Matt waved him off. "You're right." He turned back to Henry. "A little taller than me." Matt demonstrated a dodging motion with his own head. Once Henry had the height and motion correct, Matt pointed him to one corner of the room. Matt moved to the center to begin the poomsae pyongwon, a series of movements, punches, and kicks in tae kwon do that are used to give an acrobatic demonstration of fighting skill. His white cotton shirt made a sharp snap every time he executed a punch, making them seem even more powerful than they were.

When Matt completed the poomsae, he stepped within ten paces of Henry and then moved at him with a spinning roundhouse kick. His foot connected squarely with the padded target in Henry's hand. Matt followed with another sidekick before Henry could drop the target, then spun around and connected again with an upward-angled sidekick. The head was torn from the pole and went flying into the wall. Matt turned to Franklin and Thomas.

"You don't plan to attack us?" Franklin exclaimed, more than half serious.

"The board," Matt said, motioning for them to get ready. Matt smiled as he watched them work together to brace themselves.

Franklin said, "I don't know what to expect here, but—"

Matt shouted, "Ki yah!" and snapped the board with a perfect sidekick. Franklin's piece flew from his hands and landed behind him and Thomas stared at the broken piece of wood he still held in both his hands, shocked. Matt had snapped it cleanly.

"You get a lot of power when your legs are aligned like that," Henry observed.

Matt nodded. "It's taken a lot of practice."

"This is to confront Levi Payne?" Thomas asked tentatively.

"I'll defend my family if I have to," Matt replied.

Henry could see that Matt's demonstration had shocked Thomas. "These Oriental fighting styles are impressive to watch," he explained, "but they are mostly for defense."

"Men don't practice such skills never to use them," Thomas declared.

"Swordplay is similar," Henry explained. "The practice required to maintain the skill builds the control to use it only in defense. Ruffians haven't the discipline to develop such skills."

Thomas thought for a moment. "Can you teach my sons?" he asked.

Matt nodded. "Your daughter, too." The words felt reckless as soon as they left his mouth.

Thomas stared back hard. "It would be shocking to see such violence from a lady."

"Ladies should be able to protect themselves just as well as men," Matt said.

"I regret putting this in your head," Thomas replied.

CHAPTER 44.

PERMISSION

Matt felt like Thomas was trying to look into his soul as they gathered themselves to leave Henry's store and pick Will up for lunch. The older man scrutinized him as Matt slipped on his shoes and pulled his waistcoat back over his tunic. When Matt was dressed, they moved in unison out the front door with their large parcels while saying goodbye to Henry.

Matt's vision flashed as they drove through the streets of Richmond. Would he meet Levi Payne in the street today? He scanned the houses and businesses that lined the thoroughfare. He'd been here before, but not in his dreams. There were one or two horses within sight. *There aren't enough.* Nothing looked like the future he'd dreamed.

"Where's Will?" Matt asked, trying to break out of the trance that was trying to engulf him.

"His room is rented until his marriage," Thomas replied. "We'll find him there."

****

It was a ten-minute ride to Will's apartment. He was waiting on a porch bench. "Where's everyone been?" he shouted, walking out to the wagon. "It's been an eternity."

"Mr. Miller was demonstrating his fighting skills," Thomas said as he contemplated Matt yet again.

"Kicking and such!" Will exclaimed. "Is this Dr. Franklin?" He stuck his hand out before the man could jump from the wagon. "Pleased to meet you, sir."

Matt smiled and waved.

"My friend," Will said, shaking Matt's hand.

Matt gave him a warm smile. "We got our wedding clothing," Matt said. "We'll certainly look more handsome than the groom."

"I hardly believe you can beat this," Will said, pointing to his face.

"Get in," his father said, "before we ride off and leave you to eat with your looking glass."

They stopped at the King's Tavern to discuss "official wedding business," which included a jovial discussion of clothing, food, and ladies. Matt hadn't seen Franklin smile as much as he did sitting there with the two Taylor men. The man seemed to be enjoying Southern society, Anglicans and all.

They dropped Will at his apartment after lunch and drove back to the Taylor farm. Immediately after they arrived, Thomas took Franklin out for a ride in the countryside on two young mares Matt had never seen before. Matt found Grace and they headed in the opposite direction on her stallion, Silver Star, and Thunder. Scout went along, much to the dismay of Duke, who was left back at the farm, tied with a leash. The puppy barked until they were out of sight.

When they returned, the ladies cooked dinner and then the whole family, including Thomas's brother David and his wife, Faith, ate behind the house on their large wooden banquet table. They finished the night with a Bible reading and prayers, and then David broke out the playing cards. Franklin was a wholehearted participant in every activity. When darkness finally came, everyone retired to their rooms. Franklin had Will's room, while Matt looked forward to spending the night in the barn.

"Can I walk you over, Mr. Miller?" Thomas said. He immediately saw the look of discomfort on Matt's face. "'Tis nothing bad."

"Of course," Matt replied.

As soon as they stepped outside and closed the door, Thomas said, "I wish to discuss my daughter." Scout traipsed behind them, crossing in and out of the shadows that formed as the lantern swung slowly in Thomas's hand.

"Sure," Matt replied simply.

Thomas stayed silent until they were comfortably sitting in the hay barn on the bench that was Matt's bed. Matt could see Thomas's face clearly in the lantern light. "I'll not say I'm delighted with this clandestine pact you've made with my daughter," Thomas said.

"I meant no disrespect, sir," Matt replied. "I've worked this last year to be worthy of your family."

"I had a long conversation with Dr. Franklin today. He had many favorable things to say, aside from the fact that you've much to learn."

"I've heard him say that of almost everyone," Matt replied. It was true.

"He claims you have a successful and growing business."

Matt nodded. "It should be operating and growing itself soon."

"Are you ready to ask for the hand of my daughter?"

"I don't make that kind of money yet," Matt replied. He motioned around the barn to emphasize his point.

"My daughter is too stubborn to consider another man. Either you make a formal commitment, or I shall forbid you to have contact with her."

"Are you giving me permission to marry your daughter?"

"You have my permission to ask for her hand, yes."

Adrenaline coursed through Matt's body, and he set his suddenly shaking hands down on the bench. He had looked forward to this moment for almost a year, but now that it had come, all he could think of was the challenge that lay ahead.

"You don't seem delighted," Thomas said.

"It's faster than I preferred."

"I'd like to announce your betrothal on Saturday."

"That soon?" Matt said, surprised. He felt like someone just told him he'd won the lottery even though he didn't remember buying a ticket. He was both suspicious and speechless.

"For a man of letters, you're surprisingly slow to understand."

"I still have a business to build," Matt said soberly.

Thomas shrugged. "We would intend for a year betrothal with a wedding after harvest."

"Does Grace know?"

"It's your responsibility to approach Grace."

"What's changed?"

"You've come back a singular man, and you've made influential friends."

"I was in the right place at the right time, I think," Matt said, laughing.

"You've an angel guarding you," Thomas said. "I know that much to be true."

"I wish he'd make things a little easier, then," Matt replied.

"A man's life is only hard work. It's taken me most of my life to come to terms with that. It made it easier for me to hear it from someone older, so there you have it."

"Let me show you something," Matt said. He reached into his pack and pulled out his wallet. He opened the small leather case to reveal the gold and sapphire ring. He handed it Thomas.

"You expected this?"

"Hardly," Matt replied. "I carry it to remind me of why I'm working."

Thomas handed the ring back to Matt and stood to go. He patted the dog on the head. "I missed you, Scout." He turned to Matt. "It's been good having you here again, son."

CHAPTER 45.

MRS. WILLIAM TAYLOR

Matt checked his pocket to feel the small lump the sapphire ring made in the wool fabric. He'd check it and forget that he'd checked it every ten minutes. He was nervous. They'd rehearsed the wedding at the church twice the day before and he'd mastered all his duties. He wished they could've done the same thing with his engagement. He'd need to propose at the church sometime before or after the wedding so that Thomas could announce their engagement at the reception. The questions circled around and around in his head. Where should he ask her? Should it be right before the wedding or afterwards? What if the opportunity never presented itself? He wanted to shout.

The Taylors were walking Thomas up the steps to St. John's when Matt decided to get it over with. He was walking side by side with Grace, who he knew would disappear soon after they entered the church to tend to Graine. It seemed like the perfect opportunity. *My God, she looks beautiful.*

"Everyone," Matt said loudly. "Could we please stop?" He said it loudly enough that the people behind him froze.

"I'd like to do this in front of friends and family." Matt looked down to acknowledge Franklin. "I've gotten permission." Matt acknowledged Grace's parents and watched them nod in return.

Grace was surprised. "Mr. Miller, what?"

Matt fumbled in his pocket. *There it is!* He pulled the ring out and went down on his knee there on the top step of the church. People in the churchyard hurried over to see the commotion.

"Grace Taylor," Matt said. He focused on asking the question loudly so that everyone in the churchyard could hear. "From the first day that I saw you, I dreamed that you'd someday be my wife. I'm asking you in front of your family, your friends and before God. Will you marry me?"

She looked down at him. He saw the tears well up in her eyes. She put her hand out for him to take but was silent. The crowd grew impatient.

"Daughter," her mother said from the bottom of the step. "You must answer. Do you say yea or nay?"

Grace looked down at her mother, surprised. "Of course," she said.

"Of course you'll answer?" Matt asked. "Or of course you'll be my wife?"

"Of course I'll be your wife," she replied. She put both her hands on her waist impatiently. "After all that has happened and how long I've waited?"

"I still have to ask," Matt said. There were chuckles in the churchyard. Matt whispered, "Give me your hand."

"Why?"

"Give it back," Matt whispered louder. She reluctantly held her hand out and he slipped the sapphire ring on her finger. It matched her blue dress. It *was* the same dress he'd seen in his dreams. She now had a brilliant smile on her face. *She expected the proposal, but not the ring.*

"Oh!" she said. "It's beautiful." There were more chuckles from a crowd that had gotten steadily larger. Matt stood up, and Grace took the opportunity to kiss him strongly on the lips. She looked sideways, caught herself, and stepped away. The fact that she was now hopelessly embarrassed endeared her to those looking on. They both turned to the crowd, and there was a roaring applause.

Matt closed his fist and gave a barely visible fist pump, and the crowd applauded again. "Thanks, everyone," he said. He took Grace's warm hand in his and they turned to walk into the church.

"I can't wait to show Graine," Grace said. "'Tis a beautiful ring."

"Surprised?" Matt asked.

"Only that Father would agree so early. You have no way to support a family."

"Of course I do."

"I'll not believe it until we're safely married." She dropped his hand. "I should help Graine." He watched her walk to the back of the church and disappear. *Gorgeous creature!* Matt looked up at the ceiling of the church. He was trying to take in everything he could to remember this day. He whispered a thank you.

"I knew you had it in you," Will said quietly as he stepped to stand beside him.

"What about you? Nervous?"

"I think you'll make a fine brother," Will said.

"No, about your wedding night."

"Why should I be nervous?"

Matt could barely hear the quiver in Will's voice. "It's going to be hard to live up to all that bravado," Matt said.

"You should be building my confidence," Will whispered, "rather than tearing it down."

The Reverend Michael interrupted them, directing them to the front of the church.

The wedding was mostly a blur to Matt. He went through the motions but was preoccupied with thoughts of Grace and the day when he'd walk down the aisle in this same church to marry his beautiful fiancée. The thought of his wedding night filled him with desire. He snapped out of his daydream when the church roared in applause as Thomas and Graine were finally announced as man and wife.

The range of reactions Matt saw in the different family members was priceless. Thomas was happy to have it done. Mary looked sad to see her first son finally become a man with his own family. Robert and Judith Martin, Graine's parents, looked tickled beyond belief. Etiquette had dictated that they wait until their oldest daughter was married before their six younger daughters could be betrothed. Graine had been in no hurry to find a husband because of her involvement in managing her father's business. Matt wondered who would run it now that Graine was married and living on the Taylor farm.

CHAPTER 46.

DOUGLAS BROWNE

The Martin estate was wrapped up in so many bows and ribbons that it looked like a big Christmas present. Thomas, who always took great pleasure in joking about the immensity of the Martins' home, tapped Matt on the shoulder as they walked closer. "We'll be adding a building or two to the farm by the time you're to be married, but if you expect this, I should think it will require another year or two."

"Or five, I think," Matt smiled. "We'll get there." He looked around, taking in the opulence, confident that the Taylor farm could someday be as impressive. *Taylor-Miller farm. Ha!*

Matt hadn't realized, though, how big an event this would be for Richmond and the surrounding countryside. The Martins had many friends in Virginia, and their guests included business associates, local politicians, clergy, and the entire congregation of St. John's Church. Horse people, associates and friends of the Taylor Family were there as well. Also in attendance were two scientists from Philadelphia, at least one of whom happened to be an author and postmaster general of the American colonies. Judging by the attention he was getting, either Franklin's reputation had preceded him or the Martins had announced his presence in advance. Matt suspected that it might have been both.

Less appreciated by Matt was the fact that Franklin was already famous across the colonies for the things he'd done before getting involved in creating a new country. His reputation was firmly established for his scientific experiments, inventions, and the publication of *Poor Richard's Almanac*. Because of the breadth of his experience, Franklin had the enviable ability to move freely and comfortably among townspeople, farmers, businessmen, and the very wealthy.

The wedding party, including the parents, was shown to an elevated platform at the front of the reception. People were mingling below, trying to get situated as they found their name placards at the tables. Well-dressed black servants wandered through the crowd with trays of food and wine. Thomas and Graine sat talking at the center of the elevated table, seemingly unaware of the controlled bedlam taking place a step below them.

Matt would catch Grace's gaze every now and then. He liked the fact that she was looking down often at the ring. She was moving her hand, probably trying to get it to sparkle in the afternoon sun. Matt had chosen the ring with one idea in mind: that Grace would think of him every time she saw it. Seeing how she was looking at it now, he felt like his plan to keep her attention was working.

Robert Martin stepped up on a small riser, rang a bell, and waited for everyone to take their seats. He talked briefly to the newlyweds while everyone found their tables, and then rang the bell again. "Welcome, everyone," he yelled to the crowd. The murmur lowered as more people sat. "Welcome, everyone," he repeated loudly, "to the wedding of my oldest daughter."

He went on to talk about Graine, how much he loved her and how proud he was of the lady she had become. He finished by wishing the new couple God's blessing. Last was his tribute to the King of England, which took almost as much time as he'd spent talking about his daughter. He expressed his gratitude to the king and his pride in being a loyal subject of the Crown. It was enough to make Matt wonder if Robert Martin might have trouble when relations with the mother country became strained.

Thomas spoke next. "I'd like to thank our gracious hosts, Mr. and Mrs. Robert Martin. A man dreams his whole life of the day that his son might marry a lady like Graine. We've heard that my son is a charming man, often too charming for his own good." The crowd laughed. "God must have been on his side to convince this beautiful, challenging, and intelligent lady to marry into our family. This is more than I—we—could've hoped. They're an attractive couple and we wish them a blessed life. We'll be building them a new house on our farm and they will hopefully be starting their family very soon." He went on to talk about his son and what he was like growing up, then finished by offering congratulations to the newlyweds. The gathering went up in a roaring applause.

Thomas waited for a moment and then went on. "Mr. and Mrs. Martin and the young couple have given me permission to make one other announcement. My daughter Grace has been formally betrothed to Mr. Matthew Miller of Philadelphia." Thomas motioned to them and Matt stood up simultaneously with Grace. Wild applause filled the crowd again. "Many changes are afoot in the

Taylor family. May God bless us all." Thomas waved and sat down, followed by many others who spoke on behalf of either the bride or the groom. Some were long-winded, and it went on for almost an hour. There was a collective sigh of relief when lunch was served and Robert Martin ended the tributes.

Many people came by to congratulate Grace on her engagement. Matt was satisfied to see more than a few women take a closer look at the engagement ring. People also came to introduce themselves to Matt, either because he was a member of the wedding or because of the engagement. It was the usual party conversation, but he did get the opportunity to talk to a few businessmen. He tried to inconspicuously scribble their names down on a piece of paper in his pocket whenever he got the chance. He was especially focused on anyone who might be interested in selling his tablets. Grace hovered in and out the entire afternoon She would come find him to dance and then disappear to talk with her friends. The newlyweds flitted about the reception. They were an attractive couple, and it made Matt smile to think he might have had some part in getting them together.

The party was winding down at about the same time the sun was setting in the horizon. There was great fanfare as Thomas and Graine got into the carriage that would take them to a country home on the river for their wedding night, then to Williamsburg and off to the coast for a few weeks. There had been a commitment from both families that the young couple be given every opportunity to produce a grandchild. Looking around at the estate and at the Taylor and Martin families, Matt was sure they would be very lucky children.

As Matt watched the couple's carriage drive away, he saw Thomas wave him over. Thomas was talking to another older man.

"I'd like you to meet Douglas Browne," Thomas said as Matt walked up to them.

Matt reached his hand out.

"Congratulations on your betrothal," Browne said. "You're blessed to become part of such an esteemed family."

Matt nodded. "I recognize your name," he said. "You have a farm on the coast known for good breeding. There was one stallion in particular."

"Keegan. We still have him," Browne said. "He's no Shadow, despite what Thomas thinks."

"I thought Nathan Payne bought him," Matt said.

Browne shook his head. "A nasty business. I knew something was amiss as soon as he came to my farm."

"I bought him," Thomas said. "I'm going to the coast tomorrow to bring him home. It's a full day's ride, and I need company. I usually take Will."

"Seeing the beauty of your new daughter," Browne said, "I'll be surprised if Will ever returns." All three men laughed.

"I can come," Matt said. "How long?"

"A few days, I think," said Thomas. "I'm sorry to take you away from Grace, but we can accommodate the lost time when you return. The boys can do her chores."

"Sounds like a deal," Matt said. He didn't think he had a choice. It seemed like something a future son-in-law should do to ingratiate himself to his new family.

Browne broke in. "Thomas, something you should know. There's a mare at the Norfolk auction that you should see. She's a perfect match for Keegan."

Matt interrupted them. "What's at this auction?"

"More horses in one place than anywhere else in Virginia," Browne replied excitedly.

"The Paynes will be there," Matt said.

Thomas shook his head. "They've bought so many horses already."

"Trust me," Matt replied. "They'll be there."

CHAPTER 47.

NEW TACK

Matt had once visited the Indiana State Fair. It was the closest thing he'd experienced to the livestock auction they were now attending. Every manner of animal was being bought and sold by Virginia farmers. They left Keegan on the Browne farm and would pick him up on the way back to Richmond. Thomas hoped to be able to buy one other horse, the silver mare named Aida that Douglas Browne had mentioned.

Matt thought back to his impressions of Douglas Browne. Up until yesterday, he could only imagine Browne from the stories told by the Taylors. Now that he'd met him in person and seen his farm, the man had taken on legendary dimensions. He had plans within plans when it came to bloodlines, and Matt imagined Browne didn't have enough years in his life to be able to complete his quest for the perfect horse.

The Browne farm was a good contrast to the Taylor farm, helping Matt put the latter into perspective. He couldn't say if one was better than the other, but he certainly was surprised by the quality of the Browne horses. Some of them looked like they were genetically enhanced or taking steroids. Browne had significant influence over Thomas when it came to breeding, and Thomas deferred to him as a respected mentor. Matt had the impression that good horse breeding was the sole purview of the Taylors. Now, having met Douglas Browne, Matt knew who the real breeding genius was in Virginia.

Browne was supplying the whole state with breeding stock. It didn't look like he spent much time selling to people who just rode horses. He had inherited money from his father in England, so he had no monetary incentive. He worked with animals because they were his passion, and when he did sell, he charged as much as the market would bear. He was a very religious man and there were some hint that he was also a mentor to Thomas in this regard. Thomas respected him more than anyone Matt had seen since they'd met.

Matt and Thomas were walking through the separate areas of the auction, gazing at the livestock. Matt stopped to look at the chickens. He'd never seen so many exotic-looking birds. Thomas had to pull him away from the cages.

"You want to fight chickens?" Thomas asked.

"They're cool to look at," Matt replied.

"The boys told me 'cool' was something you were around ladies," Thomas said.

"Too complicated to explain," Matt replied.

They walked through the people who congregated around the horses. When they finally saw Aida, Matt had to consciously keep himself from making ooh and ah sounds. She was an impressive silver animal that stood about seventeen hands. They knew from Browne's description and envy that she would be a remarkable animal, but her rich coat and her strong line had to be seen to be appreciated.

Thomas took his time looking over the horse and explained each observation to Matt like he was conducting a class. It soon became clear to Aida's owner that Thomas knew his way around a horse, so he stepped out of the stall to talk to another man. "Tack comes with her," the owner called, pointing to a bench. "I've no way to get it home."

Thomas and Matt walked over to inspect the bridle, leather straps, and saddle. "My saddle needs to be replaced," Matt said. "I'll give you a few pounds."

"That's a ten-pound saddle if I ever saw one," Thomas said.

"I'm not the same man you found under a bridge," Matt replied.

The older man smiled. "We'll speak." He said this in that perplexing manner he had where Matt could never tell whether he was joking. Grace had inherited this ability from her father, and Matt found it equally maddening in her.

Thomas tapped Matt on the shoulder and motioned that they should leave. They were in the auction bay in time to watch Aida enter the ring. She shuffled like a warhorse, kicking up dust from the dirt floor. Matt, who had lingered behind Thomas, stepped to the edge of the bay to join his future father-in-law as three other men moved into the opposite side. Matt didn't know whether to be surprised or satisfied that the future he'd dreamed had come to pass. He was facing Nathan, Levi, and Paul Payne. All three had their eyes on the horse.

Levi, who had been following the animal's lines from head to tail, found himself unexpectedly staring into

Matt's eyes at the end of his inspection. Matt watched Levi's scrutiny turn to surprise and then to a cold calm that sent a chill through Matt. Despite his conviction that a confrontation with Levi was unavoidable, the reality of it was more than unnerving.

"Her price just went up," Thomas said when he saw the Paynes. "Ignore them."

"It's likely to happen no matter what I do."

Thomas stared hard. "We're far from home, and God willing we'll have two more horses. Neither one of us can afford to get hurt."

Matt knew that a direct confrontation with Levi ended in a fight. His pistol was in his pack on Thunder, but like everywhere else, you didn't take out a pistol and shoot an unarmed man. The only way he could prevent the confrontation was to physically avoid it. Nathan gave Matt an arrogant nod and Matt returned the man's gesture.

A number of others had gathered at the fences to the auction bay. The start of bidding broke their stares temporarily. Nathan raised his hand to make the first bid. Another man, leaning against a back wall, raised his hand, and the auctioneer responded in kind, trying to increase the bids to the next level. A few others raised their hands and the bid rose. Matt could see Nathan looking over at them with some expectation.

"If nothing else, we'll make him pay twice as much as she's worth," Thomas said as he finally raised his hand.

"Forty-five pounds," the auctioneer called. People were stepping away from the ring now.

The man leaning against the back wall raised his hand again. "Fifty pounds," the auctioneer said.

Thomas leaned over to Matt. "Daniel Helsby," he explained. "He breeds here on the coast. He'll have some limited fortune his wife has allowed."

Matt watched the Paynes. Levi was either staring coldly back or talking to his brother, Paul. It looked as if they were arguing. "How many times have you bid against the Paynes?" Matt asked Thomas.

"I've lost count," Thomas replied. "I actually want this one." He smiled as he raised his hand again. "Nathan has spent a small fortune on questionable animals."

"Is he out of money yet?"

"He's either very wealthy or very mad."

Thomas raised his hand to make another bid and was countered by Nathan to bring the price to sixty pounds. Matt watched as Daniel Helsby left his wall and disappeared into the crowd. Thomas stepped away also, pretending he was done bidding, and the auctioneer twice called out the final price. Thomas moved forward again and raised his hand to bid sixty-five pounds. He smiled at Nathan.

Levi and Paul were still in a passionate disagreement and no longer paying attention to the bidding. Only Nathan remained focused on the horse.

Thomas raised his hand again. "He has more horses than he knows what to do with."

Nathan bid seventy-five pounds.

"Going...going...going," shouted the auctioneer.

Thomas raised his hand and said, "Eighty." He stared straight at Nathan, waiting for his bid. Nathan tapped Levi on the shoulder and said something to his boys, and they walked away in unison. There was no one left. When the auctioneer finally said, "Sold!" and pounded his gavel on the counter, it echoed like a thunderclap.

"Well," Thomas said, "we have ourselves a very expensive mare, and Nathan has retreated to fight another day." The Paynes were nearly out of sight across the auction area, already looking at another horse.

Matt relaxed and turned to Thomas as he shook his head in a scolding fashion. "Eighty pounds?"

"They call that mad money in Philadelphia," Thomas said. "We got a free saddle."

"It's like I told you," Matt replied. "Buy one, get one free." The older man smiled, remembering their conversation of many months before.

Aida's owner was saying goodbye to her in the bay. He was obviously very happy with the price he'd gotten. Thomas pulled out his purse, counted out gold coins, and paid the auctioneer, then turned around and took the horse by the harness.

Matt glanced over at Thomas and said, "I'll get the saddle while you finish." He turned and walked out of the auction area. He planned to grab the saddle and collect Thomas and the new horse, and they'd be off to the Browne farm to pick up Thomas's prize stallion, Keegan. Training or not, Matt had no desire to confront Levi here on the coast. He hurried to the stables, collected the saddle and other tack, and started walking quickly back to Thomas.

"I never expected you here again." Levi was standing in the road, blocking his path.

Matt looked around to see that there was wooden fencing on both sides of the road. The thought went through his mind to drop the saddle, hop the fence, and escape. He shook his head with a resigned smile and gave Levi a disappointed stare.

"You're going to ruin my day," Matt said. "Aren't you?"

"Go back north where you belong, and neither of our days will be ruined."

"We can do this another time when we're closer to home."

"You're not going back to Richmond," Levi said.

CHAPTER 48.

VIRGINIA SOIL

Matt slid the saddle under the fence on the side of the road. He suddenly felt exhausted. It was like the feeling he got when he hiked to the top of a mountain; he had almost reached the top, but the journey had tired him out beyond belief.

"I hear you brought another Northerner with you," Levi said.

Matt didn't answer. He slowly removed his jacket, folded it, and tossed it on top of the saddle. He turned his head around, trying to see something, anything he recognized from his dreams. There were hints all over, but he couldn't put it into a coherent picture. *I'm lying bleeding on the ground.* A warm shiver went up Matt's back and his mind lit up as adrenaline saturated his body. Matt looked to the sky. *Help.*

He stepped purposefully a few times to get a feel for the ground. He'd worn a light pair of shoes today rather than boots because he'd suspected this might happen. He'd practiced many times with this same set of shoes, and they let him move and kick well.

"You'll need to stop me here," Matt said. Levi didn't answer. He was already walking forward. Some distance behind Levi, Matt could see a few people coming to watch the fight.

Matt smiled as Levi charged at him swinging, and he easily deflected the blow and chopped at the man's stomach. Levi charged again and Matt repeated the move with the same effect. It felt different from the last time they fought. He'd trained for the man's style. Matt's reactions were sharp and his body felt like a stretched rubber band, ready to snap in any direction. Levi charged him a third time like a freight train. Matt faked a blow to make him dodge like Seamus had shown him, and then he swept his feet, sending Levi crashing to the ground. Levi was breathing hard.

The weariness Matt felt was almost overwhelming. *Why am I so tired?* "Levi," Matt said. "I'm a better fighter than before."

Levi ignored him and charged again. Matt stepped aside to trip him, but his motion was partially blocked by the wooden fence, preventing him from fully dodging the punch. Levi connected with a fist across the side of Matt's face. It wasn't a solid hit, but it sent him staggering backward. *Uh-oh!* Matt felt the familiar hazing of his vision and knew he didn't have long before it would completely fade. Matt looked up into the sky. *I need you, if you're there.*

"You'll need more than heaven to help you, you Northern bastard," Levi said.

Matt could now barely see him through the grey as his vision dimmed. *This is how I die.* Matt moved forward and went after Levi, knowing that he had very little time before his vision was completely gone. He stepped through a spinning sidekick and hit Levi squarely in the side of his head. Levi dropped to the ground briefly but then climbed to his feet, shaking off the blow. *It's like he's made of steel.* Matt's vision was completely grey now. He waited for the blow that would send him to the ground to die bleeding. *Levi doesn't have a knife.*

There was a vision that flashed in his mind. Now he remembered. He'd seen this before. *Can I use my memories?* He saw in his mind that Levi would swing, so he ducked and connected with a fist into Levi's stomach. Events were unfolding in his brain. His memories of the future were running in real time.

"Next time I hit you, Levi," Matt said, "I intend to kill you." He reached up with his thumb and forefinger and tried to squeeze the grey haze away from his eyes. His head was pounding and the future was flashing in place of his vision. The high-speed camera had taken over and his eyes refused to work. He faced Levi using only his future vision to guide him.

"You won't leave here," Levi said. He advanced. Matt's memory popped and he saw a man walk between them. Matt stepped back. Was he real? He looked within to see the face of Paul Payne. The sound of Paul's voice confused Matt. *Is this voice only in my mind?* The headache increased, and the visions were fighting for more and more of his consciousness. Matt couldn't separate reality from his dreams, and he stood there, helpless.

"We've all had enough!" Paul said. He was grabbing his brother's shirt, trying to pull him away. Levi smacked at his hand. Paul's voice ripped Matt back to the present and all he could see again was grey.

"He'd ruin us if he could," Levi yelled.

Matt stood there trying to make out the two images in the cloud. His vision flashed in his mind again. Levi charged and Matt saw him fake to his left. Instinct and images were enough to allow Matt to swing to his rear and land a blow, and then step away before Levi could retaliate. This enraged his opponent.

Paul Payne followed his brother and put him in a head-lock. He shouted, "Enough!" Levi broke out of the hold, turned, and punched his brother hard in his face, sending Paul crashing into the fence.

Matt tried to focus his internal vision so he could use it, but Levi came crashing on him before he could figure out what was going on. Matt spun to kick the grey blob that charged; he connected hard but was hit twice in return and sent to the ground. Matt righted himself and faced the direction of the sounds. Matt had hurt Levi enough that he'd backed away. His internal vision flashed again. He could see a bloody-faced Paul Payne charge from where he'd landed and collide hard with his brother. The future Matt had in his mind showed them in rapid motion and struggling.

When they separated, Matt heard Levi say, "What?" Matt saw a knife buried in Levi's belly, and a long cut where Paul had forced it sideways. Levi dropped to the ground.

"Stop it!" It was Nathan Payne. Matt could barely make out his shape in the grey. He backed away helplessly, reaching for something to hold.

"Matthew?" He felt Thomas pull him to the side. Matt reached out and grabbed his arm, trying to steady himself against the onslaught in his mind. "What's wrong, boy?"

Matt held desperately onto Thomas's arm. "I'm blind," Matt lied. He wasn't blind. He could see the future. Matt watched Levi lying in the road as his blood drained onto the dirt. His brother stood over him, watching while his father held his oldest son.

"Why?" Nathan wailed up at Paul. "Why would you do this?"

"He killed Kathryn," Paul said. He said it calmly and coldly, like there was no argument.

"It was an accident," Nathan said. "It was only an accident."

"No, he was jealous," Paul said. "He spooked the horse. He knew the barn door would do it. He took her away from me."

Thomas stood there holding Matt steady as he listened to the two men discuss his oldest daughter's death. Matt looked into his memory to see Levi Payne take his final breath as the last of his blood drained into the red Virginia soil.

CHAPTER 49.

STANDING ON THE PORCH, KNOCKING

Thomas placed his hand on Matt's shoulder as he guided him to the horses. He'd reach out and correct Matt's path to keep him walking in the right direction. Matt was starting to see silhouettes again. The memories and visions that flooded his mind when he was fighting with Levi were fading. Thomas was uncomfortably silent as they threaded though the livestock buildings, but it didn't make Matt any more comfortable when he finally did speak.

"You're blind?"

"Blind is the wrong word," Matt replied. "I can't see right now. I've had headaches since Levi's men jumped me on my way back to Philadelphia. I lose my vision for a few hours."

"What're you talking about?"

"Levi sent three men to follow me. They beat me, left me for dead, and stole Thunder and all my things."

They reached the corral where the three horses were being kept. "Sit," Thomas said.

"The colors are starting to return. I'll be ready to ride in half an hour or so."

"You were beat and left for dead?"

"That's the simple description." Matt told Thomas the story of how he was hit and thrown over a cliff, his horse and things were stolen, and how he managed to get most of it back.

"They stole everything?"

"I got half of it back. They managed to spend ninety pounds in Wilmington in only a few days. All those nice clothes I had, gone!"

"Why did you never tell me that Levi sent someone after you?" Thomas asked.

"It was my problem. I didn't want to pull your family—Grace especially—into my battles." There were more flashes of light in Matt's eyes. If the blindness was similar to what he'd experienced with Seamus, it would last another hour or so before the flashes of grey were entirely gone. He could feel the synapses firing in his head and overloading his visual cortex. "I knew I'd confront him eventually. I wanted to sneak out of here today, though."

"You were convinced you were going to fight as soon as you saw him."

"I know," Matt admitted.

"Are you going to be able to ride?"

"Let me sit until the scales fall from my eyes."

"You've been attending church?"

"Not as much as I should."

"Who does?" Thomas said. Matt could now make out the man's smile. "I force myself to go every Sunday."

"What?"

"I've a hundred things to do on the Sabbath." The older man was quiet then, thinking. "I'd want to know if it ever happens again."

"I didn't want to burden you," Matt repeated.

"Let me make that decision," he said matter-of-factly. "You need to trust us should you desire to be a member of this family." There was an awkward silence, and Matt was relieved when Thomas was the first to speak. "How much longer until Franklin comes to retrieve you?"

"Another week."

"Make the best of it, then," Thomas replied. "Spend some time with Jonathan. The boy spoke more about you than Grace. He can ride now."

"That kid changes my entire perspective on the world."

They talked about trivial things for half an hour.

"You ready?" Thomas said finally.

They stood, walked to the horses, and headed to the Browne farm to pick up the stallion. Matt's vision had mostly returned by the time they collected the fourth horse, and he tried his best to hide his throbbing headache as they traveled home.

"You haven't said anything about Kathryn," Matt said about halfway through their journey.

"I've made my peace with God," Thomas replied.

"Even after today?"

"I'll not relive my daughter's death. It's been too hard on my family—I've been too hard." There was anguish in his voice. He looked up into the sky. "I miss my daughter." He was quiet as he regained his composure. "The Lord has given me much. I pray now for Nathan and regret what has become of our relationship."

"What happens now?" Matt asked. "Does he step back and rethink?"

"I've no idea. The loss of his son will devastate the family and the business. You brought out the worst in Levi, but I allow that sometimes I wished my own sons were as passionate about their business. Levi's passing will be a great loss to the Paynes." He paused to collect his thoughts. "How do you feel?"

"Tired...relieved," Matt said. "Never imagined that I could make someone that angry."

"You do seem to affect people in a dramatic way," Thomas said. He chuckled sadly.

****

They arrived back at the farm before dark. Everyone was busy with chores, so Thomas checked on Mary in the house and then he and Matt walked the new horses to the stable. Grace was spreading straw in one of the stalls. She came out to inspect the animals.

"He's more beautiful than I imagined," she said, looking at the stallion. She ran her hand down the horse's side. "You're beautiful," she repeated to the horse.

"Name's Keegan," Matt said.

Grace finally noticed his face. "You're hurt!" She moved closer. "I'll get Mother. What happened?"

Thomas, who had been gazing at his daughter in silence, walked over and hugged her quietly. "God blessed me with two beautiful daughters. I'm proud of the lady you've become." He let her go.

"What happened?" Grace repeated. She looked pleadingly first at her father and then at Matt.

"I'll tell everyone after chores," Thomas said. "But for now, you should know that Levi Payne is dead."

"Dead?" Grace looked over at Matt. "Was this you?"

"It was Paul Payne," Matt said.

Grace stood there, stunned.

"Mr. Miller needs that cut cleaned," Thomas said.

"I'm done anyway," Grace replied. "Come on, dear." It was the first time she had called him anything but Mr. Miller or Matthew. She reached firmly for his hand and led him out of the barn to the house. "You were fighting again?"

"Trouble has followed me ever since I met this family."

"Oh!" she said. "It's our fault?"

"Kind of."

"Was it Levi?"

"Yes," Matt answered.

"Were you involved in his death?"

"Yes," Matt repeated.

Matt decided not to give any more details, and Grace decided not to ask. She guided him into the house and sat him on a kitchen chair. He watched her move back and forth from the sink and sat in silence as she worked on his face. She smelled like barn, horse, and woman all at once. As she leaned over him and her hair dragged across his arms and face, he remembered what he was fighting for.

CHAPTER 50.

1771

It was darker than it should have been for this time of day. David had predicted rain, and his storm clouds had already covered the sky. Scout and Duke moved their greying heads back and forth in unison, watching quietly as the men loaded the last few boxes onto the wagon.

"That all, then?" one man asked. The three men from Wilkins' Shipping stood there waiting for Matt's reply, distracted by the squad of British soldiers moving closer on the horizon. Soldiers were passing by the farm frequently these days, coming and going from the frontier. Matt did his best to ignore them when he could. He was hoping to get the shipment on its way before he had to deal with the unwanted visitors if they did decide to stop.

The shipping wagon, pulled by four horses, was packed full with boxes of Miller Head and Stomach Tablets. It was the biggest horse-drawn vehicle Matt had ever seen. He hadn't expected the whole shipment of tablets to fit, but surprisingly, they managed to pack them neatly into the cargo area.

"I think that's everything," Matt finally answered, sneaking a glance at the soldiers to gauge the time he had left to get the wagon moving. He reached to take the form the man was holding, walked it to the inkwell, signed and returned it.

"It's probably best you're out of here before they arrive," Matt said. "I don't want this shipment delayed by whatever act they've passed." He rolled his eyes for emphasis.

"Suit yourself," the man said. He reached out his hand. "Another wagon will be here on Friday."

"Tell Zeke I said hello," Matt replied.

They got up on the wagon, situated themselves, slapped the reins, and moved quickly to the gate. Matt lingered there, watching the wagon and scanning the horses on the farm. They'd nearly tripled the number of animals since he married Grace. They were becoming good-humored rivals with the Brownes on the coast, each trying to outdo the other. The Taylors' reputation went far beyond Virginia, having placed animals on almost every wealthy estate in Virginia and the Carolinas. They had regular customers as far north as New York. Matt's brother-in-law, Will, had made it his personal challenge to add horse dealers to their network. They couldn't breed enough animals to keep up with demand. Subsequently, the price of their stock had risen dramatically.

As Matt watched the soldiers get closer, he cringed thinking of the attention the farm had generated over the past few years. The Taylor farm had become rich and influential in Virginia based on both horse breeding and medical supply manufacturing. Unfortunately, Matt was learning that being rich and influential wasn't always appreciated by those with political power. The simple fact that weighed constantly on him was that the farm and the horses were going to be hard to hide when the trouble started. The English soldiers who passed the farm regularly were a constant reminder of the coming storm.

The dogs barked as the soldiers rode through the front gate, and Matt got that disappointed feeling he always did in his stomach when dealing with something he didn't want to do. He'd had the smallest, most remote hope that the men would continue past the farm into Richmond.

Matt stepped between the dogs, put his hands on their heads, and said, "Quiet down, boys." This was more for himself than the animals. Most people in the colonies needed to practice some sort of calming ritual when dealing with English soldiers. They watched the captain leave his men and trot up the drive. Both dogs growled as he approached.

Matt turned to see Grace, who was now standing on the porch holding the baby. Johanna was already five months old. Matt thought back to their conversation over eight years ago when he joked about having ten children. He was surprised to find that Grace had taken him seriously. It was a different time indeed! Five down, five to go. She was his friend, his partner, and his lover, and he orbited around her. A wave of sorrow overwhelmed him at the future he had seen in his dreams—the one he couldn't tell her about. How much would he sacrifice to keep his sun shining? If he had to make the choice right now, he would sell his soul for five more years.

Matt shook the thoughts from his head and motioned for Grace to take the children inside. Grace had seen the soldiers too and had already begun cleaning up quilts and toys. They'd been through this same charade a number of times since the Quartering Act.

The captain nodded hello as he approached. "We need lodgings for two days," he said, "along with morning and evening provisions."

"Richmond is another half mile down the road," Matt said. "It's usually boring for young men out here."

"I want them away from trouble," the captain declared. He pointed to the hay barn. "We'll take that building." It was English law that, as a farm owner possessing large buildings, Matt was responsible for housing and provisioning English soldiers as needed. Matt nodded. The captain motioned to his men, who trotted to the hay barn and began to dismount. "Our animals should be kept in that pasture," the captain said, pointing.

"I'll need to move my horses out," Matt replied. "It will only take a moment." The last thing Matt needed was for five years of breeding to be undone by sharing a pasture with a bunch of English cavalry animals.

"We've been riding all day," the captain insisted.

"It will only take a moment," Matt repeated.

"How long until we can get food?" the captain asked.

"We'll slaughter a pig."

"My men are hungry."

"I understand," Matt replied. He tried his best not to get irritated. It was like being stopped by the police for speeding in his own time. No matter how much you might disagree, you acted respectfully and nodded politely. He had to remind himself, too, that this wasn't the man who would be responsible for burning his home to the ground.

The captain was looking now at the pasture and all the thoroughbred horses. "Some look fit for King George himself," he said.

"We do our best."

"Where's your well?" the captain asked, already on to something else.

Matt pointed to the side of the hay barn. It was the same well he had used when he awoke here for the first time many years ago. It took him back to the younger man he once was and the rash decision he'd made to stay.

"We'll pull some food together," Matt said.

The captain reached into his pocket and tossed a purse to Matt. "That should cover the two days." He pulled his horse around and trotted to the barn to join his men. Matt had a collection of purses in a drawer in the house. He'd long since stopped opening them. In his mind, it was better to believe falsely that the English officers were paying the compensation prescribed by law than to verify their lack of integrity. He watched the soldiers situate themselves, made a point to calm himself again, and then turned to find David or one of the boys to round up the horses. They too were becoming used to dealing with English soldiers.

The fact that things were only going to get worse weighed heavily on him. The incident in Boston was now being called a massacre, and the events Matt expected to lead to the American Revolution were being checked off his list, one by one, as regular as the ticking of a clock. Matt's theory that all his monkeying around in the cosmic soup might somehow change history was being discredited. The universe went unhindered despite his best efforts to the contrary, seemingly unaffected by anything he was doing in his small part of the world. Even Franklin appeared unchanged by things Matt had told him about the future and was going about his business like he was following a script written from an American history book. Nothing had changed at all! People were beginning to take sides, including his brother-in-law.

Will had taken to spending long periods in England. The only time he visited the farm was to gather new horses to distribute to wealthy business associates and politicians across the colonies. Will cared little for the daily operations of the horse farm. Matt suspected that the high price they were getting for these animals was coming directly from the Martin business. A well-bred horse, delivered into the hands of an influential man, opened doors wide to any businessman willing to take the step.

The Martins' business had grown substantially since Matt moved to Virginia, and this was in large part due to Will's contributions. Richard Martin was treating Will like the son he'd never had. The one thing that did bring Will back to the farm was his growing interest in politics, and he'd begun debating Matt on every visit. Will had become an intense loyalist since marrying Graine and as far as he was concerned, the Crown could do no wrong, and the colonies could do no right.

Matt looked up at the dark clouds and blinked away drops of rain. The storm was almost upon them.

The End of Book Two

LETTER

London, England, March 21, 1771

My Dearest Matthew,

Fondest greetings from London. I must apologize for the poor stewardship I have demonstrated as of late concerning my correspondence. There is no excuse save for the constantly changing dynamic regarding Parliament's opinions of the American colonies, which has frequently occupied my time. I have been and will always be an advocate for the continued good will between England and her citizens across the sea.

Presently, there are many in England who support the incorporation of the American colonies into the government, with a representation similar to others in the kingdom. I hold out still that these prominent men, one or two that I call good friends, may yet initiate a process that alleviates an objectionable condition so keenly protested by the American colonies. I have hopes that the American colonists may soon find themselves sharing the same voice in Parliament as any other citizen of Great Britain.

Having read the preceding, I know that you must think I am on a fool's errand and presently wandering about the mother country in a state of bewilderment. This would especially be the case upon considering our shared knowledge of your somewhat fortuitous arrival in the Virginia Colony. I promise you that I am in full control of my faculties and am guided daily by your unique insight in all my dealings with the English government. That said, to live with myself, I feel I must use this insight to smooth relations between a mother and her most promising child.

Enough of politics! I should say that I am quite impressed by the royalties that I am receiving from Miller Head and Stomach Tablets. You should also know that the last shipment received here in London was applauded by every colleague with whom I had the pleasure to share this wonderful medicine. I have often boasted of our friendship and am proud of any influence I may have had in your success.

Speaking of success, I had an opportunity recently to dine with your relations William Taylor and Robert Martin. Both have developed reputations of some prominence here in London. If I had not been previously aware that these men were Virginians, I would surely testify that they are longtime residents of this great city in which I now reside.

I have saved the most significant news for last with the knowledge that this revelation will cause you some concern and may wholly occupy your thoughts. Parliament was quite taken yesterday by an impassioned speech presented by none other than Patrick Ferguson, the man for whom we have searched so long. He has become a businessman of consequence here in London and now has the ear of men who may have the ability to influence the workings of the Crown. I will report on his activities and motivations as they are presented to me. Though I cannot presently imagine a purpose for you to cross the ocean and apply yourself in a similar pursuit, your role as a protector of Virginian interests may dictate such a course of action. I will keep you informed.

As always, your loyal friend,

B Franklen

Made in the USA
Middletown, DE
18 July 2020